"You're late."

Emma hurried af … lking away from the air …

"The traffic was at … "

He barely glanced … when he spoke. "Is that how your company has been run up to this point? Standing people up and offering flimsy excuses? No wonder your boss agreed to this merger."

These words were like a slap in the face. She halted briefly and then propelled herself forward and ahead of him so that he was forced to follow her in the direction of the car park.

"It was unavoidable," she said. "You don't understand what driving in Paris can be like."

"It can't be any worse than New York City," he countered, "and I've always managed that just fine."

"This is not New York. The sooner you realize that, the better."

"Believe me," he ground out, "I am all too aware of the distinction."

She didn't wait to see if Cole Dorset followed. He called after her, but she didn't stop, not until he finally used the company name.

"Aquitaine!"

She halted and turned, waiting for an apology.

"Here." He passed her the smaller of his two bags and kept walking.

Dear Reader,

I have something to confess. I've never been to Paris. But for years now, I've heard my Francophile sister wax long and poetic on the allure of the most romantic of European cities. I've received postcards during her visits there featuring images of statues and paintings, streets and cafes. She's gifted me with *macarons* and left me voice messages entirely in French (even though I don't speak the language). So when I began to create the characters for *The Paris Connection,* it was easy to envision Emma, a woman who left behind the familiarity of the United States for the attraction of France.

And through Emma, I learned to love this city I've never seen, just as she sets out to convince her boss, Cole, of its beauty and charm. From Cole's first appearance in my novel, *Gentle Persuasion,* I knew when he truly fell in love, he would fall hard, and he needed a city that could accommodate that experience.

With Cole and Emma's journey, I came to realize that Paris is a place for dreamers, a city steeped in both history and romance, and that it is best appreciated by those who understand affairs of the heart. It is a feeling, as much as a place, that reminds us of the thrill and joy that come with falling in love.

Whether you've ever visited France or not, I'd love to hear your thoughts about Cole and Emma's story and the city at the heart of *The Paris Connection.* You can email me through my website at www.cerellasechrist.com.

Cerella Sechrist

HARLEQUIN HEARTWARMING

Cerella Sechrist

The Paris Connection

ISBN-13: 978-0-373-36668-2

THE PARIS CONNECTION

This edition published by arrangement with Harlequin Books S.A.

For questions and comments about the quality of this book, please contact us at CustomerService@Harlequin.com.

Printed in U.S.A.

CERELLA SECHRIST

lives in York, Pennsylvania, with two precocious pugs, Darcy and Charlotte, named after Jane Austen literary characters. She has won various competitions and a scholarship for her writing, which includes devotionals, full-length plays and novels. Her debut novel, *Love Finds You in Hershey, Pennsylvania,* recently rereleased with Harlequin Love Inspired. Cerella divides her time between working in the office of her family's construction business and as a barista to support her reading habit and coffee addiction. Her novels exhibit her love for both the written word and food in fiction. You can find her online at her website, www.cerellasechrist.com, where she pens *Literary Fare: Fiction & Food,* a blog for readers.

Books by Cerella Sechrist

HARLEQUIN HEARTWARMING

23–GENTLE PERSUASION

Dedicated to my sister, Carissa:

If my life were a novel, you'd be everyone's favorite character. Thanks for being one of the best parts of my story.

CHAPTER ONE

A BLARING HORN caused Emma Brooks to cringe as she cut a sharp right and narrowly avoided sideswiping the vehicle next to her. She quickly accelerated past the tiny smart car and sped through the roundabout in an attempt to get ahead, only to slam on the brakes when another car cut her off.

"Ah! Crazy Parisian drivers!"

She jerked the wheel and quickly eased into a rare car-length gap as she continued heading in the direction of Charles de Gaulle Airport. She checked the time and bit back a groan. She was already twenty minutes late with no end to the Paris traffic in sight.

"*This* is why I travel by *métro* in the city," she announced to the empty car. She had lived in Paris for ten years and had never learned to embrace the daredevil driving of the French. She used to tell her ex-husband, Brice, that if she wanted to take her life into her own hands, she'd go swimming with sharks or take up skydiving. In her opinion, both of these options presented less risk than getting behind the wheel in her adopted city.

Another car came up suddenly from behind, sliding alongside her so close that she could have sworn only a sheet of paper would have fit between them. She knew better than to stop, though. The best thing to do in Paris traffic was to keep going and pray that the tide would just flow around you. Why, oh why, had she not told her boss, Julien, to send someone else to the airport?

She sighed. A stupid question. She knew why—because she didn't want to disappoint her mentor, and she certainly didn't wish to appear less than competent when it came to navigating the city. After all, she needed that edge to hopefully one day reclaim the promotion she'd been promised. The promotion that now belonged to the fellow American she had been sent to pick up. This reminder only rankled further. In a perfect world, she would be happily ensconced in the CEO's office of Aquitaine Enterprises, the executive recruiting firm she worked for. Instead, she was risking her life in a European version of go-kart driving to welcome the man who'd been awarded the position in her place.

New York businesswoman Lillian Reid had reached out to Julien six weeks ago about the possibility of joining her firm, Reid Recruiting, with Aquitaine. After several negotiations and a trip to the United States, Julien had announced the very thing Emma had cautioned against—they would be joining forces with the American company to create an international presence. He had thought she would be pleased. After all, not only was she American born and bred, but she still retained her citizenship there. She had always made it clear that while she loved Paris and considered it her home, she still did, and always would, consider herself American first and foremost. In light of that, she had been hard-pressed to explain to Julien her dissatisfaction with this merger. It went beyond her promotion tanking. She didn't like seeing Julien have to share everything he'd worked for over the years. He had been good to her, especially after her divorce when she'd struggled to balance her job and the responsibility of a newborn daughter. He had watched out for her. Now she wanted to return the favor.

Focusing on the line of traffic before her, she craned her neck to try to see ahead. Cars stretched out in every direction, and she was now—she consulted the time once more—twenty-five minutes late. She had thought about calling the office to alert them she was running behind, but in her nervousness about picking up the company car that morning, she'd left her cell phone on her desk. And there was no way she was going to try to pull out of this mess just to call in and let Julien know about the delay.

No, she'd just have to offer her apologies once she reached the airport and hope the new boss was understanding. After all, as her former mother-in-law always said, with her typical *c'est la vie* mind-set, "Why worry about a little delay?"

COLE DORSET CHECKED his watch for what he estimated was the eighteenth time and ground his teeth together. Where was this Emma, the woman who'd been sent to pick him up from the airport? He had called in to the office twice now and been reassured both times that she was on the way. But the meeting with the board of directors and company employees was set to take place in thirty minutes, and he was still stuck in the waiting area outside customs at the Charles de Gaulle Airport. His tension grew as he impatiently felt the minutes ticking by. This was not the auspicious beginning he'd hoped to create on his first day. It was bad enough he'd been sent to this country but now, after the long plane ride, to be kept waiting like this…

It was well beyond the limits of his frayed patience. Moving to Paris was not his dream. That desire had belonged to his ex-girlfriend, Ophelia. Then she'd broken up with him, left the company and moved to Hawaii to marry the man she'd been sent to recruit. Losing Ophelia was difficult enough—though he still wasn't certain if he'd been in love with her. They'd been together for four years; their lives had become intertwined. And while she had moved on, he was still left at loose ends, sent to take on the role that was meant to be hers. It seemed a grossly unfair consolation prize for what he had lost.

Agitated by these thoughts, Cole stood and began pacing the aisles in the waiting area. He made another sweep of the room, searching for a woman who fit the description of Emma Brooks. It wasn't much to go on. Any of the medium-height women with long, dark hair could have been her, but it was evident that most of them were waiting for friends or loved ones by their relaxed postures or the way they toyed with their phones. He'd been expecting someone in professional attire, with a sign to indicate she was his liaison.

Had he missed her? The line for immigration and customs hadn't taken any longer than anticipated, but perhaps she'd been waiting and, for whatever reason, assumed he wasn't coming? But the receptionist at Aquitaine had reassured him Emma would be arriving shortly. He pulled out his cell phone and debated calling Julien. He hardly wanted to appear the helpless American, especially given his new position as CEO, but at some point, he was going to have to accept that he'd either been stood up or a miscommunication had occurred. The thought rankled.

What sort of incompetency left the new boss stranded in the airport on his first day? It didn't bode well for the future of this enterprise. What had Lillian been thinking, merging her company with a foreign one?

Well, he knew the answer to that. She'd been smart to join with a firm already established in Paris. Such a move only served to strengthen both businesses. Reid Recruiting would tap into a market that already held contacts and a solid reputation overseas, and vice versa for Julien's firm. Cole's only objection had been when Lillian had promoted him from senior executive recruiter to executive director and CEO of the Paris firm. Despite his protestations, her wishes were clear—if he wanted his career to advance any further, he would accept the promotion and move to Paris. He had worked too long and hard at Reid Recruiting to see his future there stall now. And so, here he was, travel-weary and already homesick for New York, wondering if his American counterpart had simply abandoned him and whether he had made a mistake in accepting Lillian's directive.

In any case, it didn't matter. It was too late to go back now.

Turning away, he gathered his luggage and moved toward the exit where ground transportation was advertised in both English and French. If Aquitaine wasn't coming to him, he'd simply have to go to them.

EMMA HURRIED FROM the car park and toward the elevator leading to Terminal Two. She couldn't bear to look at her watch even once more, didn't want to consider how late she was.

Emerging from the elevator, she rushed toward the secure waiting areas where passengers were funneled after clearing customs. It had been ages since she'd gone through that procedure, not since she'd returned to the United States four years ago for her mother's funeral. Between raising Avery and her job with Aquitaine, there never seemed to be enough time to take a trip, though she knew she needed to make it a priority at some point in the future. She wanted Avery to experience her mother's homeland, not just in words and pictures but physically. Enough time to think about that later, though. Right now, she had to track down her American boss and welcome him to the country.

She reached the waiting area and scanned its occupants, trying to pair the inhabitants with the photo of Cole Dorset she'd seen on the Reid Recruiting website. None of the arrivals quite matched the image of the polished, blond-haired man she'd halfheartedly committed to memory.

Steeling herself, she glanced at her watch and gave a small gasp of dismay. She was forty minutes late. Where could he be? There was no time to waste. She moved farther into the waiting area and began navigating her way around luggage and the rows of seating.

"Excuse me, Cole Dorset? I'm looking for Cole Dorset? Cole Dorset." She felt like a fool, especially when several people shifted in their seats and grumbled annoyance.

Well, it couldn't be helped. She straightened and cleared her throat.

"If a Mr. Cole Dorset is in the waiting area, please, come this way!"

She received a few blank stares and a ripple of interest before most of the passengers went about their business. She huffed in annoyance. Now what?

"Okay, think, Emma." If she were stranded at an international airport and grew tired of waiting, where would she go? She looked around, but nothing in particular stood out to her. He hadn't gotten stuck at customs, had he? Likely not. He'd probably decided to go on without her.

She turned. The train? No, he was from New York. He'd be more apt to choose a taxi over a train, wouldn't he? Exiting the waiting area, she headed back in the direction she'd come. She only hoped he hadn't left already. What in the world would she say to Julien if the new boss showed up at the office without her?

COLE WAS NO stranger to cities, and he certainly had no problem dealing with cab drivers. But the bombardment of English and French that assailed him when he approached the taxi stands only served to stretch his already frayed patience and overwhelm him further. He began asking the cost of fares and felt a rise of desperation. The amount of euros to the La Défense business district was appalling. His presentation was in ten minutes; the cab ride would take around thirty. He didn't have time to argue with cabbies about their inflated rates.

Though not normally given to nervousness, he felt his palms growing slick with unease. How was he going to navigate through this and still manage to offer up a confident presentation to the board and staff? For just a short moment, he felt as though he were a child once more, being shuffled from one foster home to the next, with all the ensuing emotions of uncertainty and doubt filling him up.

Resolutely, he shrugged off this reaction. He hadn't been that helpless boy for a very long time. And he was not about to let a little cultural uncertainty trip him up.

He was just getting ready to hand his bags over to one of the more pesky drivers when he thought he heard his name. Pausing, he turned, wondering if his anxiety had driven him mad.

"Cole Dorset!"

He finally saw her, dodging the taxi drivers jockeying for her attention and pushing through a cluster of tourists as she headed in his direction. His first thought was *beautiful* as he took in her long, wavy, dark hair and perfectly clear skin with cheekbones just lightly tinted pink from exertion. As she drew closer, he could appreciate her trim figure clothed in a pewter-colored business suit that flattered the dove-gray of her eyes immensely. When she finally reached him, she let out a breath and offered a brilliant smile.

"Emma Brooks." She held out a hand. "Managing director of Aquitaine Enterprises and your liaison in assisting with your transition to Paris. Welcome to France."

All thoughts of her beauty fled in the wake of this introduction. This was the woman who had kept him waiting for the past forty-five minutes. She was the reason he would have to explain his tardiness to the board of directors, starting him off at a disadvantage in a company where he knew no one, had no allies.

He glanced at the hand she extended and pointedly refrained from taking it.

"You're late."

EMMA HURRIED AFTER the new CEO as he began walking away from the taxi stands.

"The traffic was atrocious, even by Paris standards," she said, defending herself against his abrupt observation.

He ignored this statement as he looked left then right. "Which way to the car?"

She pointed and then struggled to keep pace beside him when he began walking in the direction she'd indicated. "I'm not used to driving in the city. The *métro* is much more efficient."

He barely glanced over his shoulder when he spoke. "Is that how your company has been run up to this point? Standing people up and offering flimsy excuses? No wonder your boss agreed to this merger."

These words were like a slap in the face. She halted briefly and then propelled herself forward and ahead of him so that he was forced to follow her in the direction of the car park.

"It was unavoidable," she said, loud enough for him to hear without her turning around. "You don't understand what driving in Paris can be like."

She stopped short of pointing out that, had she driven any more recklessly to get here, she might not have lived to pick him up at all. His attitude was intolerable.

"It can't be any worse than New York City," he countered, "and I've always managed that just fine."

She halted at these words; because of his

clipped pace, he was unable to stop in time and stumbled into her. She found her feet and took a step away from him. "This is not New York," she announced. "The sooner you realize that, the better."

"Believe me," he ground out, "I am all too aware of the distinction."

"What's that supposed to mean?"

"It means that I would never expect this sort of thing to happen at Reid Recruiting, back in America."

"Oh, for the love of— So, I was a little late. The first thing you need to learn about the French is that they're not as tied to schedules as Americans are."

"A little late?" He consulted his watch. "I waited for forty-five minutes while you took your time getting here."

"I told you, there was a lot of traffic." Rather than continue arguing, she turned and started in the direction of the car park once more.

She didn't wait to see if Cole Dorset followed. He called after her, but she didn't stop, not until he finally used the company's title.

"Aquitaine!"

She halted and turned, waiting for an apology regarding his rudeness.

"Here."

He passed her the smaller of his two bags and kept walking.

DURING THE CAR ride to the Aquitaine offices, Cole grudgingly noted that perhaps his liaison's excuse was valid. Parisian drivers took to the road like race car stars. They wove in and out with little regard for the vehicles around them, sliding so close that, a time or two, Cole found himself cringing in anticipation of a collision. He never said a word about this to Emma, who drove in steely silence, focused on the streets before them. The traffic was abominable, and at times, they proceeded at little more than a crawl.

As the time for his presentation to the board came and went, he pulled out his cell phone to call the office and let them know he was on his way. Emma said nothing, and he didn't bother to speak to her.

He kept his gaze out the window, trying not to focus on the cars around them but rather taking in the sights of his new home. He noted the Arc de Triomphe, a monument more impressive in person than any of the pictures he had seen could convey. Not that he would admit that aloud, of course. He had no desire to be in this city and was determined it would not stir his curiosity in any way. It was his own small rebellion. But Emma must have noticed his absorption in the structure because she suddenly spoke.

"The Arc de Triomphe's eternal flame is rekindled every night, to honor the soldiers who died in both world wars. There's a museum inside, and the price of admission includes access to the top. The views aren't quite as spectacular as the Eiffel Tower, but they're still pretty amazing."

In the distance, he caught a brief glimpse of the Eiffel Tower, that well-known symbol for romantics everywhere. He scoffed aloud. After Ophelia's rejection and finding himself here in her place, the iconic monument didn't exactly inspire feelings of happiness.

Emma must have noted his grunt of annoyance because he sensed her turn toward him.

"Look, I really am sorry I was late."

He didn't respond.

"I'll explain to everyone that it was my fault."

He felt a bit of his frustration ease but not by much. "Don't bother," he replied. "The receptionist at the office said it's no problem, and Julien has already told them there's been a delay."

She seemed to be considering saying something more, but a particularly rabid driver on the left caused her to inhale sharply and keep her attention fixed on the road.

It was just as well. He wasn't in the mood for conversation, especially with this woman who had kept him waiting, even if it wasn't completely her fault. His mind was on other matters—how he was going to adjust to life in a foreign country, even a cultural metropolis such as Paris. He would miss the familiarity of New York and the life he'd left behind there.

But things had changed in recent months with Ophelia's departure. Their breakup had put him on this course, and he was resigned to his fate.

Like it or not, Paris was his home now. He might as well learn to make the best of it.

WHEN EMMA ARRIVED at the Aquitaine offices with Cole in tow, she found she could not quite meet Julien's eyes. She was afraid of what her mentor would say to her if he knew how she had spoken to their new CEO. Her assignment, after all, was to welcome Cole Dorset to France and their office, and things had certainly gotten off to a rocky start.

"Cole, it is a pleasure to see you again."

Julien extended a hand to the younger man and smiled warmly.

Cole placed his hand in Julien's and apologized for his tardiness, but Julien waved away the apology. "The board was understanding. We've been looking forward to your arrival."

The two exchanged further pleasantries as Emma looked away and in the direction of the conference room, where the board of directors and the staff had presumably already assembled.

"Emma?"

She turned her attention back to the two of them as Julien spoke her name.

"Have you filled Cole in on the details of the meeting?"

She swallowed, ashamed to admit that after their rough start that morning, she hadn't bothered to bring her new boss up to speed.

"Um...well, we didn't really get the chance...." She trailed off.

"Emma, I tasked you with giving him the details—"

Cole raised a hand to stall Julien's reprimand. "It's not her fault, Julien. I'm sure Emma will be happy to handle my introduction and explain my lateness while you fill me in." He gave her a smile that was more smug than friendly.

With Julien present, Emma tried very hard not to glare. Despite her best efforts, she knew her frustration must have shown because Julien studied her severely, his lowered eyebrows revealing his displeasure.

"I suppose she will have to since she has done you a disservice in failing to update you as to the board's feelings. Most are in agreement with the merger, but a few are waiting to see what you have to say concerning the benefits of Aquitaine joining Reid Recruiting."

Cole frowned at this, and though she shouldn't have, Emma felt a tiny bit triumphant. If Cole Dorset thought this job would be easy, he was mistaken. It would have been better if Julien had given the promotion to her, as he had promised.

As if he guessed her feelings on the matter, Cole turned toward her, his hazel eyes cold, as though blaming her for some of the board members' doubts.

"I am sensing an undercurrent of hostility between you two," Julien noted.

But rather than say anything more about her, the infuriating new boss grinned and clapped Julien on the back.

"Nonsense," he insisted before smiling at Emma. She had a feeling Cole could be quite charming when he wanted to be, but at the moment, all she felt was irritated. "I'm sure Emma and I will be the very best of friends."

COLE HAD TO admit that the morning's aggravation was nearly worth it to witness Emma's glare as Julien turned his back on the two of them. She clearly chafed at the position she found herself in, and he couldn't help feeling a certain satisfaction at her misery.

After all, he certainly didn't want to be here. He thought again of Ophelia and how her departure had forced this promotion into his hands. He wondered if she was still happy in paradise with her new husband. Though he wished her no ill will, the idea of her experiencing wedded bliss still left the faint taste of bitterness in his mouth.

But witnessing Emma's frustration helped lift some of his own. At least he wasn't the only one suffering in the wake of this merger. Still, he couldn't help feeling just a touch guilty for how he'd reacted that morning. He hadn't known how bad the traffic could be. Perhaps he should have scheduled his introduction for later in the afternoon, giving himself more time to reach the office after his arrival.

Too late now, though. The damage had already been done. Besides, he doubted Emma would have warmed to him even if he'd been holding a bouquet of roses when she'd first appeared.

"You're translating for me during this meeting, right, Aquitaine?"

She slid a glance his way. "Yes. Is that a problem?"

"As long as you translate my exact words instead of making up your own, we should be fine."

He couldn't help smiling at the offended little gasp that escaped her lips just before they entered the conference room.

DESPITE THE TEMPTATION to do exactly what he had warned against, Emma translated Cole's words from English to French exactly as he spoke them. Most of the Aquitaine board and employees spoke both languages fluently, but for the few who only knew French, Julien insisted on a translator.

Emma wondered if Julien had known ahead of time how compelling a speaker Cole Dorset was. He stood before the Aquitaine staff with seemingly unshakable confidence, charming them with his greeting and then managing to seem both humble and self-assured as he related a story about his travel experience and a cultural faux pas he'd blundered into on the flight from JFK airport in New York to Charles de Gaulle in Paris. If she had met him in this meeting, as the others were doing, perhaps she could have liked him—or at the least, found him tolerable despite the fact that he'd stolen her promotion. But if first impressions were everything, then she and Cole had absolutely no foundation upon which to build their working relationship. She wondered if Julien would consider assigning someone else to be Cole Dorset's babysitter. After all, she already had a child to care for.

One glance at Julien's face provided the answer, however. He was watching her carefully, his gaze intent, and she knew he suspected that she and Cole's first meeting had not gone as well as planned.

Well, she'd done her best to explain why she'd been late, and if he hadn't been so intent on faulting her punctuality then maybe things would have progressed more positively. Her thoughts scattered as everyone in the room laughed, and she suddenly realized she had broken off translating several moments before. Cole waited for her to catch up, and the belated laughter of the French-speaking personnel served to highlight her distraction.

She glanced at Cole to indicate he should continue and found him frowning at her. He hesitated for only a moment before he began speaking once again.

For the rest of the presentation, she forced herself to pay attention, and each time her mind started to wander, she refocused it on Cole. By the end of his explanation of his new role and the benefits of this merger, she felt uncomfortably aware of the man's presence, from his easy gestures to the smile that was quite alluring when it wasn't marked by smugness.

She found herself depressed as Cole finished, and her coworkers erupted in enthusiastic applause. Traitors. Couldn't they see how he was working them over? Were they so easily swayed by his handsome face and charming banter? She stood as employees rushed to the front of the room to converge on their new boss; but she remained in her corner, wondering if she could safely escape or whether Julien would chastise her if she bailed right now.

Her curiosity was quickly answered when Julien approached.

"What happened between you and Cole this morning?"

Julien knew her far too well to believe any sort of lie she might concoct. "I was late. He was rude."

Julien sighed. "I know this is difficult for you, Emma, but for the sake of your job and for this company, you must try to embrace this merger."

"Accept," she corrected. "I will try to accept it, but I refuse to embrace it." She folded her arms around her midsection and restarted the conversation she and Julien had been having for weeks. "We didn't need them. We were doing fine on our own."

Julien shook his head. "I've told you, the market has become too competitive. To ally with the Americans is to open up doors of opportunity for both of our companies. I should think you'd be glad to be joining with your countrymen. Lillian Reid is refreshingly frank about business. She is a remarkable woman, having built her firm from the ground up after her husband died. And all while raising a young daughter, too. You should appreciate that, given how hard you've worked to establish yourself while also being a mother to Avery."

Emma suppressed a sigh. Yes, she should

appreciate the similarities in her own life to Lillian Reid's history. It was not the first time Julien had tried to sway her with this argument.

"I doubt Lillian Reid was ever promised a promotion and then had it taken away from her and given to another." She glared in Cole's direction as she said these words. She felt gratified when her rival seemed to sense her stare, raised his head and met her eyes, frowning at the dislike she hoped she was conveying.

Julien cleared his throat. "You go too far, Emma," he warned, his voice harder than she had ever heard it. "You lost the promotion, yes, but be grateful you still have a job at all. Lillian and I negotiated fiercely to retain most of my staff rather than bring in her own people from New York. Cole Dorset's placement as CEO was the only demand she would not release. She insists he is the best and brightest of her firm."

She opened her mouth to argue, but Julien's nearly imperceptible headshake forced her to swallow the words.

"You will learn to embrace this, or you will become a consummate actress and pretend that you do. You are liked and admired here, Emma—by everyone. You have risen in the company, and I treat you well—nearly like the daughter I never had, *oui?*"

She dipped her head in agreement, feeling ashamed for her ingratitude.

"The others will look to you for their cues on how to behave. And if you do not treat Cole as your superior, then neither will they. It is why I insisted you be his liaison within the branch. The two of you working together will strengthen this merger and cause Aquitaine to remain in the forefront of the executive recruiting field. Do I make myself clear?"

Emma's gaze shifted to Cole, watching as he laughed with one of the more prickly members of the board. How had he managed to charm everyone in his few short hours here?

"Emma."

Her attention jerked back to Julien.

"Do we have an understanding?"

She swallowed. "Of course, Julien," she replied. "I'll support the merger in any way I can."

Julien relaxed. "*Merci.* Now, I would like you to show Cole to his new office as well as give him a tour of the building."

"Certainly," she managed to choke out. Julien turned to go.

"Julien." She called him back. "I'm sorry."

"It is forgiven. But do not do anything that will make you have to utter those words again."

CHAPTER TWO

EMMA SPENT THE rest of the morning showing Cole around the Aquitaine offices. By unspoken agreement, they said as little as possible to one another outside of topics related to work. The questions he asked were good ones—about the day-to-day operations, their strongest recruiters, their largest clients and competitive markets. Despite her dislike of him, she had to admit that Cole Dorset seemed well versed in the area of executive recruiting. She supposed she could see why Lillian Reid had called him her "best and brightest," but she still harbored serious reservations on whether Cole could do the job as effectively as she would have.

During the latter part of the morning, Cole asked for a few minutes with each of the top-level recruiters, so Emma began the rounds of the senior offices with him. Before they approached each one, she gave him a brief summary of that particular recruiter's special skills, fields of expertise and any personal interests.

Once again, she was forced to grudgingly admit how Cole used her words to his benefit. He was a sponge when it came to the information she fed him, retaining facts and using them to establish camaraderie with his team.

At Marc Benoit's door, he commented on the skiing hobby Emma had mentioned before they entered the room and then spent nearly twenty minutes listening to Marc enthusiastically describe his winter vacation to the Swiss Alps.

He greeted Aurora Fontenot with a grin and handshake, noting the framed canvas hanging on her wall and acting shocked when she blushingly confessed she had painted it herself.

Standing outside Louis Terrell's office, he congratulated the senior recruiter on his placement record and remembered all three names of the man's children along with his wife's charity efforts.

She hesitated on the threshold at Giselle Bisset's office. Giselle was her friend, but the woman was an unbelievable flirt. She wasn't sure how to warn Cole about Giselle's never-ending quest for dates. She opted instead to share Giselle's passion for French fashion and her specialty of media relations, and was duly impressed when Cole easily deflected Giselle's attempts at flirtation by repeatedly steering the conversation back to her niche.

Though she was loath to admit it, Cole's people skills were undeniable, and Emma could see why Lillian Reid must have found him valuable, both as a recruiter and now as a leader. Seeing his talents up close, however, only served to remind her of what she had lost—the promotion and the opportunity to be standing in Cole's place at this very moment. Fortunately, after a morning filled with introductions and a catered lunch for the whole floor, he'd asked to spend the afternoon alone in his office to review some files pertaining to the merger. She suspected he also had to update Lillian Reid on how things were progressing, but she was more than happy to leave him to it. She spent the rest of the day in her own office, catching up on her work. When the day was over, she wanted nothing more than to erase her memories of the past twelve hours, eat some dinner, take a hot bath and curl up on the couch with Avery for the evening.

She arrived home to her apartment and

hung her bag on the coatrack as she announced her presence. "I'm home!"

Entering the living area, she sighed at the sight of toys scattered across the floor and cushions pulled off the couch. A makeshift fort of pillows and blankets—and was that her favorite shawl?—blocked her entrance to the hallway. She tore down the obstruction and continued toward the bedrooms, calling for her daughter and Melanie, the au pair who had come to live with them two months before.

Though Emma had chosen to remain in France after her divorce from Brice, she didn't want Avery to forget the American side of her heritage. The au pair system was the perfect way to balance Avery's cultural experiences. After all, it was how Emma herself had first come to Paris and fallen in love, by signing up as an au pair straight out of college. She had merely been young and looking to see some of the world before settling into a career, but her time in the city had stolen her heart, as had Brice, and by her twenty-third birthday, she had found herself married and living as an expat in this country.

Emma wanted her daughter to be bilingual, so she insisted Avery speak only English when at home. Having an American nanny only reinforced this. Plus, Emma got to share her enthusiasm for her adopted city with a new au pair each year. The au pair system set a maximum amount of hours caregivers could work each week, leaving them free to explore the city and make friends in their free time. During the summer, Melanie watched over Avery through the day, and Emma got to spend time with her daughter in the evening and on weekends. Once nursery school started in another couple of weeks, Melanie's duties would shift to getting Avery ready for school and then watching her in the afternoons until Emma got home from work; the au pair would also watch Avery all day on Wednesdays, since schools had off that day in France. Melanie would still have most evenings and weekends free to spend the time as she wished.

"Avery? Melanie?" Emma called as she picked a pillow up off the floor.

"We're in here!" Melanie called from down the hall.

Emma entered her daughter's bedroom to more chaos—scarves looped around the bedposts, their ends trailing down to the mattress, where the sheets had been stripped from the bed and a picnic blanket spread out instead, along with Avery's tea party set.

To her credit, Melanie looked up with an apologetic smile. "Sorry about the mess. Avery said she'd never made a pillow fort before."

Emma waved this apology away. Avery was five years old and extremely well-mannered—at times, frighteningly so—but children were children, and playtime should be a happy mix of wonder and chaos.

"We'll get it cleaned up before dinner," Emma said. "Now...where is my daughter?"

A tiny, dark head could be glimpsed from the other side of the bed.

"Have you given her to *Madame* Bernadette in the apartment downstairs?" Emma asked Melanie with a wink. "*Madame* likes her, but Avery talks so much, Bernadette may not want her and might try to give her back."

A muffled giggle could be heard across the room, and Melanie grinned at Emma's acting.

She sighed dramatically. "Well, I hope Bernadette is nice to her. It is a shame you gave her away because I was going to make cheese omelets for dinner, and they're her favorite."

The tiny figure suddenly popped up from the side of the bed, her hair fluttering in strands across her face and her lips wide in a smile. "Melanie wouldn't do that, *Maman!*"

"Ah." Emma raised a finger, and Avery quickly corrected herself.

"I meant, Mom."

Emma moved toward her daughter as Avery came around the bed and waited for her greeting. Emma leaned down, brushed her nose against her daughter's and then kissed the top of her head—their standard homecoming exchange.

"Did you two have a good day?"

Avery nodded, but Emma looked to Melanie for confirmation.

"We did," Melanie agreed. "Except that Avery insisted we have a tea party before cleaning up our fort in the living area."

"Well, she'll have to clean it up before dinner."

Avery looked up at her with pleading eyes, but Emma shook her head. "You should be full of tea and cakes, so surely you can't be hungry," she teased.

Avery smiled and swayed back and forth. "They weren't *real* tea and cakes," she reminded. "It was make-believe."

Emma tapped her nose affectionately. "Oh, okay. In that case, I'll begin the omelets right away while you put away your toys." She turned to Melanie. "You're joining us for dinner, right?"

Melanie shook her head. "I'm meeting some other au pairs, if that's all right. We're taking the train to the Loire Valley next weekend, and we're working on our itinerary."

"Of course. You'll love the Loire Valley. It's beautiful."

The two chatted about Melanie's upcoming trip as Emma began to make dinner. Then Melanie helped Avery finish cleaning up the living room before she went to her room to get ready for her evening out. She let Avery watch her apply her makeup as Emma finished up dinner.

Emma was just plating the omelets when the phone rang. Setting aside the skillet, she went to answer.

"Hello," she greeted the caller. "This is Emma speaking."

"Allô," came the reply, and Emma felt herself tense as the familiar voice of her ex-husband sounded over the line.

"Brice," she said, making an effort to keep her tone reasonably pleasant.

"How are you?"

"I just finished making dinner for Avery. Would you like to speak with her?" She knew the answer before she even asked, but she was forever hoping Brice would take more notice of his daughter.

"Ah, yes, well, that's what I'm calling about, *chérie*."

She gritted her teeth against his persistent use of the endearment. They had been divorced for five years, and he still, out of either habit or more likely to irritate her, insisted on tossing the word into every other sentence.

"I am not your *amour*," she reminded him for the countless time and wished he would get on with it.

He ignored her tone and forged ahead. "Yes, well, I just wanted to say that I will be unable to spend next weekend with Avery as I said I would. Other plans have come up."

Emma leaned against the wall and closed her eyes. Brice had begun seeing someone new in recent months—Christine—and it seemed his time with her always superseded any plans with his daughter.

"And what if I should need to reach you?"

He chuckled, the tone faintly bitter. "Why should you need to reach me, hmm? We never speak unless it concerns our daughter."

"And even then, the conversations are rare."

She could tell her goading had annoyed

him because his voice was clipped when he replied.

"You were the one who wanted to have the child, Emma. I told you we were too busy for such commitments."

The words pierced far more deeply than she would have admitted. "I don't regret my choice," she murmured in reply. "Avery is a greater blessing than I might have imagined."

"Oui," Brice sneered, his disdain leaking through the phone line. "And it's why you chose her over me."

Emma's shoulders sagged with weariness. "It was never a competition, Brice. I could have loved you both."

"But you didn't."

His resentment was clear, and she didn't have the energy nor the desire to argue with him. Brice had chosen to believe her love for him should outweigh her love for their child. He wanted to be the center of her attention. She had fought with him to keep the baby once she learned of her pregnancy, but after Avery was born, things changed. Her entire world had homed in on that single, delicate life she held in her arms. Brice had seen motherhood dawn upon her…and he had never forgiven her for it.

"Very well. I will tell her you send your love."

"If you wish."

In truth, she had not even said anything to Avery about spending a weekend with her father. She had long ago learned not to get her daughter's hopes up where Brice was concerned.

She had been about to ask if Brice wished to reschedule when she realized his end of the line had gone dead. Releasing a sigh, she returned the phone to its cradle and went to tell Avery it was time for dinner.

COLE DORSET SAT across from Julien Arnaud and watched in awe as the man attacked his dinner with a Frenchman's gusto. Steamed mussels dredged in a butter, garlic and lemon sauce; sautéed sweetbreads with a spicy tomato ragout; a salad of crisp apples, fennel and walnuts; and *pommes frites.*

Cole found dinner with Julien as much entertainment as sustenance. After several moments of being watched, the other man finally seemed to realize he was an object of attention. He raised his head and dabbed at a drop of butter on his chin.

"Is something the matter with your meal?" He gestured toward Cole's partially eaten entrée of stuffed ravioli with broad beans and white asparagus. It was the only vegetarian dish on the restaurant's menu.

"Not at all. It's delicious." And it was, but Cole found his appetite lacking after his first day at the Aquitaine offices. He was tired and a tad homesick, as well, but he would not admit it to Julien.

"Are you sure you would not prefer the foie gras? As I said, it is excellent here."

Cole shook his head. "I'm a vegetarian."

Julien only shook his head and smiled. "You cannot live in Paris and not eat meat."

Cole didn't argue with the man. Truthfully, he didn't have anything against meat. It was only that years ago, when he had first been interviewing for a job with Reid Recruiting, he had somehow inadvertently claimed to be a vegetarian. The statement had impressed Lillian Reid, and so he had stuck with the deception all these years. He had never even revealed the lie to his longtime girlfriend, Ophelia, since she was Lillian's daughter. But occasionally, when he thought he could get away with it, he would find a restaurant where he was sure not to run into anyone he knew and order the thickest, juiciest steak he could find. But meat was the last thing on his mind at the moment.

"Perhaps I ate too much earlier. Emma was very thorough in making sure I sampled as much of the food as possible at today's luncheon."

"Ah. Or perhaps she took away your appetite, mmm?" The question was rhetorical, of course, but Cole jumped on the opportunity to discuss the woman further.

"I'm afraid she doesn't like me very much."

Julien waved this statement away with a twirl of his fork. "*Non.* Emma is only wary of you as she is of most men since her divorce. Not to mention that your job was meant to be hers before the merger went through...and Lillian demanded otherwise."

Cole felt a stab of curiosity. "Emma was supposed to have the CEO position?" No wonder she was a little touchy where he was concerned. Lillian hadn't told him she was slated for his promotion. "Is she still your preferred choice for the job?"

For the first time since their food had arrived, Julien put down his utensils. "She has proven herself extremely capable as managing director. And she is an excellent recruiter," he admitted. "I think, however, that you are, as well."

Cole reached for his wineglass and sniffed the rich Burgundy appreciatively before taking a sip. "You said she's divorced. Then she's single?"

Julien leaned back and eyed him with speculation, a smile tugging at his lips. "Why do you ask? Do you find her attractive?"

Cole chafed uncomfortably and looked away. "I've only recently moved on from a long-term relationship myself, so I can assure you, Julien, that I have no interest in romance at the moment. I am fully committed to the merger of our two companies. Anything else would merely be a distraction. I trust that Ms. Brooks is likewise committed to her job."

"Hmm." The sound Julien emitted caused Cole to suspect the older man did not believe him. "Emma is very talented. She balances her career along with being a single mother."

"She has a child?"

Julien nodded. "Yes, a daughter, and the father is little involved in their lives, so she takes on all the burdens of being a solo parent. Emma is a very special sort of woman." Julien's expression hinted that Cole would do well to take an interest in her.

But he shook his head, wanting to avoid any extracurricular entanglements. "I'm sure she's lovely, but I can't imagine getting past your Emma's thorns to find any sort of petals beneath. She's prickly, that one."

"Not prickly. Only cautious. She has a good heart, but she keeps defenses in place to guard it."

Cole didn't wish to discuss the pretty but thorny lady's heart. "Defenses aren't a problem as long as she recognizes that I'm her boss now."

Julien frowned but didn't argue. He took a long sip from his wine and then reached for his fork once more. "Speaking of bosses… have you spoken to yours? Is Lillian pleased with everything you saw today?"

"As long as I'm satisfied, then Lillian should be."

"And are you?"

Cole considered this for a moment. The day had gone better than expected, given how his morning had started off. He could offer up no specific complaints, and yet, he found that *satisfied* wasn't really a word that applied at the moment. He hadn't wanted to come to Paris, and though he knew he was there to stay, he still wasn't happy about it.

"I think we're off to a pretty good start," he said instead.

Julien frowned at him, seeming to sense his reluctance on the topic. "I have spoken to Emma, if that is the issue, and she was most sorry for her tardiness this morning."

Cole felt his lips twitch. “I’m sure she was.”

Julien blotted his lips with his napkin and then laid it aside. “I am eager for this merger to succeed, Cole. I wouldn’t want to disappoint Lillian. Please, let me know if there is something more I can do to assist in this transition.”

“Of course.” Cole was too tired by the events of the day to say anything else on the subject, so he raised his glass instead.

“Here’s to…new beginnings.”

Julien reached for his wine. “*Oui.* And to your future in the City of Light.”

Despite his misgivings on that score, Cole clinked his glass to Julien’s and drank.

THOUGH COLE SETTLED into his position with relative ease, and Emma assisted him as required, the occasional argument still arose during his first week with the Paris branch. There were a multitude of minor wrinkles to be ironed out with the transition and decisions to be made as they overhauled the firm’s operating model. Emma spent most of her mornings providing information for Cole, from company background to files. She also relayed any cultural differences she thought might be pertinent. Inevitably, at some point during their day, they'd find themselves in the thick of a heated discussion.

Friday was no exception. Cole and Emma were in his office, reviewing some of the company's long-standing accounts, when Giselle tapped on the door. Looking up, Cole gestured for her to enter.

Giselle looked at Emma. "Emma, we have an issue with Arrow Tech Media's CCO position."

Emma suppressed a sigh. The negotiations to secure Arrow Tech's top choice for the chief content officer role had been fierce, but Giselle had assured her everything was all wrapped up, and the candidate was ready to sign the contract.

"If you'll excuse us, Cole," she said to her boss, "we'll just discuss this in my office."

To her annoyance, Cole pushed back from his desk and looked up at where she stood over him.

"There's no need for that. I'd love to sit in on your conversation, if you don't mind. It will give me an even better feel for the day-to-day here."

Emma forced a smile to her lips. "I'm sure that's not necessary. You have so much on your plate already that—"

"Emma." He stopped her with his own

forceful smile. "Why don't you take a seat?" He gestured to the chairs in front of his desk and then looked to Giselle. "You, too, Giselle."

Giselle caught Emma's eye as they each settled into a seat.

"Now, what seems to be the problem?" Cole asked.

Giselle filled Cole in on Arrow Tech's search for a new CCO. The candidate they'd chosen, Andre Delacroix, was highly qualified with an exceptional track record. Several attempts had been made by other recruiters to entice him away from his current position, but thus far, none of the offers had been tempting enough. Giselle had been tenacious in her efforts to secure him, and two weeks previously, he had finally agreed to sign with Arrow Tech.

"And now?" Cole asked when she finished giving him the background story.

Giselle fidgeted, an action Emma rarely witnessed where her friend was concerned.

"I just received word that his current company has counteroffered, matching the salary offered by Arrow Tech. Delacroix no longer wants to sign with them."

Emma released her breath in a rush and

then tried to rein in her frustration. Counteroffers were always tricky in this business.

"Have you alerted Arrow Tech to the situation?"

"I have," Giselle responded. "They'd like to make a counteroffer themselves."

Emma sighed a second time. "All right. Find out the terms and write up the offer. We'll present it to Delacroix on Monday."

"No, we won't."

Emma jerked her head around as Cole entered the conversation. From the corner of her eye, she saw Giselle do the same.

"Excuse me?"

"We're not going to advise our client to counteroffer just because the guy got greedy. It would be in bad form."

Emma stared at him, but he stared right back, his coolly assessing gaze unflinching.

"You can't be serious. We've come too far to lose this guy now. He's a genius, one of the most sought-after executives in all of Europe."

Cole made a face. "Yeah, I've heard that one before."

Emma tensed. "What's that supposed to mean?"

Giselle cleared her throat, and Emma shifted her gaze as she saw Cole do the same.

"Giselle, perhaps you could give us a moment to sort this out? I'll let you know once we've made a decision."

"Of course." Giselle acquiesced and made her exit, clearly eager to avoid being caught in the middle. She closed the door behind her, and Emma faced Cole again.

"Delacroix is brilliant. If we place him, it's a huge feather in our cap."

"Maybe so, but I'm not going to begin my time here by promoting that sort of action."

Emma ground her teeth together in frustration. "Listen, I don't know exactly how different recruiting is on the other side of the ocean, but over here, counteroffers are simply a fact of life. If the client is determined, you make a counteroffer of your own."

Cole waved a hand in dismissal. "Of course I know how it works, but that's not how Aquitaine is going to do business, now that it's part of Reid Recruiting."

She felt every protective instinct she possessed rise up within her. "You may be the CEO, but don't you think that kind of business model is something that Julien should approve?"

Cole shook his head. "I'm not saying we'd never advise our clients to counteroffer, but what I am saying is that if this Delacroix is as cagey as Giselle indicated, then throwing more incentives at him isn't going to do any good. The man clearly prefers the company he currently works for and was probably using us just to get an increase in salary."

"Don't be ridiculous."

"Oh, I'm being ridiculous?" He raised his eyebrows. "Aquitaine, we're not going after this guy like we're single and desperate for a date. We're better than that."

"We?" She scoffed. "You just got here, remember?"

He scowled, and she realized how petty she sounded.

"I'm sorry," she apologized. "I just don't understand why you're so adamant on this. What's the harm in counteroffering? The worst that can happen is that Delacroix rejects it, and we're back to square one. If we don't even offer, we're already there."

Cole fell silent as the seconds ticked by. He leaned forward, resting his elbows on the desk, as though about to share something confidential. Emma scooted her chair closer.

"Emma, have you ever heard the term 'the heart wants what the heart wants'?"

Her breath caught at the way he spoke these words and their close proximity as they each leaned over the desk.

"Yes, I have. It's attributed to Emily Dickinson."

"Then she knew what you don't seem to grasp. If Delacroix wants to stay where he's at, no amount of additional incentives or salary will sway him. I witnessed the same thing recently, when we tried to negotiate Dane Montgomery out of retirement."

Emma remembered the name from her background research on Reid Recruiting, when Julien had first mentioned the merger. Montgomery had been a star in the advertising universe before he left the corporate world to run a coffee plantation in Hawaii. Reid Recruiting had negotiated him out of retirement and back to New York to work for Bianca Towers, international hotel-chain heiress, but Montgomery had soon renegotiated the terms of his contract and returned to Hawaii to work for Towers from the islands. She briefly recalled Cole's name being attached to the situation, but the more prominent figure had been Lillian Reid's daughter, Ophelia, the lead recruiter on the assignment.

"So what?" Emma countered. "As I recall, that situation was a success in the end. Montgomery still works for Towers. He just does it on location at his coffee plantation."

Her summation didn't seem to impress Cole in the least.

"Obviously. But my point is that Montgomery wanted to stay where he was at, and upping our offer didn't really change that. Sometimes, you have to let the heart take charge. If Delacroix really wants to switch companies, offering more money isn't going to make a difference either way. If he's unhappy with his existing employer then our current offer should be satisfactory. And if he's just using this as a means to increase his salary, we're not going to give him any more leverage."

She found his reasoning flawed, but she knew it was pointless to say so.

"You have a daughter," Cole went on. "Hasn't she ever tried to play you against your husband?"

"Ex-husband," she automatically corrected. "And how did you know I have a daughter?"

"Julien told me. Anyway, hasn't your daughter ever asked you for something and then gone to her father to see if she could negotiate a better deal?"

"Avery is not that sort of child, and I resent the implication that she could be that devious."

He sighed. "I'm sorry, Aquitaine. I didn't

mean any offense. I'm sure your daughter is a lovely girl. I'm only pointing out that candidates know how to play these games as well as we do."

Still rankled by his theory, she shrugged. "You're the boss," she offered by way of submission, though she knew her tone said far more than her words.

He frowned but didn't comment.

"I'll inform Giselle." She stood to go.

Her hand was on the door handle when he finally spoke. "And I trust you'll present things to Giselle in such a way that she recognizes this was a *mutual* decision."

She replayed Julien's warning in her head, about supporting Cole and the merger, and injected a sweetness into her words that she didn't feel.

"Of course. I would never even think of implying otherwise."

Cole narrowed his eyes as she plastered on a blatantly false smile and left the room.

CHAPTER THREE

EMMA ENTERED THE Aquitaine offices on Monday morning with a new outlook. Spending a weekend with Avery had done much to restore her attitude. She had played games with her daughter, caught up on some errands and taken Melanie with them to the market. She'd even found time to read a couple of chapters in a new novel she'd purchased. She walked into Aquitaine with a lighter step and smiled pleasantly as she approached her office and found Henri, one of the janitorial staff, watering the plants nearby.

"*Bonjour,* Henri."

The man's eyes lit up at the sight of her. He had once told her that she was the only Aquitaine recruiter who bothered to speak to him. The rest worked around him as if he wasn't even there.

"*Bonjour,* Emma."

"Did you enjoy your weekend?"

He sighed. "I went to see my daughter's ballet recital. I had hoped to take her and my son to dinner afterward, but my wife refused, saying they had other plans."

Emma felt herself frowning with sympathy. "Oh, Henri. I'm so sorry. If it's any consolation, things should get better. Those beginning stages of divorce are when both parties feel wounded and betrayed. Hopefully, she'll ease up in time."

Henri appeared skeptical, despite her reassurances, but she couldn't blame him. She remembered how much hurt she'd experienced when she and Brice had been in the first phase of their divorce. Her situation was different from Henri's, though, in that Brice had wanted nothing to do with Avery and had accepted whatever custody terms Emma chose to lay out. She'd been hopeful he'd eventually exhibit more enthusiasm, so she'd allowed for him to take Avery every other weekend and some holidays, but he rarely took advantage of the offer. Henri, on the other hand, seemed to be struggling in the opposite direction. It pained her to know how much he wished to be with his children and to witness how his wife continued to withhold them.

"How are the custody hearings coming along?" she asked. To her dismay, Henri's mood seemed to sink even further.

"She is suggesting I only get one weekend

a month, a week in the summer and no holidays. With my background, I am not sure I have a chance of more. There is a lawyer who feels he can help, but his fees are exorbitant."

Emma knew that Henri had once had an issue with gambling. His habit had never become as damaging as some, but it had been enough to cast a black mark upon his character, one that his soon-to-be ex-wife seemed to be using to her full advantage.

"If you need money, I could loan you some," Emma offered, but Henri was already shaking his head.

"No. I owed enough to friends after I recognized my gambling addiction. I vowed never to borrow a single euro again."

Emma nodded with sympathy and then noticed that the conversation nearby, in one of the smaller conference rooms, was growing to a steady buzz. She ignored it for the moment.

"Enough about me. How was your weekend?" Henri asked.

"Very nice." She hesitated, unwilling to mention Avery in light of Henri's own plight.

"And how is Avery? You haven't shown me any pictures lately."

She relaxed since he broached the subject first.

"She's grown at least three inches in the past few weeks. She's going to be as tall as her father one day."

Henri clucked his tongue, presumably at her mention of Brice. He slid a glance around. "And the new American boss? What do you think of him?"

She hesitated, choosing her words carefully. Henri might only be the janitor, but Julien's warning on Cole's first day had been clear. She would support the merger and CEO. "I think Cole is the perfect person to manage this company for the days ahead."

"He has a very flashy smile," Henri observed.

Emma smothered a laugh. "Yes, that's true." Cole's smile was certainly something of note. It made his handsome features even more attractive.

"Everyone here just beams whenever he comes around. I hope you plan to challenge him, keep him sharp," Henri remarked.

She grinned at this idea. "I should tell him you said so."

Henri's head jerked up in alarm. "I do not think—"

"It's all right, Henri," she assured him. "I won't say a word to him. But I promise, I'll do my best to keep him on his toes."

The hum of chatter in the conference room was unmistakable now and growing by the second. Emma turned her head in that direction.

"What's on everyone's mind, that they're talking so much?"

Henri gave another shrug. "I overheard a few things—that Julien is arranging some sort of company getaway."

Emma furrowed her eyebrows. Julien had initiated plans without consulting her? It was unlike him.

"I better go see what they're buzzing about." She paused before leaving and reached out to give Henri's arm an affectionate squeeze. "Good luck with everything. Let me know how things go."

He nodded and turned back to his work as she moved down the hall and toward the conference room. She entered to find a small group of the top four recruiters chattering excitedly and passing around what looked like colorful brochures. Julien was nowhere to be seen, but as she prepared to move farther into the room, she felt an arm brush hers; she looked up to see Cole Dorset, tall and striking as ever, studying the room at large.

"What's going on in here?" he questioned without looking at her.

She forced her gaze away and back to the group before them. "I don't know. Henri said something about a company getaway."

"Henri?"

"The janitor," she replied with distraction.

Cole fell silent so she dared to look at him once more. He was staring at her.

"You're friends with the janitor?"

She stiffened. "It's not like we go to lunch every day, but we're friendly, yes. Why?"

"No reason. I just…never thought about being friends with the janitor."

She looked away from him. "Well, maybe you should. Henri's really nice."

His voice sounded amused as he replied, "Maybe you're right." He waited a beat before speaking again. "By the way, we heard from Delacroix this morning. He's decided to take the job with Arrow Tech after all. I guess he really was unhappy enough with his current company to make a switch."

She felt a jolt of surprise at this news.

"What the heart wants, remember, Aquitaine?"

She didn't reply. After another pause, she felt his touch, warm and solid, beneath her elbow as he began to steer her farther into the room. "Let's see what Julien has gotten us into now, shall we?"

She didn't protest how he moved her along, and when his hand finally dropped away, she found that she missed the gentle touch.

"Good morning," Cole greeted everyone.

The room suddenly fell silent as they turned to face their new boss. "Um...*bonjour?*" he tried again, and Emma nearly rolled her eyes at how the group broke into smiles and returned Cole's attempt at the French greeting.

"Everyone seems particularly cheerful for a Monday morning," he remarked. "Does it have something to do with that?" He pointed a finger at one of the leaflets.

Giselle handed it over, and Emma was forced to ease closer to Cole in order to see what sort of information the literature contained.

Scenic pictures of woodlands, a dining hall and rustically chic suites were splashed across the glossy paper beneath words advertising the *"Château Bonnaire: an idyllic, team-oriented retreat center for professionals."*

She felt Cole shift uncomfortably beside her and clear his throat. Ah. She realized the brochure was entirely in French, and Cole had no idea what it said.

"A team-oriented retreat center for professionals?" she prompted. "Where did you get these?"

"Julien," Louis informed her. "He said to look it over, and that he'd be back shortly."

"Is Julien sending us on a retreat?" Aurora questioned.

Emma looked at Cole and found his frown mirroring her own. If Julien had chosen to send them on a retreat, he hadn't informed her…nor Cole, it seemed.

"I'm sure Julien will be back soon to enlighten us," Cole offered.

"You mean, you don't know?" Marc asked.

Emma felt Cole stiffen beside her at the implication he was clueless as to the goings-on at the very company he was meant to be heading.

"You know Julien enjoys his little surprises," she jumped in to spare Cole having to reply.

"Emma is correct."

They all turned at the sound of Julien's voice. "I decided to surprise you. I thought it would be good for you all to get away for a weekend, as a team. To get to know your new leadership." He dipped his head in Cole's direction.

Excited murmurs rippled through the group, but Emma watched Cole carefully. He frowned in dismay, obviously not quite as pleased as the rest of the group. Little wonder, given that Julien hadn't clued them in to his plans beforehand. She slid her gaze in the older man's direction, but he did not seem to recognize that he had possibly caused offense.

"Julien," she murmured, but he was too busy beaming in reaction to his other employees' responses to the news.

"Julien," she repeated more forcefully. His eyes found hers, and she frowned. "Could we speak for a moment in your office? Please?"

His pleased expression faltered, and she noticed his eyes shift from her face to Cole's. "*Oui*. Certainly."

The others didn't seem to pick up on the unease clouding around their American counterparts as Julien led Cole and Emma from the room. As they arrived at Julien's door, Emma reached out and laid a hand on Cole's arm, leaning in to whisper softly enough that Julien would not hear.

"Give him a chance to explain."

Cole glanced at her briefly and then nodded before stepping into Julien's office. Emma closed the door behind them.

"Julien, why wasn't I consulted about this decision?"

Julien frowned at Cole's question. "I'm afraid I don't understand."

Emma stepped forward before Cole could speak again. "Julien, I think you should have informed Cole of your idea before announcing it to the others. He— We both," she corrected, "were at a loss in there."

Julien's eyes suddenly widened in understanding. "Ah, I am so sorry." He shifted his gaze from Emma to Cole. "I apologize, to both of you. I only thought a retreat might be a helpful way for you to get to know your team and give them the opportunity to embrace you as a leader." Julien took a step forward and addressed Cole. "It was utterly thoughtless of me. I have been so used to making all the decisions as owner of the company, I forget that as my CEO, you should be allowed to take the lead."

From the corner of her eye, she saw Cole relax. "It's all right, Julien. No harm done."

He didn't say so, but she knew that if it hadn't been for the rocky start between them, he might not be so on edge.

"But I'm not sure if this is a good idea. Won't the board find a weekend at a château a bit extravagant?"

"As board chairman, I can make those kinds of decisions. You leave the board to me."

"But shouldn't our efforts be focused on the company and making sure our clients are still confident in our abilities after the merger?"

Julien waved a hand. "It is only one weekend. It will be the perfect opportunity to learn each other's strengths. You will find it invaluable, I promise you."

Emma was surprised when Cole turned to her.

"What about you? Do you think this is a good idea?"

She found her jaw sagging slightly in surprise that Cole had asked her opinion. Snapping her mouth closed, she looked from Cole's hesitant expression to Julien's hopeful one and then back to Cole.

"Yes, I think it's a good idea." She straightened her shoulders before speaking again. "It will solidify your position as our boss."

He eyed her a moment more before nodding. "All right, then. When did you book this retreat for?"

Julien smiled proudly. "You leave on Friday."

EMMA DEFTLY GRABBED a bottle of perfume out of Avery's fingers as her daughter ran from her bedroom. She tossed the fragrance into her cosmetic bag as Jacqueline shook her head.

"She has so much energy. I grow tired just watching her."

Emma reached for a blouse and folded it neatly before tucking it into her bag. "She's really excited that you'll be watching her this weekend. She's been looking forward to it ever since I told her you'd be coming." She moved toward her former mother-in-law and took her hand. "Thanks for agreeing to babysit while I'm away. I'd have hated to ask Melanie to change her plans for the weekend."

Jacqueline squeezed her fingers in return. "It is my pleasure, dear. You know I am always eager for a chance to spend time with my granddaughter."

"I know, but I'm sure it's still a bit of an inconvenience, taking the train from Le Mans into the city on such short notice."

Jacqueline waved this consideration away. "Only an hour's ride."

Just then, Avery sailed back into the room. She was dividing her time between watching Melanie pack for her own trip to the Loire Valley, and "helping" her mother prepare for the corporate retreat. Jacqueline reached out and managed to catch her granddaughter in her arms. Avery giggled and squirmed as her grandmother dropped kisses all over the crown of her head. She released Avery, who planted a kiss on her grandmother's cheek before rummaging through Emma's cosmetic bag. She pulled out a container of blush and ran toward the mirror to apply some.

"Besides," Jacqueline went on after the interruption, "I would gladly take the train for twelve hours if it meant a weekend with my granddaughter."

Avery turned with a grin, one cheek covered in a swath of pink.

"Avery, put that back," Emma chastised and then reached for a pair of sturdy shoes.

Jacqueline eyed the contents going into the bag.

"This trip was unexpected, was it not?"

Emma shrugged. "I don't know how long Julien's had it in mind, but he didn't consult me ahead of time. Nor the new CEO."

Avery, with her cheeks so pink it looked as though she'd been sunburned, dropped the blush back into the cosmetic bag resting on the bed and then skipped out of the room once more.

"Did you ask Brice," Jacqueline finally ventured, "if he would be willing to watch Avery this weekend?"

Emma couldn't meet Jacqueline's eye, so

she kept her attention focused on the remainder of her packing. She knew it disappointed her that her son didn't exhibit more care for his daughter.

"He had other plans, I believe." She didn't explain that this was to have been Brice's weekend with Avery anyway, and that he had canceled, as he so often did.

Jacqueline expelled a long sigh. "One day he will recognize what it is he takes for granted. I am always telling him that at some point, he will have to grow up." The sadness in Jacqueline's tone caused Emma to reach out and squeeze her former mother-in-law's shoulder. Jacqueline reached up and touched her hand.

"Don't worry. As long as Avery has you, she has all the love she needs."

Jacqueline shook her head but wisely chose to let the matter drop.

"Tell me more about this retreat and everything you will be doing. It sounds delightful."

Emma filled her in on the activities listed in the estate literature, as well as Julien's attempts to unify Cole with his senior recruiting team.

"Are you looking forward to it?" Jacqueline often asked her the most pointed of questions.

"A little bit. It will be fun to get away. I only wish I could bring Avery along."

"Don't even think of depriving me of a weekend with my granddaughter."

Avery padded into the room right on cue, wearing what Emma recognized as one of Melanie's hats. Emma went to her daughter and scooped her up for a kiss before turning back to Jacqueline.

"You may wish you could have switched places with me by Sunday. I have a feeling this little one is going to keep you quite busy."

Jacqueline opened her arms, and Avery wiggled free of her mother to vault herself into them.

Emma watched them and wondered if her words would be truer for herself. What if this weekend didn't go well, and she found herself wishing she had stayed home with Avery instead?

THE NEXT DAY, Emma stood before the eighteenth-century château and simply stared. The others were unloading from the van they had rented to bring them from the train station, their voices overlapping in a melody of excitement, but she was transfixed by the elegant stone facade with diamond-grid windows in front of the circular drive. The exterior of their weekend home displayed an air of old-world charm coupled with new-world adornment in the form of a contemporary white entry door and topiary shrubs in classic stone pots. She relaxed a bit, seeing this inviting atmosphere. She may have been uncertain about the trip to the countryside—feeling guilty for leaving Avery in her grandmother's care and uncertain about spending so much time in Cole's company. But now, seeing the welcoming sight of the château, she thought perhaps the next few days might not be so bad.

As the others came up behind her, they began to offer compliments on the grounds, equally as enamored with their surroundings as she was. They dropped their luggage on the lawn as Marc approached the front door and Cole came up behind her.

"Not too bad," he remarked from beside her, "but I thought it would be bigger. Like a castle."

Emma resisted the urge to laugh. "A château served as a manor house for the landed gentry. Though some were large enough to be castles, many were simply large country homes, such as this one."

Just then, their host opened the front door in response to Marc's knocking.

"*Bonjour!* I am René Denis," the man said in French. "I assume you are the party from the city, Aquitaine Enterprises?"

Emma quickly translated this for Cole as Marc politely requested the gentleman switch to English, if possible, in deference to their American boss.

"*Oui,* but of course. Come, bring your bags and place them in the front hall so I can give you the tour."

They each hefted their luggage and followed Marc into the cool interior of the house. Leaving their bags in the entry area, they were given a quick overview of the château's first floor. There was a lounge area with quaint furniture and wooden beams adjacent to a game and TV room, a Provençal-style kitchen with a cozy table for intimate meals, as well as a larger dining hall and laundry facilities in the back of the house.

René explained the schedule of meals and then suggested they retrieve their luggage and follow him up to the first floor. There were a total of six bedrooms, each with a private bath, meaning everyone would have their own room. They quickly claimed their quarters and René announced he would give them a half hour to unpack and settle in before they should join him in the kitchen for lunch and then further orientation.

Left to their own devices, they retreated to their respective rooms. Emma was glad to have grabbed one of the middle-size bedrooms near the top of the stairs. Rather than unpack, Giselle joined her. They commented on the beauty of their surroundings.

The view from Emma's bedroom window revealed a spacious stone-paved patio as well as a glimpse of a sparkling lake. Emma had also read there were hiking and bicycle trails, a nearby outdoor activities course, a forest chapel and, of course, the lake for swimming and fishing.

"We must tell Julien this should be an annual event," Giselle announced as she stretched out on Emma's bed.

Despite the charming setting, Emma remained skeptical on that score. "Let's wait and see what's in store for us before we sign up for anything regular," she said.

"Don't be so worried, Emma. It's going to be a perfect weekend."

Emma hurriedly hung her clothes in the wardrobe and placed her cosmetic bag in the bath. She checked her watch. "I'm going to call Avery before lunch and the orientation. I'll meet you downstairs in a bit."

"Suit yourself," Giselle replied with another stretch and peered out the window once more as Emma grabbed her cell phone and headed for the door.

EMMA ENDED THE phone call and allowed her shoulders to sag with relief. Now that she had spoken to both Avery and Jacqueline, she felt as if she could enjoy the rest of the day. She wasn't accustomed to leaving Avery for a whole weekend at a time, and she'd grown a little uneasy during the train ride as she imagined everything that could happen in her absence.

Now that she had heard Avery's voice and received Jacqueline's reassurances, she determined to lay her worries to rest and focus on the retreat. She was just pocketing her phone as she turned and caught sight of Cole coming around the side of the house.

"Checking in with your daughter?"

"Yes," she admitted and then noticed he was holding his cell phone. "You?" She gestured.

"Just letting Julien know we arrived."

They came to a stop at the château's front door. "It's a lovely estate, and René seems like a competent host. Julien must have done his research," he observed.

"He always does. Julien is decidedly thorough."

Cole eyed her after this statement. "I never meant to imply he isn't."

Belatedly, she realized how defensive her words had sounded.

"I admire Julien," Cole went on, "and despite any misgivings I might have about being in France, I'm honored to be working with him thanks to this merger."

"I'm...glad to hear it since I'm pretty fond of Julien myself."

The conversation stalled, and Emma folded her arms awkwardly.

"So, you ready for this?" Cole asked.

"I guess so. How about you?"

Cole shrugged. "After lunch and the orientation, René said our first activity will be at a nearby ropes activity course. He said the purpose of the exercise is to give us 'the opportunity to bond as a team and find our spirit of camaraderie.'"

Emma couldn't help grinning at how Cole repeated René's words, imitating the man's French accent.

"Sounds like René is determined to unite us." She didn't add that he might have his work cut out for him. While she got along with her coworkers well enough, none of them had ever participated in an event like this and certainly not with the intention of bonding with a new boss.

She cleared her throat. "Did Lillian ever send you on a corporate retreat before?"

He shook his head. "This is a first for me. I have to admit, I'm curious to see how it goes."

"Me, too."

Just then, René opened the front door and called them in for lunch. Cole gestured for her to go ahead of him into the house, and she followed René into the château's dining room.

Lunch was served on a table laid with chipped, antique plates and elegant silverware wrapped in linen napkins. Thc dishes were simple but delicious: quiche Lorraine with salty bacon and creamy egg custard nestled in a puff pastry; salad with crisp, fresh vegetables in a tangy red wine vinaigrette; and several varieties of cheese along with still-warm, round loaves of peasant bread and a jar of local honey.

Famished after their train ride to the countryside and further transportation in the rental van, the Aquitaine recruiters descended on the luncheon with ferocity. When they had finished, René clapped his hands and asked that they follow him outside for their orientation.

Emma shuffled toward the door along with the others and emerged into the early afternoon sunshine bathing the stone patio in the back of the house.

René began by reiterating his welcome from their arrival and proceeding with a grandiose speech about the importance of teamwork and their united purpose in the next couple of days together. Emma yawned, feeling full after lunch and warmed by the sunshine, and wishing she could just return to her room for a nap. But as Cole had already told her, René had other plans for them.

"We will begin this afternoon by driving to a nearby activity course where you will establish the foundation of your teamwork exercises by utilizing the ropes. Following this afternoon's activity, there will be some time for personal reflection and then dinner, followed by various team-building games."

There were a few murmurs of interest as they all wondered what sort of games might be in store.

"Tomorrow morning, we will have breakfast on the patio, after which we will move to the lawn for the archery portion of our exercises."

"Archery?" Emma bit her lip. She wasn't sure she liked the idea of her coworkers wielding weaponry.

To her right, Marc snorted. "What is this, medieval mayhem? How is using a bow and arrow going to bond us?"

René frowned at the interruption. "I would ask that you please take this weekend and its activities seriously. Your employer has arranged for you to be here and expects results. You can only achieve the harmony of teamwork if you are open to the exercises."

Giselle, in her typical flirtatious style, winked at their host. "I am fully prepared to embrace the possibilities, René."

This declaration appeared to startle the man, and he rushed to continue highlighting the activities for their stay. Though she continued to keep one ear tuned to the orientation, Emma couldn't help observing Cole and thinking about their brief conversation earlier. She had meant it when she'd said Julien was very thorough. She was sure he had weighed the options and done the appropriate research before sending them all on this retreat. But given how she had questioned his recent decision to merge his company with

Reid Recruiting, she couldn't help wondering if Julien was losing his edge.

And what if trying to force them all to bond with their new boss was a mistake?

CHAPTER FOUR

EMMA FELT THE tug and vibration of the tightrope beneath her and quickly redistributed her weight to accommodate the shift. Behind her, she sensed Aurora struggling, her arms flapping wildly. They were only a few inches off the ground, but it was still a struggle to remain balanced.

"Easy, easy…" René coached from the sidelines. "Work in harmony. Together."

From farther down the line, Emma recognized Marc's scoff. "Easy for you to say. You're still on solid ground and not relying on these idiots to stay balanced!"

Emma inhaled sharply at Marc's criticism but didn't tear her eyes from Cole, whose back remained poised and straight in front of her. He made the exercise seem effortless, and she felt a swell of irritation at the sight.

From several feet away, René clucked his tongue at Marc in disapproval. "*Monsieur,* it is a team effort. You must anticipate each other's movements, must be as one—"

"If you say 'as one with the rope,' I'm going to tear this thing off the stakes and strangle you with it."

"Marc!" Emma blurted out, embarrassed by her coworker's vehemence.

"It's all right, René!" Emma heard Giselle call from farther down the line. "I'm sure you would do a much better job than Marc if you were to join us. Care to take his place?"

Emma tore her gaze from the task of balancing and shot it in René's direction. She found him frowning in disapproval.

"You are all out of sync with each other. You must aim for cooperation. Understanding. Coordination. See how your boss holds his position?" René gave a nod of approval. "You must look to him as your example."

Irritation flickered in Emma's chest.

"Sacré bleu," Marc muttered. "He has the easiest position in the entire line."

For the first time since the exercise began, Emma saw Cole's back stiffen in front of her. He turned his head to speak over his shoulder. "Want to switch places, Marc?"

"Absolutely."

Marc jumped off the rope and to the ground so unexpectedly that the rest of them shifted and flailed, reaching out blindly to maintain a balance they could not re-create.

One by one, they fell off the line and onto the ground mere inches below.

Cole was the last to waver, and if Emma hadn't reached out without thinking, grabbing him to maintain her balance, he might have remained steady. Her momentary fumbling, though, caused him to stagger with the rest of them, and both she and Cole jumped to the ground at the same moment.

She stumbled, and he quickly turned and caught her, his hands firm but gentle on her waist to keep her upright.

"Careful there," he murmured.

As she collected herself, she looked up into the concerned depths of his hazel eyes. She stared for a moment, caught in his watchful gaze. She jerked to awareness seconds later as she realized how tightly she gripped his forearms and how his hands remained on her waist.

"Oh, um, thanks," she muttered and released him. His own hands dropped back to his sides.

"No problem. I guess we all need a bit more practice."

"Not me."

Emma turned away from Cole to see Marc dusting off his pants. "I am done with these circus acts."

"Marc," Cole said, his tone soft but warning. "Julien sent us here for a reason."

"Well, then, Julien can come out here himself and see what a waste of time this is. How is balancing on a tightrope going to improve how we work together? The rest of us have known each other for years. No offense, Cole," he rushed to add, "but wouldn't the company be better served if we each devoted ourselves to what we're already good at?"

René grumbled. "My program is of the highest caliber. It works, if you only give it a chance."

"I just did, and I can't say I was impressed."

Emma watched as René's mouth flattened to a straight line. "With such attitudes, it takes time to form the bond."

Emma caught Giselle's eye and saw her own concern reflected in her friend's gaze. Cole must have seen it, too.

"René, would you be so kind a host as to give the rest of the group a quick tour of the other activities here while I have a word alone with Marc?"

René's expression remained peeved.

"Please, René," Emma spoke up, "I know we would all love to see what other opportunities there are in a course such as this."

Her plea seemed to soften their host slightly.

"I thought the rope bridge looked fun," Aurora added.

"My kids would go crazy here," Louis put in. "They'd love it."

Giselle sealed the deal by moving to René's side and tugging at his stiff arm until she could weave her own through it. "Of course, you must show us!"

He finally relaxed. "Very well, if that is what you wish. Please, follow me."

Aurora and Louis trailed after Giselle and René, but Emma lingered for a moment.

"You, too, Emma," Cole said. "Join the others. Marc and I will be along shortly."

Emma's gaze shifted between the two men, from Marc's sour expression to Cole's neutral one. She gave a little shrug, decided it was Cole's job to see to Marc and followed the others, refusing to allow herself a backward glance.

COLE WATCHED UNTIL he was certain the others were out of earshot, and then he turned his full attention to Marc.

"Not a fan of the tightrope, huh?"

"Children's games," Marc spat.

Cole shrugged and then crouched down to test the tautness of the rope. He tugged on it and watched as it vibrated from the touch.

He sensed Marc watching him so he turned his head and looked up.

"You have to admit, though, it's not a bad exercise. Trying to get us to work in rhythm? It's a good icebreaker, a nice method to get you comfortable around your new boss."

Marc appeared slightly chastened. "My apologies. You are not the problem."

Cole stood and brushed his hands against the hem of his T-shirt, dusting off the dirt from the rope. "I'm glad to hear it. I'd hate to think that display just now was solely because of me."

Marc shook his head. "Sometimes I find myself short of patience where my coworkers are concerned."

"Oh? How so?"

Cole watched as Marc shifted his eyes away.

"It's okay, Marc. You can be honest."

It seemed to be the invitation Marc was waiting for.

"Aurora is a mouse. She's not cut out for work as a recruiter. Giselle is more interested in finding dates than placing recruits. Louis isn't so bad, so long as that wife of his isn't calling him at his desk all day long. And Emma. Don't even get me started."

Cole felt a stab of curiosity. "What about Emma?"

Marc sneered. "Julien's little lackey. She's his favorite, and it shows. She doesn't have half the talent I do, and yet, she's the managing director and was slated for promotion before you came along."

Cole thought how appropriate it was that this conversation was taking place beside a tightrope, where each step had to be measured carefully. He felt as if he was still balancing on that thin line.

"Her record speaks for itself," he pointed out. "Her satisfaction rating with her clients is impeccable. Her recruitments love their placements at their new jobs, and the companies who hired them couldn't be happier."

"Of course. But her talents are no better than my own. Why should she have the opportunities to advance when they are denied to the rest of us?"

"The rest of us?" Cole repeated. "Or denied to you specifically?"

Marc released a rush of breath in a quick huff. "The old man plays favorites. He gives to Emma with one hand and withholds from me with the other. And he thinks sending his supposed top recruiters on a little holiday is going to unite us?" Another scoff. "I had hoped, with your coming, that matters could be set right."

Balance, Cole reminded himself. He was an outsider here, new to this country and this office. Was this Marc's attempt at a corporate coup? If so, he'd approached the wrong man. Cole had no intention of overthrowing Julien. He was still president and chairman of the board, even if Cole did now possess daily operational control.

"I think you're going to have to be a bit more specific in what you want me to do," Cole said.

He watched as Marc took a step back, turned and walked a few feet and then came back to stand before him. His agitation was evident in how he met Cole's eyes and then quickly looked away.

"Emma has made her dislike of you clear."

Cole eyed him but said nothing in response to this.

"She left you waiting at the airport on your first day. Things were tense between you."

Marc had been paying far more attention to the situation between him and Emma than Cole had realized.

"We simply had a few misunderstandings at first. She had a good reason for being late to pick me up on that first day." Despite the initial tensions, they had formed an unspoken truce, and he felt compelled to defend her.

Marc made a face. "Traffic? She has lived in Paris for ten years. She should know to allow the appropriate amount of time to reach the airport."

Cole felt a ripple of irritation run through him.

"Marc—" Before he could get another word out, the other man began speaking again.

"It's curious, though, isn't it?"

Cole stopped. "Curious? What's curious?"

"Emma. And Julien."

Cole reared back in surprise. "What are you saying, Marc?"

"Well." Marc shifted from one foot to the other, ran a hand through his hair and then paused to rub the back of his neck. Cole felt his impatience growing.

"Marc? Just say whatever it is that's on your mind."

Marc dropped his hand. "It is no small matter, though, and I need to be certain I can trust your discretion."

Forcing himself to relax his posture, Cole nodded. "I understand your concerns, but that's what this weekend is for—to build trust between us all."

He waited as Marc eyed him for several seconds. "I believe you are trustworthy, but it is a delicate consideration."

Cole gritted his teeth and tried to be patient as he waited. Marc obviously had something to say; Cole needn't push him to say it.

Marc drew a breath and then slowly exhaled it. "All right. Have you considered that perhaps there is more between Julien and Emma than they would have you believe?"

Cole blinked. "Are you suggesting…?"

"I think they are in a secret relationship."

Cole couldn't stop himself. He burst out laughing at this idea but soon cut it off when he saw how Marc stiffened. He couldn't help wondering if this conversation was staged in some way. He looked away from Marc, his gaze sweeping the forest around him. The activities course contained several different areas where other groups and instructors were engaged in various exercises, but this particular corner of the ropes course remained isolated from the rest. There were a handful of people gathered around an instructor many yards away, but here, he and Marc were alone. No one was listening in, at least that's how it appeared. He shifted his focus back to the man before him.

"Sorry, Marc, but no. I don't believe that's

the case." He thought about Emma, her classic beauty, and then Julien's round form, a product of too many years of a gourmand's indulgence. He could not imagine Emma and Julien together. The idea was preposterous. He had to give Marc credit, though; the man possessed far more imagination than he would have thought.

"You are thinking of superficial considerations, I can see," Marc stated as he crossed his arms over his chest. "But imagine Emma's advancement—he was prepared to name her CEO before your company took over. How does someone as young as Emma move up so quickly?"

Cole shook his head. "She's not much younger than you or me. Why shouldn't she advance quickly? Is it because she's a woman?"

"Do not be ridiculous. Only consider the signs. Julien favors Emma, more than the rest of us. It would make sense she has seduced him."

Emma? A temptress? Cole was hard-pressed not to break into laughter once more. And yet, Marc's words had done what he supposed was their original intent—planted the smallest seed of doubt. It was obvious to him how fond Julien was of Emma, but he hadn't thought it was rooted in anything more than affection.

"After her divorce, Julien was very solicitous of her situation. He played a *very* personal role in her affairs, if you understand my meaning."

Oh, Cole understood all right. There were no cultural barriers to what the man implied. But couldn't Julien have simply cared for Emma as a friend and mentor? The thought of the two of them together, in that way, made Cole feel faintly sick, though he wasn't entirely sure why. It was just that the two seemed so mismatched physically. Then again, he studied Marc, wondering if any of these accusations stemmed from the man's own jealousy for a woman as lovely as Emma. He discovered that the idea of her with Marc, who was much better matched to her in both age and appearance, still left a twisting knot of disgust in his abdomen.

This entire conversation had become ridiculous.

"What Emma and Julien do in their free time is none of our business. I suggest we focus on our purpose for being here."

Marc seemed to finally sense Cole's annoyance and backed off. But only slightly.

"Of course, of course. She is your managing director, and you will be required to work closely with her. You wish for things to run smoothly. I understand."

"I'm so glad," Cole said, wondering if Marc would pick up on his sarcasm.

"Only, what if..." Marc trailed off, and Cole sensed he was making an attempt to lure him in.

"What if...?" he prompted Marc to continue.

"What if you didn't?"

"Didn't what?" Cole asked in growing exasperation.

"What if you didn't have to work with Emma?"

Cole said nothing.

"It is no secret that she was not in favor of this merger. She argued with Julien several times over it. If she continues with that opinion, it will affect her ability to perform her job. And her dislike of you is obvious."

This point caused Cole to cringe slightly. Her dislike of him was obvious? Sure, they'd gotten off to a rough start, but he thought they had moved forward since then. She'd been pleasant enough during their travels that morning as well as in the hours since their arrival at the château. Was Emma really still that averse to his presence?

"And?"

"And if you argued that her views are threatening the success of the merger, surely the board would allow you to replace her."

"Replace her with…you?"

Marc beamed, and Cole felt as though he were the dim-witted student in class who'd finally grasped the solution to the equation.

"*Oui.* As your managing director, I would be your guiding hand. Aquitaine could continue to grow in its partnership with Reid Recruiting, and together, we could provide a level of success this company has never before seen."

"Ah. I see."

And he did. He could fully see Marc for what he was—calculating, ambitious and utterly untrustworthy.

"So, you think you could manage things better than Emma?"

Marc already had an athletic figure with broad shoulders and a lean waist, but now he puffed his upper body up in a display of confidence. "Absolutely. I will do whatever is required to ensure your, and the company's, success."

"Mmm. Except for the teamwork thing."

Marc's swollen posture deflated a bit. *"Excusez-moi?"*

"The teamwork thing. You remember? This retreat? The entire reason we're here?"

Marc frowned, seeming every bit as dense as Cole must have appeared to him several minutes ago. Cole sighed.

"I appreciate the offer, Marc, and I recognize that you are a valuable asset to this firm. As such, I'm sure you understand that this merger is a tricky thing, and I wouldn't want to do anything to jeopardize it or this team."

He watched as Marc's determination seemed to wilt.

"I see."

"I knew you would." He reached out to grip the other man's shoulder and squeezed gently. "Just keep doing your job, Marc, and I'm sure the appropriate promotion will come in time."

Marc cleared his throat and straightened. "I assure you, Cole, I will not fail you. And if Emma should—"

"Then I know where you stand," Cole cut him off. "Now, I think it would be best if we returned to the others, don't you? Make a real go at this teamwork building, since it's something I want as much as Julien does. Okay?"

Marc nodded, and Cole released his shoulder with a final squeeze.

"I'm glad we understand each other," Cole said.

EMMA HAD BEEN watching for several minutes, wondering what Cole could possibly be saying to Marc. When the two finally came into sight, she felt her shoulders relax with relief. At last, the retreat could continue. She wondered what had caused Marc to behave so poorly. At times, he could be arrogant and even a little rude, but rarely did he react with such lack of restraint. What had gotten into him?

It seemed she wouldn't find out from Cole, who approached them with a neutral expression.

"Thanks for waiting, everyone. Did we determine what exercise we're going to try next?"

Emma's gaze shifted to Marc, who seemed much less irritable than he had been when they'd left him. And yet, there was something in his demeanor—though she couldn't determine what—that left a faint uneasiness in her stomach.

"René has given us the full tour," Giselle announced, and Emma turned her attention back in time to see her friend touch their host's arm flirtatiously. She shook her head in amusement and decided to put Marc's tantrum out of her mind.

"Excellent," Cole said. "Why don't you lead the way, Giselle?"

The group moved toward the bridge area where several different types of rigging were strung out between the trees. A few were of typical board and rope construction but others looked a bit more challenging, such as one made with loops of cord running in U-shapes from one elevated platform to another.

As they reached this area, René turned to face them. "As mentioned when we first arrived, this next exercise will require you to break into pairs so that one participant can serve as what we call a 'spotter' for another. Do you all remember the role of a spotter?"

Giselle raised her hand, as eager as any schoolgirl. "A spotter is like a safety net for their partner on the ropes. If their partner falls from the rigging, the safety harness and pulleys will help their descent back to the ground, but the spotter should be prepared to assist in guiding their drop."

"Very good, Giselle."

Emma smothered a laugh as her friend batted her eyelashes in the face of René's praise.

"And how does a spotter help guide the drop?"

Giselle's hand shot up again, but René turned away from her.

"Aurora?"

"The spotter should not try to catch their partner but rather be present and take the brunt of the collision in the hip area."

"Yes, exactly. Does everyone understand?"

"Perhaps you could demonstrate it for us?" Giselle suggested.

René faltered. "Er…demonstrate?"

"Yes, how the spotter should help catch their partner if they fall from the ropes."

"Well." He cleared his throat. "We have already demonstrated the proper handling of a falling participant."

"Yes, but safety is of the utmost importance, is it not? Can we really have too many demonstrations to assure our security?"

René sighed. "Very well." He gestured toward Cole. "*Monsieur,* if you please."

Emma watched as Cole pressed his index finger against his chest. "Me?"

"*Oui,* if you were her—" he gestured toward Emma "—spotter, demonstrate how you should catch her if she falls."

From the corner of her eye, Emma noticed Giselle frowning at how René had managed to avoid touching her yet again. Perhaps her friend had finally met a worthy adversary. She didn't have time to dwell on the thought, however, as Cole approached. He reached out his arms toward her, and she felt herself tense.

"As she is falling, the rigging will delay her descent, and you must approach her like so."

René stepped closer to demonstrate, showing Cole how to move forward with his arms extended. "You will try to take her momentum by grasping her hips."

Emma tried not to look directly into Cole's eyes, but it was impossible.

"Go on, show us," René instructed.

Cole's hands touched her briefly at the waist. René sighed.

"No. Like so."

René moved around Cole to grab his hands, forcing them from her waist and lower, onto her hips. She swallowed and tried not to fidget.

"See? You will grab your partner and help lower her to the ground. The descent may happen faster than you expect, so you will need to be watching carefully and react quickly. The most important consideration is to protect her head and neck as she falls. Place one leg in front of the other, like this, and flex your knees." René tapped Cole's legs until he mimicked their host's position.

Emma saw René turn away from them and back in Giselle's direction.

"Was that demonstration sufficient, *mademoiselle?*"

Emma didn't know what her friend said. She was too distracted by the feel of Cole's palms, lingering on her hips.

"You may release her now, *monsieur,* if you feel comfortable in the duties of a spotter."

Emma swallowed as Cole's hands remained on her body. He was studying her quite intently, and she began to feel herself blush.

"Cole," she murmured. "You can let go now."

He blinked. "What? Oh." He released her as though he'd been touching a hot stove and took a few steps back.

"Are there any more questions?" René asked as Emma forced herself to pay attention to their leader instead of keeping her gaze on Cole, who had quite deliberately turned his back to her.

"Then we will divide into pairs." René placed Giselle and Marc together, despite both of them rolling their eyes at this pairing, and then Aurora and Louis before turning back to Cole and Emma. “And since you two demonstrated so well, we will assign Cole as the spotter, and Emma, you may take to the ropes. If you will follow me, we will outfit you in your helmet and harness.”

Without any other choice, Emma turned her back on Cole and followed René.

TWENTY MINUTES LATER, Emma was regretting the idea of the activities course. René had decided that ladies should be first and had sent Giselle, Aurora and her onto the rope bridges while the men served as their spotters on the ground.

The course itself required all of her attention, and yet, she couldn’t help feeling highly aware of Cole’s eyes on her as she struggled from one rope step to the next. René called out encouragement, as did Louis, and Marc occasionally exchanged barbs with Giselle, but Cole remained notably silent. Emma found herself distracted with curiosity about what must be going through his head as he watched her fumble along.

And then there was the way he had held on to her, after René had ended the spotter demonstration and stepped away. What had the look in Cole's eyes meant? Why had he been gazing at her so intently?

"Take your time, Aurora!" René called out from below. "It is not a race. Those behind you must move at your pace. This is how you learn to work together!"

Emma brought up the rear of their line, and it suited her just as well that Aurora's steps were cautious. Finding her footing on the ropes was difficult enough without attempting to race across the bridge. She could only imagine what it would be like if Marc was in the trees with them. He would be pressing for speed, and the results would likely be catastrophic. Which made her wonder again... What had Cole said to him? They had returned to the group with Cole decidedly impassive and Marc seeming satisfied. She knew her fellow recruiter could be impatient, with somewhat of an ambitious streak, but his comments earlier had been a trifle uncharacteristic. Marc usually possessed more restraint in his commentary around his coworkers. Then again, they had never been forced as a group into a situation such as this one.

"Careful, Emma," René warned just as she misjudged the rope hold in front of her. She retreated, shifting her weight to her back foot to regain her balance, but it was too late. Her distraction had caused her to move without being certain she had a strong enough hold. She felt her right foot begin to slip off the rope while she still attempted to maintain her balance with her left one.

She could feel herself losing control. "Falling!" she cried in warning, as René had instructed them. She tensed, waiting for her spotter's response to let her know he was prepared to catch her fall. Her breath caught, her balance tipping precariously. Any moment now, she'd be flying through the air. She had a vague sense of Aurora and Giselle bracing against her movement, and then Cole's voice came to her from below.

"Fall on!" came the response that signaled her spotter was ready.

With that reassurance, she let go, feeling the tug of the belaying system as it minimized the speed of her descent. The nearby trees went past in a blur of green and brown while the breeze from her fall rushed through her ears. As she approached the ground, she sensed Cole positioning himself, and then, almost effortlessly it seemed, he had her by the hips and easily guided her to a standing position.

René was ecstatic. He actually clapped his hands with delight.

"Perfect! A perfect catch! Did you see? I have never seen a beginning spotter catch a faller so flawlessly."

René went on, but Emma tuned him out. She was too caught up in Cole's stare once more. He was studying her with an expression of both curiosity and seeming disappointment. She couldn't understand what it meant.

And still, he held her as before.

"Thank you," she murmured, uncertain what else to say.

He opened his mouth as though about to speak, considered, and then closed it once more. She cocked her head.

"What is it?" she asked, her curiosity nearly overwhelming her. There was something on his mind, she could feel the question of it hovering between them.

He watched her for a moment more, his grip still firm on her hips. And then he spoke.

"Are you and Julien having an affair?"

The softly whispered words, audible to no one but her, caused her to jerk with surprise. He released her, and she took a step back, feeling her jaw grow slack at this insinuation.

And then, because it was the first reaction

that came to her, she raised her arm, drew it back and delivered a slap to her boss's handsome face.

CHAPTER FIVE

THE ECHO OF Emma's smack reverberated around them. Cole rubbed a palm over his stinging skin.

He had probably deserved that. Why had he even asked her such an inappropriate question? It wasn't as if he really believed Marc's insinuations. Maybe he'd simply wanted to catch her off guard and gauge her reaction to the idea.

He watched as Emma's expression went through a range of emotions: her mouth opened with shock, then her eyes narrowed with rage, and then they widened as she realized what she had done.

He waited for an apology from her, but none came. Still, he sensed she was mortified by her reaction. She took three steps back before she began struggling with her harness and helmet.

"Get it off," she said, quietly at first, and then when no one came to her aid, she grew more insistent. "Off! Take it off!"

He stepped toward her to assist, but she backed up again. "*You.* Stay away."

Holding up his hands in a gesture of surrender, he inched backward. René finally moved, hurrying to unbuckle the belaying attachments. While he worked at freeing her, Cole watched as she tugged at the straps holding her helmet. Her hands were shaking, he noticed.

He had to admit, her reaction pleased him. It was possible she had reacted out of surprise at being caught, but he had been reassured by the shock in her expression. Not alarm at having been found out but rather utter astonishment at the very idea of what he'd suggested.

There was nothing between her and Julien. He was certain of it. A sore jaw was a small enough price to pay for that reassurance. On the other hand, he wondered if Marc had known how Emma would respond to something like this. His gaze swiveled from where Emma still struggled to disentangle herself to where Marc stood several feet away. The other man was watching her with a smug expression, his smile triumphant. Cole felt his satisfaction deflate.

Whatever game Marc was playing, Cole feared he had fallen right into it. He looked back to Emma as she tugged her helmet off and dropped it to the ground at the same moment René released the last of the harness straps. She stepped free of them and abruptly began walking away. Cole watched her go, her head held high. Good for her. She wasn't going to let his tactless question shame her.

When he looked away from Emma, he found the men on the ground watching him. Shifting his gaze above, he saw Giselle and Aurora frozen on the ropes, their eyes round in disbelief.

"I think maybe that's enough for one day, don't you, René?"

The sound of his voice seemed to propel their host into action. "Yes, I agree. We will return to the château."

As René moved to begin helping Aurora and Giselle find their way back to the ground, Cole looked in the direction Emma had gone. He thought about following her, but then decided perhaps it would be best to give her a moment alone so she could compose herself.

Louis seemed to hesitate between joining him or going to assist René. Marc moved toward him, leaving Louis to finally shift in René's direction.

"You see?" Marc prompted when it was just the two of them. "She is unstable. Not at all an appropriate choice for a managing director."

Cole allowed a ripple of anger to run through him and then counted three even breaths before responding. "Now is not the time to discuss this further, Marc." He held the other man's eyes until Marc finally looked away. "Do I make myself clear?"

"Oui," Marc mumbled.

"Good." Satisfied that he would have no more commentary on the matter, he brushed by Marc in order to help the others. As he approached the rest of the group, Giselle was batting at René's hands, trying to unbuckle her belaying restraints instead of waiting for assistance. He stepped up to them at the same time Giselle finally found herself free. She immediately placed her face within inches of his.

"What did you do to her?" she demanded.

Cole felt his patience slowly ebbing away. This weekend seemed to be driving them all farther apart rather than creating a team spirit.

"Giselle, I understand she's your friend, but I'm your boss, and I'm asking that you let Emma and I work out our differences on our own."

Giselle's mouth tightened as he watched

her battle with the choice words he was sure she'd like to share with him. She was quite pretty, but Giselle's beauty was all makeup and style while Emma's was fresher, more simple and pure. He had spent his entire career around well-dressed and polished women. He realized that was part of what made Emma so beautiful—very little about her appearance was artificial.

In the time it had taken him to come to this realization, Giselle seemed to have come to one of her own and decided not to let the matter drop. "She was never like this before you came. Emma is the most steady, reliable person I know. Why would you try to make things difficult for her?"

He couldn't help it; a scoff escaped. "Me? You think I'm the one making problems?"

"She would not have hit you if you did not give her a good reason," Giselle seethed.

Cole could feel the temperature of his emotions rising higher and struggled to rein them back under control. "Let me worry about Emma."

"Why? So you can get rid of her?"

"I don't want to get rid of her. I like her. I like her very much, and I think she's a tremendous asset to this company."

In the wake of these words, Giselle fell si-

e of discomfort and al-
ve from Giselle to the
a half circle, staring at
had nothing vested in
med absorbed in their

ite lovely and capable
l.
h. "I know she is."
r her helmet's straps
n one deft motion. She
f her safety gear and
hands.
to her."
nd your concern," Cole
sking you to please stay
vith Emma once we're

d he knew she was torn
r new boss or comfort-
inally acquiesced with

lax a little more. "Thank
s stance toward René.
e, let's find Emma and

e argued with that sug-

EMMA WAITED FOR the others by the van, cradling her wrist as it throbbed in protest from when she had slapped Cole. When the others finally arrived, she climbed inside without a word to anyone. Cole took the passenger's seat, so Emma claimed a seat in the back, as far from her odious boss as she could get. Her coworkers filled in the rest of the vehicle silently, and Giselle sat next to Emma in a show of silent solidarity.

The fifteen-minute drive back to the château was strained, weighted by the silence, but Emma didn't care. Let the rest of them be uncomfortable. The quiet couldn't be half as awkward as the humiliation she had just experienced. Every pleasant thought she'd tried to afford Cole up to this point was now tainted by the suggestion he'd made on the ropes course.

His assumption that she and Julien were lovers was an embarrassment she could hardly bear. In his arrogance, he had taken her fondness for Julien, their shared affection for one another, and reduced it to something tawdry and clichéd.

If this was how he thought of her, how he viewed the president of their company, then how could she possibly continue to work with him? It would feel like a betrayal to herself, lent. Cole felt a twinge of discomfort and allowed his gaze to move from Giselle to the others. They stood in a half circle, staring at him. Even René, who had nothing vested in this conversation, seemed absorbed in their little drama.

"She really is a quite lovely and capable woman," Louis put in.

Cole released a sigh. "I know she is."

Giselle reached for her helmet's straps and unclicked them in one deft motion. She tugged off the last of her safety gear and shoved it into René's hands.

"I'm going to talk to her."

"Giselle, I understand your concern," Cole tried again, "but I'm asking you to please stay out of it. I'll speak with Emma once we're back at the château."

Giselle wavered, and he knew she was torn between obeying her new boss or comforting her friend. She finally acquiesced with a short nod.

Cole felt himself relax a little more. "Thank you." He shifted his stance toward René. "René? If you please, let's find Emma and return to the estate."

Fortunately, no one argued with that suggestion.

EMMA WAITED FOR the others by the van, cradling her wrist as it throbbed in protest from when she had slapped Cole. When the others finally arrived, she climbed inside without a word to anyone. Cole took the passenger's seat, so Emma claimed a seat in the back, as far from her odious boss as she could get. Her coworkers filled in the rest of the vehicle silently, and Giselle sat next to Emma in a show of silent solidarity.

The fifteen-minute drive back to the château was strained, weighted by the silence, but Emma didn't care. Let the rest of them be uncomfortable. The quiet couldn't be half as awkward as the humiliation she had just experienced. Every pleasant thought she'd tried to afford Cole up to this point was now tainted by the suggestion he'd made on the ropes course.

His assumption that she and Julien were lovers was an embarrassment she could hardly bear. In his arrogance, he had taken her fondness for Julien, their shared affection for one another, and reduced it to something tawdry and clichéd.

If this was how he thought of her, how he viewed the president of their company, then how could she possibly continue to work with him? It would feel like a betrayal to herself, and to Julien, as well. But then, she couldn't help thinking that maybe it was the other way around—maybe Julien had betrayed her by instigating this merger, by allowing this man to take her place. Perhaps she was a fool to trust any of them, and this grieved her heart most of all.

She had begun to like Cole, had started to recognize what it was Lillian Reid must see in him and why Julien kept encouraging her to give him a chance. But that newly born impression had dissolved in the face of his tasteless and presumptive question.

They were just pulling into the château's drive when her emotions began to overwhelm her. She suddenly felt as though she couldn't breathe, as though one more second confined to this vehicle would smother her with its silent discomfort. As soon as René came to a stop, she began struggling to get out, climbing over Giselle and reaching for the van's door handle.

The others let her go as she fought her way toward the door and jerked on the handle to release it. Her wrist smarted in protest at the action, but she ignored the pain as she stumbled out of the van and took in several great gulps of air before striding toward the château's front door. She had nearly reached it when he called her name. She hesitated for just a brief second and then kept going, suddenly even more desperate to escape. Her fingers closed around the door handle, and she turned it, only to find the door remained closed. Locked.

He called her name again, and she felt him moving closer toward her. No. She didn't want to see him, didn't want to speak with him, didn't want anything to do with him. She only wanted to hide from what he obviously thought of her.

But even as she pulled on the handle once more, she knew it was hopeless. She'd have to face him sooner or later. He was her boss.

Releasing the door, she turned and met his gaze as he moved onto the step beside her.

"Yes?" she questioned, keeping her voice as cool as possible.

He appeared surprised by her sudden acknowledgment, after he had called her name so many times without a response. The soft hazel-brown of his eyes seemed darker than usual, filled with some emotion she couldn't trust. It appeared almost like regret, and his frown certainly indicated some sort of distress. But she wouldn't believe it.

"Emma," he said again, and she found her stomach twisting at the sound of her name on his tongue. How did he make it sound so special? Was it the fact that he spoke with an American accent, as she did? He had never said it so quietly, either, nor with such a pleading tone. "Could I have a word with you alone?"

"No," she answered quickly. She hadn't even considered his question. She only knew that anything this man wanted from her would be met with denial.

"Emma. Please. I would like the chance to explain and…apologize."

She sensed the others gathering by the van, watching the two of them. She didn't want to give him an opportunity to explain why he had assumed such a thing about her, nor did she want his apology. But neither did she want to stand there, a spectacle for her coworkers.

Tearing her stare from his face, she shrugged. "Fine. But I'd like the conversation to be brief. I have a headache," she lied.

From the corner of her eye, she saw Cole nod. He then gestured away from the house. "Perhaps we could take a walk?"

She turned in the direction he indicated and began striding away, keeping her focus squarely in front of her so she didn't meet any of her coworkers' curious eyes. She sensed

Cole following her, though he said nothing until they were some distance from the house, weaving their way into the estate's forest on a well-worn path. She might have walked the entire distance back to the city if he hadn't said her name again in that way that made her breath catch in her chest.

"Emma."

A part of her wished to rebel and keep moving, but she knew that would solve nothing. So she stopped.

"I apologize."

She turned on him. "That's it? That's all you can say to me?"

"No," he replied, "but right now, it's the most important thing. I handled that poorly."

She gave an unladylike snort and nearly flushed in embarrassment at the sound. "I should say. What if one of the others had overheard you? Do you have any idea how that would have affected my reputation at the firm?"

"It wasn't an accusation," he defended. "Only a question."

Her expression must have spelled fury because he hastened to elaborate. "And a tactless one at that. It was ill-timed and unacceptable. I regret it very much."

He seemed genuine in his remorse. But she would never let him off so easily.

"What put that sort of idea into your head? Have I ever behaved in any way that would indicate Julien and I are more than friends?"

"No," he admitted. "You haven't."

"Then why?" she demanded.

"There was no particular reason. It only seemed a possibility, given how close you two appear and the fact that you are, of course, a beautiful woman," he said, his voice low and soothing. She didn't like it and shifted away from him.

Behind her, he remained silent as she turned her attention to the darkening light in the forest as the sun sank overhead, softening everything into dusky shadows. The path was well traveled; they could easily find their way back. But she didn't wish to leave. Not until he said something, anything, to ease the discomfort that had lodged in her chest.

"You didn't deserve such an accusation. And I'm sorry. If it's any comfort, I don't believe it. I don't think I ever did. But I had to know because..." He trailed off, and she sensed something that made her turn.

His gaze had moved toward the ground and away, as though he looked for something in the earth.

"Why?" she pressed, her voice softer than before. "Why did you have to ask such a thing?"

When his eyes came back to hers, she found them filled with frustration. "Because I don't know the rules of the game on this side of the ocean, and I have to make the most I can of what I have if I'm to succeed here."

This candid response took her aback. "There is no game, Cole," she assured him. "I'm not planning to try to wrest the CEO position from you. It's yours. I accept that. I would never… I couldn't… I'm not that sort of person."

His gaze lowered once more. "I think I knew that." He raised his eyes, and she saw the determination in them. "But I had to be sure. You understand?"

As much as it chafed at her, she did. "Yes," she admitted. "I understand."

"Then you'll accept my apology?"

She offered the shortest of nods and felt a swell of pleasure to see how his expression lightened in response.

"Good."

She moved from one foot to the other, unexplainably awkward in the face of his improved humor. Something niggled at her, as though she should pursue the matter just a bit further—try to discover why he had unexpectedly entertained the notion. But he suddenly moved one step closer to her, and all rational thought fled as she became aware of his proximity.

He reached out, and she leaned back.

"You have something in your hair," he explained, and she forced herself to remain still as he plucked a wayward leaf from the crown of her head and handed it to her.

"I'm not sure how you manage it, but you look completely at ease in the forest. Like some sort of wood nymph."

Despite herself, she felt a flutter of amusement. "Avery would like that idea—her mother as a maiden of the forest." She twirled the leaf between her fingers, admiring its veins just beginning to brown. For whatever reason, she decided to keep it, perhaps press it into her novel in her room back at the château. She held it carefully in her fingers so as not to lose it and looked up to find Cole eyeing her intently. With the last, lingering light of the forest gilding the line of his jaw, he, too, seemed to be a magical part of the woods. Though she would never say so.

She cleared her throat at the very idea of

such fairy-tale musings. "We should return. The others are likely bursting with curiosity."

He nodded, but his eyes remained on her face. When, several seconds later, he had made no move to go, she forced herself into motion, brushing by him and starting back the way they had come.

It took a considerable amount of willpower to keep from looking over her shoulder to see if he still watched her.

IN THE HOUR before dinner, Emma found herself restless enough that she headed toward the lake behind the estate grounds. She thought the quiet might help clear her head where Cole was concerned. She dangled her legs over the dock and enjoyed the feel of water swirling through her toes. She wondered if Giselle was making any progress with René. Her friend's tenacity was admirable, if somewhat bewildering. To give her credit, at least she went after what she wanted. Emma had never been like that. She'd risen steadily through the ranks at Aquitaine, but that was as much due to Julien's mentorship as to her own ambition. Even in her marriage, her ex-husband had taken the initiative. And there had been no one in her life since their divorce. Which suited her just fine. She was a single mother with a career. She didn't have time to get involved with anyone romantically.

But for the first time in years, an ache of disappointment rose in the wake of this thought. It had never bothered her before, her singleness. Her life was full, in its own way, without the companionship a relationship might bring. But the idea of that sort of connection, someone to share life's everyday joys and sorrows, suddenly stirred a strange yearning inside her.

Pushing aside these thoughts, she stretched her arms behind her and placed her hands on the dock, leaning back and tilting her face to the sky. The weather was perfect; Julien couldn't have chosen a better weekend for their outing. Her wrist still ached slightly, but it, along with her mood, had improved significantly since Cole's apology.

Her eyes slid closed, and she hummed a few snatches of *Frère Jacques* beneath her breath, a lullaby she had often sung to Avery when she was a baby.

"You're a little old for nursery rhymes, aren't you?"

Emma straightened, opening her eyes to see Marc standing over her. He sat down beside her on the dock, uninvited.

"It's just a lullaby I used to sing to my daughter."

"Isn't she a little old for that by now, too? What is she? Ten?"

Emma shook her head at the thought. "Heaven forbid. She's only five. And it still feels like she's growing up too fast."

Marc began tugging off his sneakers. "My sister has two teenage boys. She said it feels like yesterday that they were still in diapers."

This observation made her melancholy. She didn't want to think of Avery becoming a teenager. Marc placed his shoes aside and began to unroll his socks.

"I'm sure it is difficult."

"What is?"

"Being away from her so much." He stuffed the socks into his shoes and lowered his toes into the water with a gasp. "That's cold."

"You get used to it. And then it feels nice." She turned her ankles in circles, sending slight ripples in his direction. He inhaled sharply but lowered his feet in the rest of the way.

They sat in silence for a few moments. She didn't feel uneasy around Marc, but neither did she feel completely relaxed.

"This is a lovely estate," she said by way of conversation.

"It's not bad," Marc admitted. "Though a bit rustic."

"It's not *that* rustic," she said. "And besides, it has its own country charm."

Marc shrugged and kicked his feet a little, splashing water droplets. She eased away from him slightly. She wished Marc hadn't joined her. Even though she didn't mind talking to him, she felt as though her time at the lake had been much more peaceful before he came.

"So, do you feel like you're missing out on a lot of things?" he asked.

"Excuse me?"

"With your daughter," he prompted. "Do you wish you had more time to spend with her?"

She slid him a glance out of the corner of her eye. "Why do you ask?"

"No reason. Only..."

"Only what?"

"That I admire you, Emma. It must be extraordinarily difficult for you—an expat with a child and a career. It takes a special sort of person to juggle your situation."

"Oh. Well. Thanks, Marc. That's really nice of you to say."

"It is the same thing I said to Cole, when he asked about you."

She turned to look at him. "He asked about me?"

Marc nodded. "When we were at the ropes course. He had a few questions."

"What kind of questions?"

"Oh, just different things, how long you've worked for Aquitaine, how many clients you handle. That sort of thing."

"Why would he ask you about that?"

"I believe he was trying to determine your level of commitment."

"My level of… But why?"

Marc wouldn't meet her eyes. "He mentioned something about divided loyalties, in raising a child as well as holding such a high-level position in the company."

"I see. And what did you tell him again?"

"That I admire your dedication to your job, in addition to your commitment to your child. I recognize it requires a certain sacrifice on your part, but that you are extremely competent and a valuable asset to Aquitaine."

She felt a stab of suspicion. "You said all that, huh?"

"It was nothing."

"Oh, it's something." A big old pile of steaming something, in her opinion. She and Marc had never been enemies, but they weren't exactly friends, either. They had certainly never experienced enough camaraderie to warrant such a glowing defense of her. She began to view Cole's question concerning her and Julien's relationship in a new light.

"What else did Cole say?"

"Emma, everyone knows you don't want him here."

"That's not true." And it wasn't, she realized. Sure, she had been disappointed to lose the promotion, but there would be other opportunities.

"It wasn't right, for Julien to let someone else lead us."

She sighed. "Cole is an asset to Aquitaine. This merger will elevate and solidify our position in an increasingly competitive marketplace. We need him."

It felt good to say those words out loud. Better than she might have guessed.

"You've been telling Julien for weeks that it was not a good idea."

"Well, maybe I changed my mind. I think the merger will be valuable for Aquitaine. And I think Cole is exactly what we need," she repeated.

"Hmm," came Marc's response.

"What?"

"We need him? That is not what he says about you. In fact, he approached me about replacing you, when the time comes." His tone was the perfect balance of gossip mixed with apology.

"Replacing me." It wasn't a question, but Marc nodded as though it were.

"*Oui.* I told him I wouldn't think of it."

Though she made an effort to contain it, she couldn't help the curt laugh that escaped.

"It's not going to work, Marc. Cole and I may not have gotten off to the best start, but I hardly think he's planning for my departure anytime soon."

The earnest, sympathetic expression Marc had worn up to this point flattened into disappointment.

"Nice try, buddy, but I'm not going anywhere." She pulled her feet from the water and moved to stand. "And don't you ever try spreading lies about Julien and me like that again, you got it? If you want to take my job, you're going to have to be smarter than that."

And with those words, she grabbed her shoes and left Marc sitting alone by the lake, with his feet still dangling off the dock.

THAT NIGHT, COLE made certain he exchanged several pleasant words with Emma in front of the others when they gathered in the dining room for dinner, and he even went so far as to sit beside her as they took their places at the table. But he continually steered the conversation away from any inquiries regarding their conversation in the forest and was relieved when no one pressed the issue. They all seemed content to go ahead with the weekend as planned instead of dwelling on the unfortunate scene from earlier. All with the exception of Giselle, who occasionally cast suspicious glances his way. But to her credit, she treated him little differently than she had before that afternoon's outing. He wondered if Emma had spoken with her friend in the hour between their return and dinner, when they had all dispersed to either rest or wander the grounds. Cole had used the time to check in at the office and catch up on a few emails, but he didn't know where Emma had gone after they'd returned to the house.

He decided it didn't matter what Emma might have told Giselle. The retreat would go on, and, hopefully, the scene he and Emma had caused would be forgotten soon enough. And as long as Marc didn't cause any more trouble, the team-building could continue.

"They do not own the pharmaceutical sector," Louis was saying. "At least not yet."

"But it is obvious they are shifting their focus in that direction," Aurora argued. "They have been making significant inroads into the financial sector in the last year, and now they are widening their net."

Cole knew he should be more invested in this conversation as his recruiters discussed Aquitaine's largest rival recruiting firm, Léon Professional Services, but he found himself distracted by the knowledge that Emma sat beside him. Each time he turned toward the opposite end of the table, he caught sight of her in his peripheral vision and became engrossed in her mannerisms—the delicate way she forked into her fish, the elegant movement of her wrist when she reached for her wineglass. He had found himself sidetracked by the way she would take a sip and then shift her attention to whomever was speaking. He tried to keep his observations subtle, but he found he could barely pay attention to anything else, even after the meal had finished and the dishes were cleared away. Still, he caught himself sneaking glances at her.

"What about Solene?" Louis asked and looked toward Emma. "You two are still friends, aren't you, Emma? Has she said anything about her company's direction?"

Cole felt Emma stiffen slightly. "We're still friends," she confirmed, "but we…" He noted her hesitation. "We try not to talk shop too much now that she no longer works for Aquitaine."

Emma turned her attention to her lap, where her napkin still rested, and began folding it neatly. He thought about questioning her further on her friend, but before he had a chance, the conversation continued.

"It is a much more competitive market," Marc stated. "And we must be better to accommodate it. It's as simple as that."

Giselle scoffed. "It is hardly simple. We may have to be more creative than you think, Marc."

"Speak for yourself. I still have the technology sector well in hand. My placements are still considered some of the best in that field. If the consumer media market does not feel the same about you, then perhaps I could offer some pointers."

This sharp exchange barely registered with Cole. He had forced his gaze back to the tabletop, wondering how long he could keep from looking in Emma's direction. So he was rather taken aback when he felt her elbow nudging him gently in the side. He straightened and turned to find her facing the others. But clearly she wanted him to join in.

"That is why the merger with Reid Recruiting will be so beneficial to us. We're now in partnership with one of the top-ranked recruitment firms in the United States. It is no longer just us. We're part of something bigger, with increasing opportunities."

When she turned to face him, her eyes begging for his input, he found himself buoyed by her words. She had just declared herself a team player in this, had gone all in for the sake of him and this merger. Even after what he had implied just hours ago. Emma truly was exceptionally dedicated to this company. He nodded and looked around the table at each of his top-level recruiters.

"Emma makes a good point. Not only do you—we," he quickly corrected, "gain an even stronger reputation as a world-class recruitment firm, but our resources have effectively doubled. That gives us the edge we need to stay on top, as long as we keep seeking out and delivering the best possible candidates to our clients."

He watched as they straightened, taking in his words and recognizing that this was their company—he was their leader, and they were going to continue to be at the forefront of their field. He earned a reaction from each of them—Aurora straightened and lifted her head proudly; Louis squared his shoulders; Marc smirked with satisfaction; and even Giselle gave him a nod.

When he finally looked at Emma, he found her smiling in a way that let him know he had said everything she wanted him to say. Unexpectedly, he grinned back and even went so far as to reach his arm around the back of her chair, feeling, perhaps for the first time since he had arrived, that he was truly a part of things and the leader of this company.

He only had a few seconds to enjoy this feeling, however, before René appeared in the dining room's doorway.

"Is everyone ready for the evening's activities?"

Cole felt René seek him out and watched as the other man's scrutiny passed between him and Emma. Cole relinquished the back of Emma's chair and pushed away from the table, offering his assistance to help Emma to her feet. She paused briefly, looking at his proffered hand and then up into his eyes. She placed her fingers into his and allowed him to help her from the table. When he looked back toward René, he found the other man nodding at him in approval. Apparently, René thought he had patched things up rather well.

Cole hoped that he had. Because for some reason, all he wanted at the moment was for Emma to keep a good opinion of him.

CONSIDERING HOW MISERABLE she had been this afternoon, Emma had to admit that she was enjoying herself immensely. Dinner had been delicious, and she felt satisfied with the conversation and how Cole had helped her reinforce the benefits of the Reid and Aquitaine merger. Her own opinion on this score amazed her—though she had been against the joining of the two companies initially, she realized that she had somehow come to view their union as a promising thing.

She was not, however, wholly at ease. Her conversation with Marc earlier in the day and the idea that he had planted implications about her in Cole's head still rattled her slightly. And she had been all too aware at dinner of Cole's eyes on her. He couldn't possibly believe anything Marc had said, especially after they'd set the record straight with their talk. Still, she felt uncertain about the way he watched her and frequently found herself rubbing at her wrist, still remembering the ache from when she had slapped him.

Despite everything, Cole had behaved like a perfect gentleman, even escorting her outside after dinner and onto the patio, where there was a table set up with items for the evening's activities, along with chairs for their group.

René instructed them all to settle into a semicircle while he retrieved a giant inflatable beach ball from the nearby cluster of props. He directed Cole to a separate chair, facing the rest, and placed the beach ball into his hands.

"Julien instructed that this weekend was both an exercise in team-building and an opportunity for your new boss to learn more about each of you while, in turn, you get to know him. So I have taken some of the usual icebreaker activities and adapted them to your situation."

To her right, Emma sensed Giselle straightening as René moved around their circle. She suppressed the urge to roll her eyes at Giselle's obvious interest and managed to catch Cole's gaze in the process. He grinned at her, as though he shared her amusement, and she belatedly realized that, like Giselle, she had straightened at this attention. She quickly turned her focus back to René.

"To begin, we will let Cole get to know

you each a little better. He may toss the ball to each of you in turn, and when he does, I will choose a slip of paper with a question you must answer. Cole will be allowed one follow-up question, if he chooses."

On her left, Emma sensed Aurora fidgeting nervously. She turned her head and found the other woman frowning. "What sort of questions will there be?" Aurora asked.

"The list might include anything from where you grew up to how many children you have or what your favorite color is. You must all remember that your CEO is new to both this country and your firm, so while you already know multiple details about each other, he is still getting to know you. Now, are there any more questions?" René paused before stepping out of the semicircle and moving back to the table. "Excellent! Then we begin. Cole, whenever you're ready, you may toss the ball to anyone you choose."

Somehow, Emma was not at all surprised when the red-and-white striped sphere came flying toward her. She caught it easily and then looked to René for her question.

"Do you have any siblings?"

"No," she answered, forcing her attention back to Cole. "But I do have lots of cousins, back in the States."

"Cole," René spoke, "do you have a follow-up question?"

"Where in the States?" he asked.

"Oregon," she replied. "I was born and raised in a small town there before I left home for college in Seattle."

"A West Coast girl, then," he remarked.

She nodded and sensed he would have questioned her more if René hadn't prompted her to toss the ball back. Cole caught it and shifted in Louis's direction.

Louis answered questions about how he met his wife and how long they'd been married, before Aurora, Giselle and Marc each had a turn. Marc talked at length about several awards he'd won over the years before René pointedly cleared his throat, and Emma found the ball aimed back in her direction. She rested it in her lap as René read her question.

"What is your most profound childhood memory?"

She involuntarily flinched at the question, unprepared to be asked something that would strike such a personal chord. She realized Cole had caught her reaction and saw his head cock with curiosity.

"Um...what do you mean?" she asked, stalling.

"Any childhood memory that has influenced you into adulthood," René elaborated. "Whether a family member, a vacation, an award—" He quickly halted on that score, his gaze skittering to Marc and back as though he feared the other man would once more launch into his list of accomplishments.

She drew a breath. "I see. Well. I suppose it would have to be the death of my father."

Focusing her eyes at a point above Cole's right shoulder, she still couldn't help noticing how his eyebrows furrowed, as though with pity.

"He died when I was fifteen, from surgery complications. It was…unexpected. And difficult." Just how difficult, she didn't want to elaborate on, recalling the deep well of loss over the years as she had witnessed her friends on father/daughter outings and the ache she'd experienced on her wedding day when her dad hadn't been there to walk her down the aisle.

The group had fallen silent following this answer, the sound of nighttime insects creeping into their circle.

"Cole? A follow-up question?" said René.

Cole studied her, as though he had quite a few more things he'd like to ask. She was relieved, however, when he shook his head. She tossed the ball back, and he caught it, holding her gaze with his own for a moment, before shifting toward Aurora. The questions went around the circle several more times. Emma had the chance to talk a bit about Avery and even her arrival in Paris as an au pair, as well as naming her favorite movie—of course, it was *An American in Paris*—and the fact that she hated peas.

With each question, Emma sensed all of them relaxing a bit more, and by the time the game finally wrapped up nearly an hour later, she was pleased to notice that not only were they laughing and teasing with each other, but easily including Cole in the banter, as well.

As René took the beach ball from Cole, he encouraged them all to stand and move around a little since the next activity would be a bit more physical. While they stretched and chatted, Emma noticed René laying out squares of multicolored carpet in a rectangular shape along the patio's pavers. Once he finished, he called them over and asked each member of the group, with the exception of Cole, to stand on the squares. They took their places, with Louis and Aurora side by side at the front, Giselle and Emma behind them and Marc standing on his own at the back.

"For our next activity, you will have the opportunity to learn more about your boss through the popular game Two Truths and a Lie."

"Oh, I know that one," Giselle announced.

"Then you know how it's played. Cole will offer three facts about himself, and you must choose which two are the truth and which one is the lie. But there is a twist to our version."

René stepped around the rectangle, gesturing to the squares of carpet beneath their feet. "For every time you guess wrong as to which statement is the lie, I will remove one of these squares. The object is that your feet must never step off the carpet. As the space shrinks, you will have to find room to accommodate each other. If one of you steps off the carpet and onto the patio, you are out of the game."

Marc scoffed. "Easy enough. How hard can it be to spot a lie?"

The rest of them all looked over their shoulders to eye Marc. No one bothered to contest this statement, but it was obvious to Emma that they all recognized the challenge. Since they knew relatively little about their new boss, anything he said could be less than true.

"Do we all understand the rules of the game?"

Emma shifted, along with the others, to face René and Cole. She found herself eager to find out what facts Cole would share about himself.

She inwardly assured herself that her interest was purely professional, but deep down, she knew it was more than that. After the past couple of weeks working together, she couldn't wait to know a little bit more about her boss.

COLE FACED HIS employees and was grateful that René had warned him about this exercise ahead of time, so he'd had a chance to consider what facts he'd like to share. Though he didn't shy away from talking about himself, neither did he invite it. His history, growing up in the foster care system and the sad story behind his birth, would only invite pity from others, something he never wanted. He usually had a ready anecdote or two to share about himself, but he always found it was good to be prepared in advance when possible.

Since René had given him the heads-up, he had a stack of statements ready to offer for this game.

"One, I had a dog named Rufus growing up."

True, though he wouldn't tell them he'd

been forced to leave the dog behind when he'd been transferred from one foster home to another.

"Two, I've never been married."

Also true, though he had proposed to Ophelia before she summarily rejected him in favor of moving to Hawaii and marrying Dane Montgomery.

"Three, my favorite book is *Fahrenheit 451.*"

Silence descended, and he could see the group working through all three of his declarations. He couldn't help being satisfied to see Marc frowning severely, his brows furrowed as he tried to figure out which of the items named was the lie.

Giselle raised her hand. "The one about the dog. That's not true."

Cole couldn't help grinning at having fooled them. "Wrong."

They uttered a collective gasp of dismay, and he sought out Emma, watching as she shifted to make room for Giselle as René removed one of the squares they stood on.

"Which one was the lie?" Louis asked.

"My favorite book is *To Kill a Mockingbird,*" Cole answered.

"Don't make it easy on us or anything," Marc muttered.

Cole kept his grin up. "Oh, I don't plan to."

"All right, ready for round two?" René asked. No one protested, so Cole continued. "One, my middle name is Bradley. Two, I have the world's rarest blood type, AB negative. Three, I'm allergic to shellfish."

Again, the group frowned in concentration. He saw Emma watching him, as though trying to discern the lie simply by observing him. He found he enjoyed the attention from her and widened his grin for her benefit. She quickly looked away, and he felt a swell of disappointment.

"Blood type," Marc declared. "He is definitely lying about the blood type. The odds are too great."

René looked to him for his response.

"Wrong again. I am, in fact, AB negative, but I'm not allergic to shellfish."

Another groan went up as René took one of the squares, and their space shrank a little more.

The game continued for the next half hour with the squares slowly disappearing. Emma guessed correctly twice, when she claimed he was lying about once having dated a famous movie star and then again about hiking through the Brazilian rain forest. But she struck out when she supposed he had never taken cooking classes. Eventually, the carpeted space for the group to stand on had reduced to around half a dozen squares with the five of them crowded up against one another. Marc became irritable with the close proximity, and Giselle snapped at him more than once.

René suggested Cole whittle his statements down to one truth and one lie to even the odds a bit.

"One, I cried at the movie *Titanic.* Two, I have deuteranopia, which is a form of color blindness."

Though he felt this one was a bit easier, the group was obviously still stumped.

"A man would never admit crying to that movie. You must be color-blind," Louis announced.

Cole shook his head. "I bawled like a baby when the ship went down."

They laughed at this, but as René moved to take away another square, they shifted more tightly together still. Marc grumbled, trying to find room, and began to elbow his way in between Giselle and Emma, who were already standing hip to hip. Cole watched as Emma tried to accommodate him, but Marc was bigger and forcefully pressed in until she was edged out. He called her name just as she stumbled backward. She tried to catch herself going down, reaching out her right hand. Her palm stopped her descent, but then she cried out as her wrist gave way, and she fell onto the patio's stones.

CHAPTER SIX

DESPITE HER EMBARRASSED protests, Cole insisted on looking over Emma's wrist. She was too humiliated to admit to him that it had been sore after she had slapped him earlier in the day. She suspected it was simply strained, but when she had landed on it, the pressure had caused it to give way beneath her. Now it was more tender than painful, but both René and Giselle agreed with Cole's insistence that she put some ice on it.

Though Giselle offered to join her, Cole declared he'd take care of it, and the next thing Emma knew, he was escorting her away from the group and back into the house, toward the château's kitchen. He helped her to the table, even after she reminded him she could walk just fine, and then made quick work of locating a plastic bag, gathering ice from the freezer and insulating it in a dish towel.

"You seem pretty handy in a kitchen," she remarked, desperate to break the silence.

He looked over his shoulder as he finished wrapping the towel around the bag of ice.

"I've been a bachelor for years. I learned to manage the basics." He moved toward the table, carrying the ice pack.

"Then you're not at all like my ex-husband, Brice," she remarked. "He can't even make coffee without someone to measure it for him."

Cole didn't respond. Instead, he reached for her hand, and she immediately jerked away when his fingers, chilly from the ice, touched her skin.

"Oh, that's cold," she murmured.

"Sorry." He rubbed his hands together and reached for her again. The touch of his fingers, warmer this time, still raised goose bumps along her skin.

"That's probably why Brice had a new girlfriend each week for a while after we divorced. He can't bear to be alone. He's one of those types of people." She knew she was babbling, but she needed something to distract her from the way Cole was cradling her wrist, turning it left, then right.

"Does that hurt?" he asked.

"Only a little. It's just a bit sore, that's all."

He picked up the bag of ice and placed it over her wrist, but to her consternation, he kept the fingers of his opposite hand along the underside of her arm, as though checking her pulse. "What do you mean, 'those types of people'?" he said.

"The ones who fear their own company."

"Oh. Those." He paused. "Maybe he missed your company when you weren't around."

Emma made a face.

"Brice might miss having someone to look after him, to feed his ego, but he never missed *me*."

"Then he didn't know what he had when he had it."

She studied her wrist, too shy to look into his eyes after this indirect compliment.

"So, is that why you and Brice divorced? He didn't appreciate you?"

"Oh, no. It was sort of the opposite. He didn't think I could love him enough, when I became a mother."

She looked up in time to see Cole's eyebrows lift in surprise. "What do you mean?"

The table was laid with a saltcellar and pepper mill. Emma picked the latter up with her free hand and began to toy with it. "Brice didn't want a child. He didn't think I could love him in the same way if I was a mother. When I became pregnant with Avery, he suggested we...make other arrangements. But she was our child, and just because he didn't want a baby didn't mean I was prepared to give her up."

She realized her body had turned rigid with this argument, as though she expected Cole to contradict her as Brice had. But she was pleasantly surprised to feel his fingers squeeze lightly in reassurance against her wrist.

"You made the choice you knew was the right one."

She relaxed. "I did. I love Avery. I've never regretted my decision."

She noticed a cloud cross his features before dissipating. "Every child should be loved like that," he murmured.

He sounded almost…wistful. "What about you?" she asked. "Do you hope to have children onc day?"

He was silent for a bit. "You know, I've never really given it much thought."

Somehow, she wasn't quite certain that was the truth. She thought about his answers during their recent game. Nothing he'd shared had been truly personal. She wondered if he'd done that on purpose.

"Hasn't there ever been anyone special in your life? Someone who made you think about having a child with her?"

She felt the ice's chill descend over the underside of her wrist as Cole pulled his fingers away. She worried that she'd offended him somehow until he spoke again.

"There was Ophelia, my ex-girlfriend."

"Lillian Reid's daughter?"

She'd heard the rumors, of course, about how Ophelia Reid had left her position at the company to move to Hawaii and marry the retired ad executive she'd been sent to recruit.

"Yes, we were together for four years. I had even proposed, but she…broke things off when she left the company. That's how I was assigned this position. It was meant to be hers, but when she left, Lillian assigned it to me instead."

"You still don't sound too happy about it."

He met her eyes, and she was caught in the warmth of his gaze. "Oh, I don't know. It might be growing on me a little bit."

She felt a flush building and directed her attention to her arm, rearranging the ice pack even though it didn't really need it.

"Tell me more about Avery," Cole coaxed, and she was grateful for the suggestion.

"Avery is perfect," she announced.

He laughed at this statement. "Well, it's not like you're biased or anything."

She laughed along with him. "Her hair's dark, like mine, but she has her father's eyes."

"That's a shame."

She jerked slightly in surprise. "What do you mean by that?"

"Your eyes are nice," he elaborated. "I just meant she'd be lucky to have that feature from you."

"Oh. I see." She cleared her throat. "Well, she enjoys tea parties, of the make-believe variety."

"Don't all little girls enjoy that?"

Emma gave a slight shrug. "I never did. I was too engrossed in books to be bothered with that sort of thing."

He nodded. "I could see that."

"I loved fairy tales," she added. "But only ones with princes and princesses. And happy endings, of course."

"It sounds like you always had good taste."

She grimaced. "No, that's not true."

"Oh, come on, give yourself some credit."

"If I had good taste, I wouldn't have chosen Brice. He barely gives a thought to Avery. How could I have chosen a man who doesn't care about his own child?" She was surprised she had asked this question of Cole, and yet, his attentive ear and kindness had caused her to let her guard down.

"I don't know, Emma," he answered. "But it's not your fault that he didn't want Avery.

And it doesn't make you a poor judge of character because you didn't see that. You did the right thing by your daughter in the end. That's all that matters."

She suddenly felt exhausted, overwhelmed by thoughts of her ex-husband and the events of the day.

"I think maybe I should call it a night." She removed the ice pack and twisted her wrist around to prove it was all right.

"It's been a long day," Cole agreed.

They fell silent. She could hear faint sounds of conversation and laughter from outside; the others were clearly still having a good time. She preferred being in here, though, she realized, in Cole's company.

"You're sure your wrist is okay?" he asked, taking her hand in his once more and moving it gently from side to side.

"It'll be fine in the morning, I'm sure." Perhaps it was his thoughtfulness and the intimacy they'd established in the past few moments, or maybe it was simply his proximity, but she felt compelled to speak openly with him.

"Cole? Maybe I owe you an apology."

"Why?"

"I didn't want you to come here," she admitted. "I didn't want the merger to happen.

I refused to believe it was a good idea, but now I think maybe I was wrong."

"It's all right, Emma. I know this merger is a tricky thing. There are a lot of mixed feelings about it."

"I know, but…" She drew a breath. "I shouldn't have judged you, before I even knew you. You're obviously very capable, and it's clear you care about the people who work for you, and you're charming and han—" She had to stop talking. Now. "I mean, you're not so bad. For the most part." She tried to keep those last remarks teasing and hoped he wouldn't notice just how much she'd given away. She was relieved when he smiled without drawing attention to her effusiveness.

"Thanks. I appreciate that." He hesitated. "And about earlier today… Again, I apologize."

"It's okay," she assured him, and then, because she had to make sure he understood, she said, "I would never behave like that, you know. For one thing, I have a policy that I never date people I work with. Julien and I are just friends."

"I know."

"He was there for me," Emma continued, "after Brice and I separated and then divorced. He helped me find ways to balance motherhood with my career. I don't know why he did it, but it was kind of him. He still remembers Avery's birthday every year. He always sends some sort of present. She looks forward to it. He's been like a father figure to me, especially since I haven't had a father of my own in a very long time."

He nodded at this, but she sensed something she'd said had bothered him. She waited to see if he would share it with her, but he finally got to his feet. She followed his actions, slightly disappointed at his lack of response.

"Thanks for clarifying things for me."

"Of course," she murmured, still uncertain why she felt he had closed her out.

"Rest well, Emma."

"Thanks. You, too."

He left the kitchen, and after another moment, she did, too.

EMMA AWOKE THE next morning feeling slightly confused by her unfamiliar surroundings. She curled deeper beneath the covers, trying to orient herself until she recalled that this was the weekend of the corporate retreat. Once she remembered that important fact, she stretched out and tugged the sheets off her head, blinking at the sunshine streaming through the window. She replayed the events of the day before, tensing over Cole's question at the ropes course and their conversation in the forest.

Twirling her wrist around beneath the covers, she was happy to feel no pain. Thinking of his apology allowed her to relax once more until she remembered how Cole had turned slightly distant at the end of the evening and how she'd tossed and turned for the better part of an hour as she'd replayed everything she'd said. She couldn't believe how open she'd been with him about Avery and her relationship with Brice. It wasn't like her to share so much, but the warmth of his fingers on her arm and the growing closeness she'd felt toward him after the team-building games had conspired to loosen her tongue.

Perhaps his coolness in bidding her goodnight had been because he found her revelations about her personal life immature and unprofessional. She lay in bed and stared at the ceiling, counting and recounting the wooden beams of the old château. Well, she couldn't take any of it back now. She might as well make the best of it and enjoy the weekend as much as she could.

She kicked off the covers and looked at the bedside clock. It was still early enough that she could probably sneak away unnoticed.

She decided to dodge the others for a while and check out the forest chapel from the estate brochure. According to yesterday's orientation, it was tucked away, just off the bike path, in the woods. Maybe some fresh air and privacy would restore her confidence.

She ducked into the bathroom for a rushed shower and dressed in a black-and-white striped shirt and corduroys. She reached for her cell phone and then stopped, deciding to leave it behind. That way, she wouldn't be tempted to respond if any of the others called to find out where she'd gone. Slinking out of her bedroom, she tiptoed down the stairs. She hesitated at the kitchen entryway, wondering if there was any coffee available, and then decided it wasn't worth the risk. She wasn't ready to face anyone, least of all Cole, just yet.

Heading for the shed where René had said the bicycles were stored, she was relieved to find it unlocked. She pulled out one of the bikes and climbed on, wheeling it toward the front of the house. She circled the drive a few times to practice. It had been several years since she'd been on a bicycle. Not since she'd first moved to France and married Brice, and they'd spent a week at a bed-and-breakfast in Vendée, where there were numerous cycling trails. As soon as she felt comfortable, she pedaled toward the forest path and entered the woods.

It was a beautiful morning, the air clean and crisp and not too warm. Occasional signs assured her she was headed the right way, and it felt good to pump her legs to propel the bicycle forward. After about ten minutes, the path widened to the right, and she could see a lane leading into a clearing. As she steered into the curve, she recognized the stone building featured in the estate literature. She drove to the end of the dirt road and came to a stop, her eyes sweeping over the charming little chapel. The stone steps leading up to the door were traced with lines of moss sprouting from serpentine cracks, but they appeared well intact. She admired the door with its gothic arch and faded stained-glass plates fitted into the top. Above these rested another stained-glass window, its colors darkened with age, and then, toward the roof, a cutout of a cross.

She wheeled her bike next to the stone steps and rested it against the building as she noticed a plaque, describing the chapel's history. Written in French, it explained that the chapel dated from as early as the fourteenth century with restorations performed in the latter half of the nineteenth century. It had seen a rich and varied past that included everything from wars to weddings. She reached out to rest her palm against the cool surface of the stone and marveled, as she always did, at France's long history. She'd always been a bit of a history buff, and while she loved American studies, her homeland's past was much shorter than that of other countries. America had been an unknown and untamed wilderness when this chapel had already stood for centuries.

She dropped her arm and headed up the steps to check out the inside. The chapel's interior was cool and inviting, with terracotta floor tiles, stained glass, several rows of wooden seats and a *prie-dieu*—or prayer desk—at the front of the room. She took a few minutes to wander the circumference of the room, allowing her palms to run along the walls in an attempt to soak up the memories contained therein. Then she stopped before a sculpture just beneath the window at the front. The small statue was aged and worn, its stone pockmarked in several places. But she admired the artist's skill in carving the lines of the supplicant's face as she raised her eyes toward Heaven.

She began to reach out to touch the clasped

hands and then stopped, not wanting to cause any more damage to the crumbly, decaying figure. Taking a step back, she suddenly sensed a person behind her, watching her. Tossing a glance over her shoulder, she saw Cole standing in the chapel's doorway.

Her memories of the previous evening came back in a rush, and she turned to face the front of the room once more. Had Cole sought her out? Or was it simply a coincidence that they'd both found themselves in the chapel this morning?

"I guess I wasn't the only one who decided to take René's suggestion," he said.

She listened as Cole stepped farther into the room, but she didn't move to face him just yet.

"I noticed one of the bikes was gone. I wondered if you were the one who took it."

"I thought it might be peaceful," she responded, still keeping her eyes on the sculpture. She could hear his steps, circling around the room. After a few seconds passed, she turned and watched as he took in the sanctuary in the same way she had, methodically, cataloguing its details. He finally stopped at the *prie-dieu* and rested his eyes on her.

"You weren't planning to join us for breakfast this morning, I take it."

"I just wanted a bit of time to myself."

"Oh." She thought she heard disappointment in his tone, and the thought confused her. Did it mean he would have missed her had she not come for breakfast?

"If that's the case, I'll leave you alone," he offered.

"No," she said as he turned to go. "No, I didn't mean you had to go. I don't mind the company."

She was surprised at herself. It would have been much easier to let Cole leave her in peace for a few minutes more.

"Well, if you're sure." He moved toward her again. "Then I'll stay."

She felt an unexpected happiness at this. He came up beside her, and they stood in quiet reflection for several minutes, studying the sculpture and the stained glass.

"You're right, it's peaceful here," he murmured after a time.

"It is," she agreed, and then she couldn't help but turn toward him. "Listen, Cole, about last night—"

"I wondered when you'd get around to that."

She looked down and fidgeted. "I'm not normally so…candid."

She felt his breath flutter her hair as he

leaned close. "I'm glad you were. It gave me the chance to get to know you a little better."

"I'm not sure I shared anything you needed to know."

"Oh, I wouldn't be too sure about that."

"Meaning?"

"Meaning I learned quite a bit about you last night."

Her curiosity got the better of her. "Like what?"

He moved forward, strolling around the front of the tiny prayer desk, his eyes roving over the ceiling. "I learned how much you love your daughter."

"I could have told you that."

"You could have," he agreed, "but it wouldn't have been the same as getting the big picture, like you gave me when you weren't as worried about what I was thinking."

She crossed her arms. "Okay, fair enough. What else?"

"I learned why Julien means so much to you."

"I thought we covered that earlier in the day."

He shook his head. "Not the same."

She sighed. "Okay, then."

He stopped moving and turned to look

at her. "And I learned you're a hopeless romantic."

She scoffed. "Hardly."

"You disagree?"

"I'm not a romantic. I'm a working mother, juggling a daughter and my career. I am the picture of practicality."

"You wish."

She gasped in indignation, though his accusation stirred something deep inside her. "Exactly what did I say that led you to this stunning revelation?"

"Nothing. And everything."

"Do you enjoy being vague? Because I can tell you, it's not an attractive quality."

"Well, we can always talk about how you called me handsome."

"I didn't—"

"Oh, but you were going to."

So, he had noticed. Of course he had, it wasn't something he was likely to have missed. "I'm sorry if I spoke inappropriately."

"You have nothing to apologize for. You were a perfect lady." He rested a hand above his heart. "My virtue is intact."

Her eyes narrowed. "You're getting off topic."

"Right." He dropped his arm back to his side. "Where were we again?"

"Explaining how you came to the conclusion that I'm a romantic."

"Well, there are the obvious signs."

She waited for him to elaborate.

"You left behind everything that was familiar to move to a foreign country."

"So did you," she accused.

"I didn't come here for love. You moved to Paris for Brice, am I correct?"

She remained silent.

"That's strike one. And when you divorced, you stayed in a city that you obviously love—though I can't imagine what makes it so special—even when there was nothing left for you here. Stop me anytime if I'm getting this wrong."

She pursed her lips. He wasn't wrong, and though she wouldn't admit it, she wanted to hear what else he had to say.

"Strike two. You fell in love with Paris, like any woman infatuated with the idea of the City of Love."

"It is so much more than that," she fired back at him. "You haven't spent enough time in the city to understand."

"I'm not finished."

She sighed. "Go on, then. I can't wait to hear what my next strike is."

He took several steps closer so that he stood mere inches away. "You won't date anyone you work with."

His proximity annoyed her, and she took a step back. "I've always had a policy of not getting involved with anyone at the office."

"Because you're afraid you won't be able to control it. You put that rule in place to keep yourself safe from...yourself."

"You don't—" She stopped. She couldn't very well say he didn't know her. After her confessions the night before, he knew more about her than she would have liked. "—know what you're talking about." She fixed her error.

"Maybe not," he agreed. He moved toward the door.

"Where are you going?"

"It's too beautiful a day to be inside. Are you coming?"

She couldn't see any reason not to, so she followed him back outside. They wandered, by unspoken consent, around the side of the chapel, and caught sight of a gated cemetery. They went to stand by the wrought-iron fence and looked over the tombstones.

"Listen, Emma. We didn't get off to such a great start."

"No," she agreed. "We didn't."

He rolled up the sleeves of the white hoodie he wore, and she admired the cords of muscle in his forearm. He must find time to go to the gym in between his hours at the office.

"I don't want you to feel bad about everything you told me last night. I'm not teasing you when I say you're a romantic. I still think you are," he hastened to add, "but that's not a bad thing. In fact, maybe you can help me figure out exactly what it is about Paris that's so special."

She took the opportunity this opening afforded to ask what she'd been wondering for a while now. "Why do you dislike it so much? You've never been to France before, have you?"

"No," he admitted.

"Then, what? Everyone falls in love with Paris."

He arched an eyebrow at her. "Everyone? I think your inner romantic is showing."

She couldn't help laughing at this. "Okay, so maybe I'm a little more enamored than most, but I still don't see what you've got against the place."

He leaned down, resting his bare forearms

on the fence. "It's not the city itself, really. It's what it represents."

She leaned against the iron barrier herself, watching him. "And what's that?"

He straightened back up. "It's just difficult, taking this position after it was meant to be Ophelia's and after she…rejected me. But I'll make you a deal. I'll try to see Paris through your eyes if you keep helping me through this transition."

She rested her arms against the rail beside him. "You mean you'll try to see things like a romantic?"

He nudged her. "I wouldn't push it."

She nudged him back. "But that's what you like about me—my pushiness."

He straightened. "Now you're just getting cocky."

She straightened, too. "Okay, then. It's a deal," she agreed.

They stared at each other. "Do you want to shake on it?" he asked with a smirk.

She rolled her eyes. "I trust you." They turned at the same time, moving away from the cemetery and back toward the front of the chapel. They climbed onto the bikes and pedaled back toward the house in companionable silence. Emma's spirits lifted as the trees flew by. She realized this was the lightest she had felt in months, ever since she'd found out her promotion was gone, and the merger was happening. Things hadn't turned out so bad after all, she realized. Maybe she had just assumed the worst. That wasn't a very romantic trait, was it?

She nearly laughed aloud as she stole a glance at Cole. A romantic. She'd never really wanted to admit she was one, but maybe Cole was right. She had come to this country looking for an adventure and gotten swept into romance instead. And then, when it had ended, she hadn't wanted to leave. Perhaps, in the spirit of romance, she was still waiting for Paris to fulfill some sort of naive fantasy.

She shrugged off this thought as they emerged from the forest path and coasted toward the front drive. She noticed Giselle outside, seemingly waiting for them. A small knot formed in her stomach, and she skidded her bike to a halt, dismounting and letting it drop to the ground.

The concern etched in Giselle's face drew her forward, desperation suddenly propelling her along.

"Is it Avery? Is she okay?"

"It's not Avery," Giselle answered as Emma became aware of Cole coming to stand beside her.

"Brice couldn't reach you on your cell so he called me—Jacqueline had a heart attack."

Emma gasped in dismay.

"Who's Jacqueline?" Cole asked.

"My former mother-in-law," she quickly answered. "She was watching Avery this weekend."

"As soon as she knew what was happening, she called Brice. He called 112—"

"That's France's version of 911," Emma distractedly explained to Cole.

"—and then Solene to ask her to watch Avery," Giselle finished.

Emma felt a complicated mixture of relief and regret, happy that Avery was safe and being taken care of but pained at the same time. Jacqueline had always been so kind to her, even following the divorce. She adored her granddaughter, and her love for the child made up for a lot of Brice's shortcomings in that area.

"Is Jacqueline going to be okay?"

"I don't know."

Emma realized that her friend's eyes shifted to Cole and then back to her. She suddenly became aware of Cole's hand in the small of her back, holding her steady. She drew strength from it.

Giselle paused before delivering the next blow. “Brice asked if you would come to the hospital, as soon as you can.”

CHAPTER SEVEN

EMMA MET BRICE in the waiting room of the Paris hospital. His face was haggard, the handsome lines edged with wear. She couldn't remember ever seeing him look like that, like something that had been wrung dry. As soon as he saw her, he stood and moved in her direction. And then, to her utter surprise, he drew her into a hug. Brice hadn't touched her since the day their divorce had gone through. But now, he clung to her as though she might try to turn around and escape.

"Hey," she soothed, trying to ease his grip slightly. "It's not that bad, is it?"

He pulled back, and she noticed his eyes were red-rimmed and swollen. Had he been crying?

"Bad enough," he replied. "The doctors say it is congestive heart failure brought on by coronary artery disease."

She felt her jaw sag. "What? But Jacqueline always seems so…so…vibrant when I'm around her."

He sniffed. "I guess she puts on a good act."

Still surprised by this news, Emma wandered toward the rows of seats in the waiting area and sank into one. She'd taken a cab from the train station and hauled her overnight bag with her through the hospital, but now she left it in the entryway as she took a seat. It was hard to believe that just a few hours ago, she'd been standing in the little country chapel with Cole, debating her romantic streak. There was a marked difference from the still serenity of that sanctuary and the muted, sterile environment surrounding her now.

Brice picked up her bag and brought it to her, placing it on the floor before settling down into the seat next to hers. She turned to face him, once again noting how drained he looked.

"Where's Christine?"

He ran a hand over his face, the sound of stubble rasping against his palm. "At the apartment," he answered. "She doesn't like hospitals."

"Well, I can't say I'm a fan myself," she replied and then paused, looking around. “Can I see her?”

“Christine?” He shook his head in confusion, and she felt a moment’s pity for him. “Oh, of course, you mean *Maman*. Not just now, she’s resting.”

She reached out to squeeze his hand in reassurance. “It’s okay. You look exhausted. Maybe you should go home and get some rest yourself.”

It surprised her when he turned his hand around, his palm meeting hers, to twine her fingers into his. “Not yet. I want to wait until she’s awake.”

“All right. Then, is there anything I can get you? Have you eaten?”

A ghost of a smile danced across his lips. “This is how you have always been, looking after me. Even when I do not deserve it.”

“Sometimes, we all need to be looked after a little. Even when we don’t deserve it,” she couldn’t resist tacking on.

The hint of a grin remained. “Maybe.”

She disentangled her hand from his. “So, what do you say? Coffee? Maybe a croissant?”

He sank lower into the seat, resting his neck along its back. She eyed him pitifully as she stood. His light brown hair was limp and disheveled, his dusky blue eyes even darker with worry. The lines that would one day age him were significantly pronounced.

"Yes," he agreed. "Perhaps coffee will help."

"Of course it will," she encouraged. "I'll be right back. Watch my bag."

She moved toward the doorway until he called her back.

"Did you want something else?"

He remained seated but straightened, reaching for her hand. He drew it toward his lips and pressed a kiss onto her fingers. She eased out of the touch as soon as she could, uncomfortable with such intimacies after so many years without any affection from him.

"Thank you for coming. I wasn't..." He trailed off. "I wasn't sure you would."

She touched his shoulder briefly, thinking of all the times he had promised to visit Avery and then failed to show up. But she wouldn't try to punish him for that. Not now, when he so clearly needed a friend. "You know me better than that, Brice."

He nodded and then leaned forward to rest his face in his hands. She squeezed his shoulder one last time before she left to find them both some coffee for the hours ahead.

LILLIAN REID SAT in her loft's living room in the predawn Sunday morning light and waited for her cell phone to vibrate. She had slept poorly the night before but felt wide awake even after such little rest. For the first time in years, she was filled with an emotion she could barely remember feeling—doubt. For someone as successful as her, it was not a pleasant or familiar experience, but she could not seem to shake it. And so she waited, somewhat ashamed of her weakness, for the call she knew would be coming.

At 5:59 a.m., she tensed, fingers curled around the phone, and as the display flipped to 6:00 a.m., she felt it begin to vibrate in her palm. She relaxed at the sight of the name—Julien Arnaud—but waited several seconds more before answering.

"Allô," she greeted him when she finally picked up. Something warm and comforting settled into her spirit when he responded.

"Allô, mon ange."

She experienced a tiny thrill each time he addressed her as his angel, though she didn't say so. "You are right on time, as usual."

"And it is not too early, I trust?"

It had been a standard exchange between them ever since Julien had started these calls following his visit to New York six weeks ago, to finalize the merger agreement of their two companies. The first time he'd called, it had taken her by surprise. He had apologized for the premature hour in her time zone, and she had assured him she was a very early riser. He had thanked her for her helpfulness during his time in New York, expressed his happiness at the merger, wished her a wonderful weekend and finished the conversation in less than ten minutes. She had hung up feeling gratified at her decision to join their firms and then moved forward with her day.

But then one week later, the following Sunday, her phone had vibrated again at exactly 6:00 a.m. Once more, it was Julien, this time with several details of clarification concerning their contract. When they had finalized a few points, he lingered on the phone, asking after her week and discussing Cole's upcoming move to Paris, admitting how much he liked the younger man and how suited he seemed to the job. They'd ended the call thirty minutes later, and this time, the conversation stayed with Lillian throughout the rest of her day before she returned to work on Monday and moved on to other business.

The third week, she had found herself awake even earlier than usual and hovering near her phone out of curiosity. At six, she'd reached for the phone as it started to vibrate and answered his call. They talked for over an hour, and Lillian found herself replaying the conversation in her head for the entire week.

By now, the sixth of these calls, she was slightly alarmed to find herself looking forward to them, anticipating them all weekend long. She should have known better than to allow them to continue with such regularity, but she had always had a weakness for men with French accents. Or at least, one particular man with a French accent—her husband, Marcel, had passed when their daughter, Ophelia, was only seven years old. Now Lillian was embarrassed to admit that she felt the same giddy anticipation for Julien's calls as she'd experienced when waiting for Marcel to return home from work all those years ago. She found it scarcely believable that she could still experience such reactions at her age.

And yet, every Sunday morning, she lingered by her phone, waiting for his call.

"How has your week been, *chérie?*"

She hesitated, debating how much she wanted to share with him. She was desperate to talk to someone, however, and Julien had proved himself a wonderful listener.

"I spoke with my daughter last night."

"Ophelia? She called from Hawaii?"

"She did. I don't hear from her as often as I'd like, so it was a pleasant surprise."

"And how is she doing since you last spoke? The coffee venture is still a success?"

"More so every day, apparently. I was uncertain about her marrying Dane Montgomery, but she seems…quite happy. And…" She swallowed.

"And?" Julien prompted.

She sighed. "And she had some news."

"Good news?"

"Well…yes, I suppose."

"You do not sound so certain."

Lillian could not explain her emotions and would not have even tried to with anyone but this man, who seemed to know her better than she knew herself.

"She said she and Dane are trying for a child."

Most people would have exclaimed happily at this, offering the standard congratulations. But as she had predicted, Julien knew better than to make such statements.

"You are not happy about such a thing?"

She exhaled slowly. "Of course I am. My daughter will be having a baby at some point in the near future."

"And you will be a grandmother."

"Yes."

Silence lingered between them.

"And Ophelia is happy?"

"Ridiculously so. I think she'll be a wonderful mother when the time comes."

"But I sense you are sad."

"Not sad, only—" how to explain what she could not understand herself? "—uncertain, perhaps."

"About what?"

"About the future. About my own future. I had everything mapped out quite neatly a year ago. My eventual retirement. Ophelia marrying Cole and the two of them taking over Reid Recruiting, running things from Paris. I would eventually join them there and live out my days in a lovely little apartment by the Seine."

"A nice daydream."

"Yes," she concurred. "A perfect little fantasy."

He did not respond immediately, so she continued. "Things have not turned out quite the way I expected."

"You miss Ophelia," he finally said.

"I do, but her life is in another place now. She's going to become a mother, and she'll have her own family there, in Hawaii, with

Dane. And I am here, in New York, wondering what I have worked for all my life. My daughter will not be taking over the business when I retire. I will have a grandchild raised on surf and sand rather than the city. What did I do with my life for the last twenty-six years? What do I have to show for it?"

"A successful international company and a daughter who was brave enough to make her own choices, as her mother did before her."

The ache in her chest eased. She knew he would have the words to comfort her. It amazed and frightened her that she knew this.

"You are a good friend, Julien," she murmured.

There was a long silence, and she felt some of her unease returning.

"Ah, *chérie.* Perhaps not as good a friend as you would like."

"What do you mean?"

"I must share some unpleasant realizations with you."

Lillian stood. She had never been one to receive bad news sitting down. "Go on."

"I fear we have a leak within the company here."

"A leak? Why?"

"On Friday, before leaving the office, I

learned that two of our candidates on the cusp of placements with our clients had unexpectedly signed with different companies. They were placed by a recruiter at a rival firm here in Paris. It was disappointing, but these things happen, as you know."

"Yes, it can be a highly competitive field at times."

"Very much so, *oui.* However, last evening, I learned of two more candidates who signed contracts elsewhere. I am still trying to learn the recruiter on the last placement, but the other was the same recruiter who stole away our first two candidates. Three by the same recruiter, and I suspect the fourth, as well."

Though she had stood to receive the news, Lillian now sank back onto the sofa. "Four lost placements?" It was a significant blow, especially on the heels of the merger. "Are we being targeted in some way?"

"I do not know. But I do believe there is a leak somewhere in the office."

"Could it be one of the recruiters?" It would make no sense. The recruiters would lose their commission by selling off candidate profiles to another firm. They only stood to gain money by the recruitments they actually placed, earning a percentage of the first year's salary when a candidate was hired.

Unless they were receiving some sort of kickback from the other company. But why bother with such underhanded tactics when they could simply place the candidate themselves? Unless it was, as she'd suggested, some sort of specific attack against the Reid/Aquitaine name.

"*Non,* I do not believe it is a recruiter here in the office."

"And Cole? What does he say about this?"

"I have not told him yet."

"Why ever not? He's the CEO—he should know this is happening. Where is he?"

"I sent him and the top recruiters on a company retreat for the weekend. I thought it would help bond them as a team and allow them to embrace Cole as their new leader."

Though she felt inclined to protest at this gesture, she had to admit she was strangely touched by it. Julien was committed to the success of this merger, including making sure that Cole was accepted at the Paris branch.

"Can you get in touch with him, let him know what's happened?"

"I can," Julien said, "but I thought I would let them see the weekend through. They can do nothing about it until tomorrow anyway. Why ruin their time together?"

Lillian suppressed a sigh. She should

know, after her years in Paris, how differently the French operated. They tended to manage things at a less frantic pace than her manic American sensibilities could accept.

"Very well," she acquiesced, "but apprise Cole of the situation as soon as he returns, so he can get to the bottom of it. The faster we discover who leaked our candidate files, the sooner we can prevent such a thing from happening again."

"Of course, *chérie*. We will have the matter in hand as soon as possible."

She allowed herself to settle more comfortably into the couch in order to enjoy the rest of their conversation. They chatted for a while about this and that, including when she might make her next visit to Hawaii to see Ophelia and how often she might fly there should Ophelia become pregnant. They touched on topics ranging from their company to the latest headlines, and before Lillian knew it, they had spoken for nearly an hour and a half. With some regret, she urged the conversation to an end.

Before hanging up, she thanked Julien, as she always did, for the call.

"It is my pleasure, dear Lillian. Talking with you is the highlight of my week."

To her disbelief, she felt a happy warmth

bubble inside her that made her feel a good thirty years younger than she really was.

"I—" She hesitated. "I feel the same," she admitted.

She hung up the phone and then lingered in the glow of the rising sun, feeling warmed, for the first time in a long time, from the inside out.

EMMA HELPED AVERY over the bottom step of the bus's doorway and handed over her *Navigo Découverte* for the fare, before finding them a seat near the front of the vehicle. Avery curled into her side as the other passengers filed onto the bus.

The day had been long, and she suspected Avery might not stay awake for the ride to their apartment, but to her surprise, her daughter straightened before the doors even closed and looked up into her face.

"Maman?"

"English," Emma gently reminded.

"Oh, right. Mom?"

She smiled, brushing her daughter's long, dark hair out of her eyes. "What is it?"

"Is *Grand-mère*—Grandma," she quickly corrected, "going to die?"

Emma felt a weight of grief settle itself in the pit of her stomach. They had spent the better part of their Sunday afternoon in the hospital by Jacqueline's bedside. Her former mother-in-law looked little better today than she had the day before, but Emma continued to hope for a full recovery. "I hope not, sweetheart. The doctors are doing their best to make her well."

"I know, but what if they can't fix her?"

For a moment, Emma regretted bringing Avery with her to the hospital. But when she'd come home late the evening before, exhausted after her return from the retreat and her time with Brice, she had been accosted by her daughter. Avery hadn't much appreciated being left with Solene for the day when she knew something was seriously wrong with her grandmother.

She looked into Avery's wide cobalt eyes, their depths searching hers for reassurance. "Don't worry yourself, sweetheart. Your grandmother is in the best possible hands, okay? And you know, I think seeing you made her feel a lot better already."

Avery still appeared doubtful. "She looked really sick." Her voice had fallen to a hush, as if she was afraid to speak these words aloud.

"She is really sick," Emma agreed. "But we're going to send lots of love her way and visit her regularly until she's out of the hospital so that she knows how much we care. And that is some of the best medicine she can have."

Emma leaned down to press a kiss to her daughter's forehead. "She loves you, you know. And so do I."

"I know." Avery relaxed a little, resting into Emma's side once more.

Emma was just beginning to feel relieved that the questions had ended when Avery came up with the most difficult question of all.

"And my daddy? Does he love me?"

Brice hadn't been at the hospital when Emma brought Avery by to visit her grandmother. She wasn't sure if he was avoiding her after the vulnerability he'd exhibited yesterday, or Avery, since he never seemed quite comfortable around her. Or maybe he had simply decided to go home and get some rest. Jacqueline had said he'd been with her that morning but had finally left shortly after the lunch hour.

Emma swept her palm over her daughter's forehead, across the crown of her head and down her back, scratching in reassurance. "You are a very loved little girl, Avery Marie. Trust me on this."

It wasn't enough. Emma felt a flicker of

dismay as Avery persisted. "But what about Daddy? Does he love me?"

"Of course he does," Emma replied, though in truth, she didn't know how Brice felt about their daughter. He had shown only minimal interest in the years since their divorce, making an appearance for the occasional birthday or outing. He had been unprepared for fatherhood. Or maybe just indifferent about it. But Emma was determined that Avery would have every reassurance she could offer her on that score.

The bus had moved forward by this point, carrying them in the direction of their neighborhood. She tugged Avery closer.

"You've had a long weekend, sweetheart. Why don't you just rest against me until we're home?"

She feared Avery might resist and press the subject, but weariness won out as the child sagged against her. Emma stroked her back throughout the ride and tried not to think on what she'd say when her daughter brought up the subject again.

COLE SAT ON the stoop of the apartment building and checked his watch for the third time. It was getting late, and he was beginning to think coming here had been a bad idea. He hadn't counted on Emma not being in. And her au pair, understandably, didn't feel comfortable inviting a strange man into her employer's home. So he had politely volunteered to wait outside for Emma's return.

The longer the minutes dragged on, however, the more he wondered what could be keeping her. As soon as the group had arrived back from the retreat, he had called to check in with Julien and been told about the leaked candidate files. To make the situation worse, Julien had recently learned the recruiter's name for the fourth stolen candidate. The person responsible for all four lost placements was Solene Thierry, a disgruntled former employee of Aquitaine but also one of Emma's best friends. Julien was particularly unhappy about Solene's involvement. Whatever bad blood was between them, it ran deep. The severity of the situation was easily apparent to Cole. A few lost candidates were one thing, but being targeted by another firm could be a declaration of corporate war. It would threaten the success of the merger and possibly his credibility as the new director of Aquitaine. At the minimum, it was a headache that needed to be dealt with immediately. And while he easily could have brought Emma up to speed in the morning at the office, he felt a restless desire to see her straightaway.

Part of this was simply because he wondered how her ex-mother-in-law was doing, and, if he was honest with himself, he wanted to know how things had gone with Brice. He knew curiosity would divide his focus for the rest of the night, so he'd convinced himself he might as well head to her place. After all, he decided it would be good to get out in the city, even the more residential *arrondissements,* on his own. So he'd flagged a cab, still not familiar enough with the bus system to attempt it, and used his phone's contact lists to track down Emma's home address.

His taxi driver was eager to put his English to good use, and he gave Cole a broad background on the Batignolles village of the seventeenth *arrondissement,* where Emma lived. The seventeenth featured many upscale residences, but Batignolles was the northeastern bohemian district, known for its hipster vibe. Though a residential area, the seventeenth still offered much to enjoy, his driver assured him, including the Haussmanian architecture and the knowledge that many of the world's most famous painters, from Monet to Degas, had started the Impressionist movement here in the late nineteenth century.

Though Cole didn't say so, these facts concerned him little in comparison to his desire to see Emma. But he was grateful for his driver's assistance when he pulled up to the curb of Emma's apartment building and explained how to find his way from there.

The au pair had not been quite as helpful, though she'd done a lot of blushing and fidgeting when he'd spoken to her. When she'd hesitated to let him into the apartment, he'd spent some time wandering the neighborhood, taking note of the architectural styles the cab driver had mentioned and trying to imagine Emma walking these streets. He made the effort to see the village through her eyes, wanting to know exactly what it was about this place that she found so special. It struck him that he had never cared much before, when Ophelia would speak of the city. Maybe his ex-girlfriend had spoken so much about Paris that it had failed to hold any significance for him after a while. But now, knowing that Emma had chosen to stay here even after her divorce, he had to confess to a certain interest about what sort of allure it held.

After he had wandered for a while, he'd circled back to her apartment building and settled himself on the steps to await her return. He thought the au pair might have looked out a window to check on him, or at least that's what he told himself when he felt as though he were being watched. But the time slid by, and he debated heading off to hail another cab until he realized that the au pair would surely tell Emma he had come. She had enough on her hands at the moment without worrying about the reason for his visit. He'd come this far, he might as well see things through.

He was just considering ringing for the au pair again and asking where the bus stop was so he could meet Emma when she arrived, when he saw her in the distance, struggling to balance a large bundle in her arms that he realized must be her daughter. He stood and hurried in her direction, noting that the girl she carried had obviously fallen asleep.

"Hey, looks like you could use some help." Without waiting for her to accept, he easily lifted the child and tucked her into his arms.

"Whew, she's heavy, isn't she?" He hoisted the girl up, and her head instantly found its way to his shoulder, her face pressing into his neck. She was petite for a five-year-old, and her tiny form fit snugly against him. The warm breath of her exhaustion brushed his skin, and he felt a stirring of protectiveness. "She's had a long day, I take it."

He turned his attention back to Emma to find her staring, slack-jawed and wide-eyed, at him.

"Oh." He realized how strange it must be to have her come home and find him waiting for her. "Sorry."

She blinked, coming to life. "Sorry? What for?"

"For showing up here unannounced."

Before she could respond to this, the girl in his arms let out a deep sigh of contentment, and Emma suddenly seemed to realize he had taken on her burden.

"You don't have to carry her. I can do it."

"Don't worry about it. I can carry her up. You look exhausted."

And she did, with dark smudges beneath her eyes highlighting how pale the rest of her face was.

"Why don't I take her to your apartment for you? Your au pair wouldn't let me in because she had never met me before."

"I'm sorry," she automatically apologized. "Melanie's been away all weekend and just got back this afternoon. I called to tell her what's been going on, but she's probably a little overwhelmed by it all."

"She's a smart girl. I wouldn't want someone watching my kid if they just let anyone and everyone into my home."

Emma still appeared bewildered as he began walking down the street toward her building, waiting a beat before she followed. She took a side entrance—a gated entryway—before leading him through a courtyard and another door into the building.

"There are no elevators," she apologized. "Many older buildings in France don't have them. If you want me to carry her—"

"I'm good. Just lead the way." He followed Emma up the stairs until they reached her floor, and down a hall to her apartment. She used her key to let them inside and called softly for Melanie, the au pair.

The girl appeared, her eyes wide as she took in Cole holding Avery in his arms.

"It's okay," Emma reassured her. "This is my boss, Cole."

"Oh, I'm so sorry," Melanie apologized, her cheeks darkening to a dusky pink. "I made him wait outside for you. He's been out there for over an hour."

Emma looked at him in surprise and then turned back to Melanie. "It's all right. You didn't know who he was."

"You did the right thing," Cole affirmed.

"It shows you're a smart au pair, not letting strangers into the house."

This praise from him only caused Melanie's cheeks to darken further. The conversation, or perhaps the sense of familiarity, caused Avery to stir, and she lifted her head to look into Cole's face.

"Bonjour," she greeted him.

"Avery, this is Cole. He speaks English," Emma told her.

"Hello," Avery said.

"Hey, there," Cole replied, somewhat amazed that the child wasn't more disconcerted to find herself in a stranger's arms.

"I was taking a nap," she informed him and then cocked her head, eyeing him suspiciously. "Are you a prince?"

He suppressed the urge to laugh. "Not quite, but you know, I was under the impression that you might just be a sleeping princess."

"The prince always appears after the princess wakes up from a long sleep," she informed him.

"Always, huh?"

She nodded, her little face serious. Her features were like a miniature version of Emma's, from the nose that pointed upward slightly at the end to the lips with the smallest of indents in their center. Only her eyes differed, their dusky blue a far deeper shade than Emma's dove-gray gaze.

"I think your mom is going to have to be careful when you're a little older. I suspect there will be a lot of princes hanging around, waiting for you to wake up."

Whether she understood what this meant or not, her tiny lips unfurled into a smile of pleasure. "You're handsome," she informed him, and he heard Emma make a choked sound. He didn't look her way.

"That's what your mom says."

"Okay, then." Emma stepped in and reached for her daughter. "I think maybe Melanie should make you some dinner and then get you tucked into bed."

"But I want to stay and talk," she protested as Emma pulled her from Cole's arms and stood her on the floor. She turned away from her mother and looked at Cole. "Are you going to stay for dinner?"

Emma jumped into the conversation. "You're more than welcome to. I'm not sure what all we have in the apartment..."

"No, it's all right. That's not why I came to see you."

Her expression creased in concern. "Is everything all right?"

He decided not to answer that question. Instead, he looked to Avery, and Melanie, taking the hint, stepped into the conversation.

"Come on, Avery, how about I make you a grilled cheese?"

The little girl resisted at first and ran toward him. She reached his side and grabbed his fingers, her little palm soft and insistent as she tugged him down. Bending at the waist, he leaned toward her so she could stand on her tiptoes and reach up to drop a kiss on his cheek.

Then, with a shy grin, she whirled away and out of the room. Cole straightened, inwardly melting at the little girl's charming actions.

Emma was staring at him when he turned his attention to her once more. He tried to keep his voice even as he spoke.

"We need to talk."

CHAPTER EIGHT

EMMA PINCHED THE bridge of her nose and tried to find her way through the cloud of exhaustion that had settled over her. She had suggested they take a walk for the sake of privacy. Leaving Melanie to tend to Avery, they had left the apartment and headed back downstairs. Emma led the way past the courtyard and back onto the sidewalk, moving in the direction of the Square des Batignolles, the large park and garden that covered nearly four acres of the seventeenth *arrondissement.* She suddenly craved its serene fountains and statues, along with its variety of trees, shrubs and flowers laid out in an English-garden style. It was one of her favorite places in all of Paris and part of the reason she had chosen to move to Batignolles following her divorce. She wanted Avery and her to have access to it every day.

Cole said nothing as they walked, and she was glad for the silence. After her visit to the hospital, the serenity of the château's chapel and her time at the corporate retreat seemed as though it had happened months ago.

They reached the entrance to the square, and she crossed over the threshold with Cole at her side. She heard him breathe in deeply, a sound filled with admiration. She stole a glimpse at his face and saw him looking toward the lake, where black swans floated around ornate sculptures. Then his gaze moved to the walkways edged with trees and lush vegetation, and then he watched a family playing a game of *pétanque,* where players tried to toss metal balls as close as possible to a wooden one in order to score points and win the game.

"Even you have to admit how amazing this is." She turned away from him and breathed in the park's air, enjoying the late summer breeze as it ruffled her hair.

"It is pretty impressive," he conceded.

"There's even a grotto and a waterfall."

He eyed her in disbelief, and she held a hand up as though taking an oath.

"Cross my heart and hope to die."

He began walking along the path, and she followed. "No need to do that, Aquitaine, I believe you. But remember, I'm from New York. I think Central Park is rather amazing itself."

She wasn't interested in debating the features of city parks, so she cleared her throat and came back to the point.

"So, what's so important that you had to come all the way to my apartment to tell me?"

"It wasn't that far," he reminded. "I haven't had a chance to go apartment hunting yet, and my hotel's just across the Seine in La Défense."

She knew that, but she still found it curious that he had taken the time to scout out where she lived.

"Still, what brings you here? You said we needed to talk," she reminded him. "Did something happen on the retreat, after I left?"

"No, it went pretty well," he assured her. "I think Giselle even managed to leave with René's personal cell phone number."

She laughed. "If anyone was going to succeed on that score, it's Giselle."

"She's tenacious. I think she simply wore him down."

"Maybe that's what makes her a good recruiter—she never gives up."

"Maybe," Cole said, and she sensed him growing more serious. "How's your ex-mother-in-law?"

She wondered if he was stalling. "She's

holding her own. She's been diagnosed with congestive heart failure. I took Avery to see her. I think it helped lift her spirits. They're hoping to release her in another few days."

"And…Brice?"

"Brice?"

"How's he doing with everything that's happened?"

She found it odd that he would ask about her ex-husband. "I think it rattled him a bit. It's always difficult to face your parents' mortality."

"Hmm."

"When my mom died a few years ago, I was a mess. It was after the divorce, and Avery was just one year old at the time. I flew back to the States by myself. My aunts had arranged the funeral. All I had to do was show up. It felt wrong, as though I should be doing something, even if it was just taking care of the final details of her life. I guess that's the difficult part—wanting to do something, even when there's nothing you can do. I mean, they take care of you your entire life, and when the end comes, you want to do the same—to kiss away the pain and wash away the hurt. But life doesn't work like that."

He said nothing, his silence stretching out unnaturally, and she suddenly felt foolish for sharing so much about herself. Hadn't he already learned enough about her this weekend? More than he'd bargained for, that was certain.

"So, what's up? You didn't come out here just to check up on me."

He seemed to come out of a deep reverie. "I wanted to see where you lived. I thought it might give me more insight into why you love this place so much."

She stopped walking and grabbed his arm to make him halt, as well. "That's hardly why you came. You said we needed to talk."

He sighed and then gestured to a nearby bench. They moved toward it and sat down together. When he turned to face her, she was struck again by how handsome he was, even wearing such a sober countenance.

"I spoke with Julien when we got back from the retreat."

"Oh?" She felt a rising swell of apprehension.

"There's a situation at the office. Several candidates we had in mind for clients were suddenly placed by Léon Professional. None of them were in talks with anyone else as of last week. So it means—"

"Someone at Léon got hold of our candidate files and used them for their own clients."

He nodded. "At first, Julien chalked it up to coincidence. Some of the candidates had to have been talking with other recruiters. But word kept trickling in of placements. There have now been four candidates who were working with our firm, waiting for negotiations to be finalized, who suddenly contracted with Léon's clients. That's too many to be coincidence."

"How did they get the candidate profiles?"

"It appears they were leaked. Someone must have given them to a recruiter at Léon Professional."

"Leaked? But who would bother? A recruiter could just as easily earn the commission themselves as sell a candidate's profile to someone else."

"It does seem far-fetched," he agreed, "unless someone is trying to sabotage this merger and the company."

She hadn't considered that. "But I thought things were going well. The retreat was good, wasn't it?"

Cole hesitated. "It doesn't necessarily have to be another recruiter selling off the information. It could be a board member, an intern..." He trailed off.

"Or?"

He shook his head. "Nothing. I'm just saying it could be anyone at the firm. Recruiter or not."

She wondered if Solene knew about this and what she'd have to say if she did. "I could ask my friend Solene. She works for Léon Professional."

He didn't say anything. She looked in his direction and found him studying her. "What?"

"That's part of the problem."

"What is?"

"These placements, all four were by the same recruiter at Léon Professional."

She felt a knot of dread forming.

"Oh? Who was the recruiter?"

He watched her carefully. "Solene Thierry."

She had known the answer before she even asked the question. It had been evident in Cole's hesitation.

"Solene," she repeated

"Yes."

She looked toward the lake, watching as a duck waddled along its edge. A few ducklings followed in her wake, struggling to keep up.

"I understand that Solene used to work for Aquitaine."

"She did," Emma confirmed.

"I heard she and Julien didn't get along."

"Solene is very independent. She wanted more freedom than Julien was willing to give."

"What do you mean by that?"

Emma debated on how to phrase her reply. She knew that however she answered, it would make Solene look less than ethical and her guilt in this matter would seem even more likely.

"She wanted to use some tactics that are considered questionable."

"Such as?"

"Using false identities to speak with hard-to-reach prospective candidates, pulling a red herring when a candidate gets a better offer, that sort of thing."

He seemed to be waiting for her to elaborate, but she spoke no further and avoided looking at him directly. She had never condoned Solene's tactics, had even found them to be a little distasteful, but Solene had taken Emma under her wing in this country and at Aquitaine. She was her friend.

"Emma."

"Yes?"

"Emma, look at me."

Reluctantly, she turned.

"You and Solene are friends. I get that. You have a certain loyalty to her."

"I'm loyal to Julien, too," she said.

"I know. I never meant to imply you aren't." He paused. "I'm not accusing you, Emma. I don't believe you had anything to do with this, and I don't know enough about what occurred between Julien and Solene to judge how deeply she's involved in our current situation. I'm asking you to help me, okay? I need help on this."

She felt a ripple of understanding. "You need me," she clarified.

"I do," he agreed without a touch of rancor. "You know the rules over here better than I do. Maybe that's why Julien assigned you as my liaison. He knew you could help me navigate these sorts of situations until I can learn the landscape for myself. There's a reason you're the managing director. I believe he placed you in that role because he trusted your abilities. And...I'm trusting you, too."

She was touched by this, by his attempt to assure her she was still a valued member of this company. "What do you need me to do?"

"You know Solene better than the rest of us."

She nodded in agreement.

"Do you think you could talk to her, find

out what she knows? If nothing else, see if you can learn how she got this information and who might be trying to sabotage me or this merger."

"I can do that," she agreed.

They discussed a few more possibilities before the light began to edge deeper into the horizon. Cole stood, offering to walk her back to her apartment before he went in search of a cab. He paused before they left the square, drinking in the sights around him. She swelled with pride in her adopted city, hoping that the Batignolles village had begun to charm him, as it had her, so he could start to see how truly wonderful Paris could be.

They spoke little on the walk back to her apartment, and though she asked again if he'd like to come up for a bite to eat, he declined, saying he knew what a long weekend she'd had.

It was true, and she knew she should be exhausted. But this past hour in Cole's presence had somehow served to revive her. Perhaps it was only the news of Solene's involvement, but she felt a little too on edge now, and she feared she might not be able to sleep for some time.

Before Cole offered his goodbyes, he stepped a little closer to her, and she found herself shivering despite the warmth of the summer air.

"Emma, I want you to know that I meant what I said back there. I'm really glad you're on my team."

"Thanks. I—" She stopped. He was so close, she could count the individual eyelashes and admire the way they framed the brown tint of his eyes that faded into green in the center. He wasn't quite smiling, nor was he quite frowning, either, but his face was relaxed, his expression casual. A dusting of scruff rested along his jaw, and she realized she liked that slightly rugged touch so much more than his clean-shaven appearance. The urge to run her palms along that stubble caused her fingers to twitch. "I'm glad you came," she murmured, the words slipping out before she could think about them too much.

"To your neighborhood? I am, too. It's… nice." He let out a small breath. "Okay, so I have to admit. It's nice enough that I can see why you love it."

"Thanks, but that's not what I meant. I meant that I'm glad you came to Paris. I think you're going to be a really good CEO."

"Oh." He looked genuinely startled by this pronouncement, but then his face turned serious. "Thanks. I really appreciate that, Emma. More than you know."

She nodded. "I better get back upstairs. Are you sure you can find your way to a cab?"

"Sure, I'm not as helpless as I look."

She laughed. "You look anything but helpless." In fact, she began to think he was fitting into this city and her own life just a little too well.

"I'll see you at the office, Aquitaine."

She waited and watched as he turned and headed down the street, unable to tear her eyes away, even when he disappeared around a corner and she couldn't see him anymore.

EMMA INVITED SOLENE to lunch as soon as she reached the office on Monday morning, but her friend was already booked with a client meeting, so they opted to go for coffee in the afternoon instead. The mood at Aquitaine was more tense than usual, as word of the leaked candidate placements got out. Cole took it upon himself to interview each of the top recruiters, trying to discern where the leak had come from, but he told her none of them seemed to be responsible or have any idea of who might wish to tarnish the company's name.

Emma was tasked with contacting the companies who had been prepared to hire the candidates, making the firm's apologies and offering up alternative résumés. Most of their clients took the news well, except for one, who threatened to transfer their business to Léon Professional Services instead. Emma offered effusive regrets and promised to handle their next placement personally. She hung up the phone exhausted after that call, and she hadn't even been in the office two hours.

She was both dreading and looking forward to her coffee break with Solene when the clock reached four. Grabbing her purse, she ducked her head into Cole's office to let him know where she was going. He was on the phone but gave her a thumbs-up and a smile that sent a rush of pleasure through her.

Hormones, she told herself. Her growing reaction to the new boss was simply the result of hormones. Or her addled brain after the crazy weekend. She headed toward the elevators and then the building's exit, making her way to the café she and Solene liked to frequent.

She arrived ahead of her friend and took the time to order them both their usual, café au lait with the coffee served in a pot and a pitcher of milk on the side with two cups. As she waited for their order, she found a table near the back of the establishment. The business was slow this time of day, but she preferred it. She wanted a relative amount of privacy for the conversation she had to have with her friend.

She settled into a seat to wait and checked her phone to make sure she had no missed messages. As she looked up, she caught sight of Solene just entering through the door, and she stood, waving to get her attention. Solene's face broke into a smile as she made her way around tables and chairs to the back.

"Why are we seated back here? I feel as though this is a secret rendezvous." She placed her cheek against each side of Emma's face in her usual greeting before sitting. Emma sat across from her, facing the door.

"I just liked the view from the back of the room. And I thought it would be nice to have a little bit of privacy."

Solene seemed to sense something in her tone because she dropped her bag to the table and eyed her speculatively. "Privacy? This sounds more clandestine with every minute."

"I'm hardly an international spy, Solene." But given the corporate espionage that was taking place at Aquitaine, this statement only served to make Emma more uncomfortable.

Before they could say anything further, a server appeared with their order and placed it on the table between them. They each took a minute to prepare their coffee before conversation continued.

"Thanks again for watching Avery this weekend, after everything that happened."

Solene fluttered a hand in dismissal. "I only hope Jacqueline makes a complete recovery. I never got to ask, though, how the corporate retreat was going before you had to come home early."

Emma took a sip of her coffee and scalded her tongue. "Ah." She took a second to recover. "It was…good."

Solene paused with her cup halfway to her lips. "Good? You sound unconvinced of that statement."

"No, not at all." It *had* been good, in her mind. But she also didn't know how she could explain things to Solene, about Cole's insinuation concerning her and Julien and the conversation at the chapel, without her friend casting a negative light on the weekend.

"And the new CEO? How are things coming along with him?"

To her horror, Emma felt her cheeks flaming, the heat spreading outward toward her jaw and neck. Solene watched with interest.

"Emma. You are smitten, aren't you?"

"Wh-what? You're crazy." She took another sip of her coffee, hoping to rein her reactions in, and scalded her tongue once more. She winced.

"Listen, Solene, there's something I need to talk to you about." She couldn't just sit here and discuss Cole or the retreat. She had to get this thing out in the open.

Solene calmly sipped from her own cup, and Emma marveled that she didn't singe her lips. But then, Solene had always been Emma's idea of the quintessential Frenchwoman. She could do anything and appear elegant and at ease, even burn her mouth on hot coffee and act as though nothing had occurred. She wondered just how often she got to see the real Solene, the one underneath the perfect veneer.

"I am ready whenever you are," Solene prompted after she had remained silent for several seconds more.

Emma cleared her throat and straightened up a bit in her seat. "Your company has been poaching our candidates."

Solene leaned back, eyes wide. "That is quite the accusation, my friend."

Her use of this appellation was not lost on Emma. They were friends. Solene was one of her very best friends, and she was grateful for how Solene had watched out for her over the years. Accusing her felt a little like a betrayal.

"I'm not trying to blame you, but I have a list…." She dug the paper out of her purse and slid it toward Solene. "You recognize all these names."

Solene took the sheet and unfolded it, scanning the list. "I do," she admitted.

"Solene, all four of those names were placed by you. And they were candidates we were in exclusive talks with. No other recruiters had approached them."

Solene lifted one shoulder in a casual shrug. "You had not contracted any of them yet."

Emma felt her stomach sink with disappointment. "Then you did poach them."

Solene sighed. "I was offered an exclusive list of candidates who were looking to be placed with companies in their field. It would have been foolish not to take it. If I hadn't, then someone else at my company would have."

"Solene." Emma felt a sting of hurt. "That

feels an awful lot like revenge against Julien."

"Oh, *chérie.*" Solene leaned forward and clasped her hand. "It was not intended that way. I was given an opportunity. It was not illegal to take it."

"No," Emma had to admit, but it was the same reason Julien and Solene had parted ways to begin with—her methods, if not illegal, hovered in a gray area at best. "But, Solene, that was a direct strike to Aquitaine, to the merger, to *me.*"

Solene squeezed her fingers tighter at this. "*Non,* you cannot think of it that way. We are friends, Emma. I would never do anything to jeopardize you."

"Then tell me who gave you the candidate names. Was it one of the other recruiters? Marc, maybe?"

Solene released her and leaned back. "No, I cannot tell you that. I promised that I wouldn't."

Emma felt a swell of frustration. "You just said that we're friends. Can't you help me out here? I was on the phone all morning, doing damage control. It's going to take us weeks to come up with suitable replacements for the candidates we lost. And you can't even tell me who at my own company betrayed us?"

Solene reached for her mug and took a sip of her drink once more. “I gave my word not to tell.”

Emma felt her jaw drop and then snapped it closed. “So *that’s* where you choose to be suddenly principled? You can blur the lines in every respect but not when it comes to naming the person responsible for selling company files?”

She didn’t even flinch. “I am sorry.”

Emma let out a sigh of disgust and leaned back in her chair. “How do I know it won’t happen again?”

Solene said nothing, and Emma stiffened. “It has already, hasn’t it? You have more names, more profiles.”

“They still have a choice, you know. Any candidate still has the opportunity to choose between the company Aquitaine offers them and the one I do.”

She scoffed. “That’s hardly fair.”

“Oh, my darling.” Solene’s voice turned sympathetic. “You know that none of this is fair. Wasn’t that the first rule I taught you when you began this business? Don’t ever assume anyone fights fair.”

“It’s true. You did warn me,” Emma conceded. “But I thought I could at least count on you to be honest with me.” She took the paper that still rested between them and stuffed it back into her bag.

"I promise to be honest with you now. Come and work with me at Léon. I've already spoken to our board chairman as well as our CEO. They're willing to interview you for managing director with a possible salary increase. It would be the same title you have at Aquitaine right now with the guarantee for promotion within a year."

Emma frowned. "Solene, why would you do that? You're still only a senior recruiter yourself."

She grinned, and Emma couldn't help feeling it was just a touch wolfish. "I like being a recruiter. I like the hunt and the negotiation. I have no desire to manage other recruiters and a firm. You're so much better at it than I would ever be. And I miss you. I want us to work together again."

As flattering as these words were, Emma still felt a niggling doubt. "And it would be so convenient, wouldn't it? To strike another blow at Julien by stealing me away?"

Solene's smile flattened. "He does not deserve you, any more than he deserved me. You should have been the new CEO. You worked harder for it than anybody, and what does he do? He bows to an American woman's wishes to install her own man in your place."

"My promotion wasn't official yet," she said weakly in defense of Julien.

"It does not matter. He betrayed you. Can you not see that? When will you learn, Emma? First, Brice, and then, Julien."

"Brice has nothing to do with this."

"No? Brice and Julien have one thing in common—their selfishness. They each expected you to sacrifice your wishes for theirs."

"They're not the same," she protested. "Julien has been there for me, many times over. He's like a father figure—"

"And he plays on your need for one." Solene cut her off.

They both fell silent in the wake of these words. At least Solene had the decency to look abashed.

For her part, Emma could only hold her head high for so long before she dropped her gaze and reached for her coffee cup. The milk had left a cloudy film across the café au lait's surface. She placed it back on the table.

"I am sorry, *chérie*. I did not mean to say that. It was not fair."

"But it's true," Emma admitted. "I miss my father. He wasn't in my life long enough, and I've always felt the lack of his presence. I worry about Avery—I want her to have a stronger bond with her father."

Solene scoffed. "She is an adorable child. Brice does not deserve her."

Emma didn't respond to this. Solene reached out and took her hand once more.

"Please, Emma. Just think about it. You and me, on the same team again. Julien would have to understand, after how he gave the CEO promotion to someone else. He has no right to keep you stuck where you are when your talents could be put to much better use."

"I don't know. Aquitaine is my company."

"It is Julien's company. Not yours. And that has never been more apparent than now, when he joined forces with the Americans and denied you the title that should have been yours. You, who have devoted so much time and skill to strengthening the company name."

Emma's uneasiness must have shown because Solene squeezed her fingers in reassurance before releasing them.

"Just think about it. You don't have to give me an answer this minute. Take a few days, a few weeks, a month if you need it. And let me know when you've made a decision."

Emma didn't see the harm in this suggestion. It wouldn't be a betrayal to Julien just to entertain the idea, would it?

"And the candidate names? You won't tell me who gave them to you?"

"I can't, darling. It would require breaking a confidence. I promised. You understand."

"Then at least swear to me that you won't use any more of them."

Solene hesitated, her gaze darting away.

"Solene? Please."

She sighed. "Very well. I promise. I will not use any more of the names on the list."

Emma knew that was the most she could hope to get out of Solene. She began to prepare herself to return to the office, wondering exactly how she was going to tell Cole that she had no more answers than when she'd left.

CHAPTER NINE

COLE FOUND HIMSELF more on edge than he'd expected as he waited for Emma to return from her coffee meeting with Solene. The entire day had been a tedious repetition of speaking with his recruiters and other office staff, doing his best to remember each one and their roles within the company, and then trying to determine if any of them might have been responsible for leaking candidate files. Nearing the end of the workday, he still didn't have a single viable suspect, and when Julien stopped by his office before he left for the day, Cole was forced to admit that he had learned nothing.

Julien took this news with a sober expression and a nod. "Has Emma returned yet, from meeting with Solene?"

Cole shook his head. "I expect her back at any moment."

Julien looked at his watch. "I cannot wait. I have a dinner meeting with several members of the board. If she has learned anything of import, send me a text."

Cole told him he would keep him apprised of the situation and said goodbye for the day. After Julien left, he turned in his chair to stare out his window at the La Défense district below and realized that he was becoming accustomed to the sight. No longer did he expect to see Manhattan high-rises when he looked outside—the view from his new office was gradually becoming more familiar.

His thoughts turned to Emma and how she was becoming someone more familiar, too. He had looked for her this morning, first thing upon entering the office. He told himself it was because she was his cultural liaison and the managing director. It was expected that he would seek her out when he arrived at work.

But now, with the late afternoon's shadows stretching across his desk and an end-of-day hush descending over the office, he had time to consider his motivations more fully and had to admit that it might not just be his and Emma's working relationship that made him take an interest in her. The sight of her smile and that cute upturned nose, the way her eyes crinkled slightly when she laughed or even the tiny indent that formed in between her eyebrows when she was displeased—each feature had grown more endearing to him. He tried to remember feeling that way about Ophelia, tried to recall the small details of her expressions and realized, to his chagrin, that her face had already become faded and blurred. Had he simply forgotten, so soon, the tiny details of her appearance? Or was it that he had never paid attention in the first place?

Whatever the case, he knew that in the short time he'd been in Paris, he could tell someone more about Emma, her quirks and reactions, her form and features, than he would be able to relate about Ophelia, who had been his girlfriend for four years.

His mind drifted along these lines, thinking about the weekend and how far he and Emma had come since their first impressions of each other. He thought about Avery and how much she resembled her mother and how adorable she'd been to speak with. He remembered how nice it was to walk with Emma in the Square des Batignolles the evening before and considered whether he should gear his own apartment search in that area. What would it be like to live near Emma and her daughter? Could they possibly meet for dinner on occasion, or even commute to the office together? He found the idea a pleasant one as a daydream, if nothing else. Before he could muse much further on such reflections, a knock sounded on his door.

He swiveled his chair around to find Emma peeking her head inside. Her appearance caused a sudden swell of happiness in his chest.

"Do you have a minute?"

He gestured for her to come inside and, for whatever reason—politeness or chivalry—found himself getting to his feet. "Hi. You're back."

She nodded. "I'm back."

Her posture was stiff, and the sleepless bruising beneath her eyes spoke of her fatigue. Her skin had a chalky pallor, and she looked utterly drained.

"You look terrible." He cringed as soon as the words were out of his mouth, and her shoulders drew back in offense.

"Thanks."

"I didn't mean—" He stopped. "I meant, it looks like you could use a good night's sleep."

"You're right about that," she agreed and stepped farther into the room. "Between the retreat, visiting Jacqueline in the hospital and this candidate incident, I think I need more than a good night's sleep. I need a vacation."

He chuckled at her honesty. "When was the last time you took one anyway?"

She sank into the seat before his desk without being invited. He sat back in his own chair as she pondered the question.

"The last time I took a vacation?"

He watched as she nibbled her lip in consideration. "You know, I can't even remember. Avery and I usually travel to Le Mans once or twice a year and spend a few days with Jacqueline, but that's about it."

"And you never go back to the States?"

She shrugged. "My life is here now. I plan to take Avery one day, give her a proper tour of her heritage, but for now…I have too many other things to consider." He noted that her brow furrowed even more deeply, her mind obviously reviewing all the other things she was supposed to be considering.

"Like finding out who gave away our candidate files?"

She made a face. "Yeah. Like that."

"Did your friend have any answers for us?"

She looked away and toward the window he'd just been gazing out of. "Not enough. She admits she got the information from someone in our office, but she refuses to tell me who gave her the names. She said she couldn't betray their confidence."

He scoffed. "She has no qualms about stealing the candidates we worked so hard to cultivate, but when it comes to naming the guilty party, she suddenly grows a conscience?"

Emma said nothing, her face becoming stony. He realized he had overstepped with his opinion and sighed. "I'm sorry. She's your friend. I shouldn't have said that."

Her expression softened slightly. "It's all right. I'm aware how this must look to everyone. Solene is just…Solene. She's not a bad person. Her values are just a little more skewed than the rest of us."

Cole wasn't sure that excused the woman's actions, but he didn't want to criticize Emma's friend and put them on bad footing again. In fact, his thoughts were going in a much different direction.

"It's been a long day," he remarked.

She exhaled, and he noted some of the tension left her body at this topic change. She rolled her head around on her neck. "It has," she agreed.

"Why don't we go out to dinner, as a reward for all our hard work?"

She brought her head back around and focused on him. "Dinner?"

Her voice was so suspicious, he leaned forward. "You do know what that's like, don't you? Treating yourself once in a while?"

"Of course. Only…who has time for that sort of thing?" she muttered.

He shook his head. "No vacations and not even letting someone treat you to dinner on occasion? Aquitaine, no wonder you're exhausted."

He stood once more and began pushing aside the remaining paperwork from his day, slotting it into trays to be dealt with tomorrow. "Come on. We'll spend a few minutes talking about work and call it a write-off."

He thought he heard a faint laugh and looked her way.

"You're pretty good at this, aren't you?" she said.

"At what?"

"Negotiating things to go your way."

He filed the last of the paperwork and came around the side of his desk. "Emma, you haven't even begun to see my negotiating skills. Now, come on. Join me for dinner." He held out a hand, and, after a moment's reluctance, she placed her fingers in his.

EMMA STARED AT Cole in disbelief. "You are positively devious," she pronounced and then spooned up another bite of her lamb and white bean cassoulet. "I'm not sure I can ever trust you again."

It was amazing what some good food and even better company could do to improve a girl's spirits. And Cole was, if nothing else, an utterly charming dinner companion. He'd been practicing his French and had apologized in advance to the waiter before making an attempt at ordering. His self-deprecation was so endearing that even their snooty server at the outdoor café hadn't been able to resist smiling and assisting when Cole stumbled over a word here and there.

He'd managed to order for both of them, but when he'd asked for *Les Tournedos Rossini* for himself, she'd stopped him.

"I think you need to keep working on your French. *Les Tournedos Rossini* is beef, topped with foie gras," she'd said.

He'd grinned, rather devilishly, she thought. "I know," he'd said and then handed the menu back to their server, who'd taken it and departed.

Later, after their food had arrived, she'd watched him tuck into the meal with a gusto even Julien would have envied. She'd let him eat for a while before curiosity had finally overcome her.

"I thought Julien said you were a vegetarian," she had said.

And then he'd explained how he wasn't, how it had merely been a pretense begun long ago and something he kept up to impress Lillian. That was when she'd declared him devious.

"Totally untrustworthy," she went on. "And if you keep eating like that—" she pointed to his plate, twirling her spoon around to encompass the meat that she knew had been dredged in butter before searing "—you're going to end up looking like Julien in no time. A true French gourmand."

Cole swallowed his bite and began cutting off another. "Don't worry, I won't make it a habit. Tonight's a celebration."

She admired him in the evening dusk, the way the dwindling light gilded the tips of his hair and softened the planes of his face. His jacket was slung over the back of his chair, and the top buttons of his white shirt were undone, the sleeves rolled up to his elbows. He wore a black vest that was absolutely dashing on him, and she couldn't help thinking how handsome he looked, relaxed but still in his professional attire. It heightened her awareness, not only of his easy and attractive demeanor but also of his good mood.

"What can we possibly be celebrating?" she asked as she placed her spoon aside and reached for her napkin. "We nearly lost an important account this morning, we're back to square one on several placements and, despite my best efforts, Solene didn't tell us a thing."

She quickly dabbed her lips and returned the napkin to her lap, avoiding his eyes as she smoothed it into place. She'd told the truth; Solene hadn't given her anything that would help the situation at Aquitaine. But she had certainly offered Emma more than she could wrap her mind around. Her head was still swimming with the proposal her friend had made.

"But you're having dinner with me. And that's cause for celebration." He raised his glass of sparkling water to her.

She shook her head and picked up her spoon once more. "You don't have to try to charm me."

"Now, why would I do that?"

Her eyes narrowed in suspicion. "I feel as though you're buttering me up for something."

He sliced into his steak with obvious relish. "You're pretty suspicious for such a young woman." He ate the bite of steak and chewed for a few seconds before swallowing. "Look, I just think we have something to celebrate, you and I. We're working together. As long as that's happening, we can figure out this candidate situation and make the merger a success."

She felt a twinge of guilt at his pronouncement. Yes, they were working together. But if she considered Solene's offer, for how long?

He put his utensils aside. "Listen, Emma, I'm just happy we're on the same page. I feel like it took us a little while to get there, with how things started off between us. But I don't know..." He reached for his fork and knife again. "I feel like you've got my back. And I want you to know that I've got yours. That's cause for celebrating, isn't it?"

His words touched her more than she would have expected. Recruiting could be a ruthless business at times, and once in a while she feared the corporate cutthroat mentality was getting to her. That maybe she wasn't the determined negotiator she had been when she'd started but rather someone too aggressive, or too ambitious. She had changed over the years, as was to be expected, but she never wanted to lose that younger version of herself entirely, the one who put others first and wasn't just focused on advancement and salary.

"Thanks, Cole."

"No problem."

She reached out, her fingers brushing against his as he pushed his plate aside. Her touch must have startled him because he looked up, eyes wide.

"I mean it. It's nice to feel like I have an ally."

His hand moved, flipping over so that their palms touched. The feel of his skin against hers caused a reassuring warmth to spread toward her wrist. "I like the feeling, too."

They held each other's eyes a bit longer, and she felt herself leaning forward, as though the earth were tilting on its axis, ever so slightly, and pushing her in Cole's direction. It wasn't until their waiter appeared, offering refills on their drinks, that they released hands. She pulled hers back into her lap and realized she couldn't eat another bite. Her stomach was too crowded with emotions to accommodate food.

"How about some dessert?" Cole suggested, his tone light.

"I can't," she protested. "I'm stuffed."

"Not even *macarons?* Giselle mentioned they're your favorite."

She had? She wondered if Cole had been asking about her or if Giselle had offered up the information on her own.

The waiter paused, waiting to see if they would order anything more. She shook her head at him to indicate it wasn't necessary, and he moved away.

"I do love *macarons,*" she admitted, "but if you're going to eat them in Paris, it's better to get them at Ladurée. They make the best ones."

"So this is serious business, eating *macarons.*"

She nodded, keeping her expression severe. "You can't just eat any *macaron* when in Paris. You have to have the real thing, the best possible kind."

"Then it's settled. We're going to have to go to Ladurée."

"Tonight?" She blinked in surprise.

"Not tonight, but I'm thinking..." He leaned back, and she felt the intensity of his stare as he studied her. She tried not to fidget beneath the scrutiny and, instead, smoothed her charcoal-gray pencil skirt and fiddled with the sleeves of her soft pink blouse.

"What if I made you a bet?"

These words grabbed her attention. "A bet? What sort of bet?"

"I bet you can't make me fall in love with Paris."

She straightened in her seat, totally unprepared for this suggestion. "Are you kidding?"

"I couldn't be more serious. Think about it. It's obvious you adore this city, and clearly, I'm in need of some persuasion where it's concerned. Why don't you take on the challenge of showing me your Paris. You can start with Ladurée, if you like. The *macarons* will be on me."

"You mean, I could show you the sights, that sort of thing?"

"Whatever it takes to make me fall in love."

The prospect both thrilled her and made her wary. She had the feeling she was already growing a little too comfortable where her boss was concerned. Spending time outside of work, showing him the City of Light, wouldn't exactly solidify any boundaries between them. And yet, the opportunity to show off her adopted home, with all its magic, was a lure she couldn't resist. She began thinking of all the places she would take him—from her favorite *boulangeries* and shops to the most iconic sights.

"When would we find the time?"

He shrugged. "Whenever. After work. The weekends. We could take it slow. After all,

I spent years learning everything that made me appreciate New York. You can't expect me to fall for Paris overnight."

She considered this. "Avery would have to join us. Melanie has most evenings and weekends off, and I'm not going to stick Avery with a sitter."

"Of course, I'm counting on it. I'm sure she has her own unique perspective. Plus, she's pretty adorable. Kind of like her mother."

The compliment made her hesitate again. Spending her free time with Cole wasn't going to make her decision for Solene any easier. But he had proven himself a pretty good source of company, and besides, Avery had seemed to like him. What harm could it do, really? If anything, it was like a favor—she could help him acclimate completely to France. Then, if she did choose to leave Aquitaine for Léon, it wouldn't be as though she'd left her job as Cole's cultural liaison unfinished.

After a bit more deliberation, she bowed her head. "All right, then. You're on."

He grinned. "Then I'll prepare to have my heart stolen."

COLE SHOWED UP at Emma's that Saturday morning at precisely eight o'clock, as they had arranged. He buzzed for admittance to the apartment building and waited for Melanie to ring him in before making his way up to their floor. He knocked on the door, and within seconds, it eased open with Avery standing on the other side.

When he held out a small bouquet of flowers he'd picked up from a street vendor, her eyes grew wide.

"For Mommy?"

"No. They're for you."

If possible, her eyes grew even rounder. "For *me?*"

"Of course. A gentleman always brings a lady flowers."

She grabbed the daisies and hugged them to her, losing several petals in the process. "Mom, look what Cole brought me!"

She ran farther into the apartment, leaving him standing on the threshold uncertainly until Melanie appeared and offered a shy grin.

"You can come inside. Emma's almost ready."

He followed Melanie inside and took an appreciative look around. Emma's apartment was exactly what he would have expected from her—simple but still elegant and inviting.

Melanie gestured toward the couch in the living area. “Do you want anything to drink?”

He shook his head. “No, thanks.” He sensed the girl was still a bit uncomfortable around him, so he tried to put her at ease. “Emma said you have most weekends off. Are you enjoying your time as an au pair, getting to take in plenty of sights?”

“Oh, definitely,” she gushed, finally opening up a little. “I’ve been to all the major sights—the Louvre, the Eiffel Tower, all those places. My friends back home are so jealous. Emma showed me around the first month, but then I met a bunch of other au pairs here in the city. We go out together on the weekends to absorb as much culture as we can.”

“How long will you stay here?”

“I signed up for a full twelve months, and I arrived just over ten weeks ago. I’ll be here throughout Avery’s school year before I head back home in June.”

“It sounds like you still have plenty of time to enjoy your experience, then.”

She nodded, and just then, Emma entered the room dressed in a simple outfit of jeans and a white T-shirt with a bright yellow scarf looped around her neck and a gray cardigan in her arms. He felt himself perking up, pleased to see her in something other than her usual professional attire. Her hair was loose as well, the dark waves tumbling over her shoulders. She appeared more rested than he'd seen her in the past two weeks. Avery padded in behind her, still clutching the bouquet of daisies and trailing petals across the carpet. Half the flowers were already bald from all the movement.

"Good morning," Emma greeted him.

Avery plucked out a flower from amidst the bunch. She held it toward Melanie. "Here, Melanie. This is for you."

"Aw, thanks." Melanie bent down and dropped a kiss on the little girl's head. "Why don't I put these in some water, huh? I think they might need a drink." She tactfully took the already wilting bouquet and headed for the kitchen. Avery followed, presumably to watch.

Cole turned back to find Emma smiling at him. "That was very nice of you. She's never had anyone give her flowers before. I think you might just beat out Melanie for her favorite person this week."

"I thought maybe she'd appreciate it. Don't all girls like to get flowers?"

"I guess they do," Emma admitted.

They grew silent, having run out of preliminary things to say, and Cole cleared his throat a trifle awkwardly.

"You look lovely, by the way."

"Oh, really?" She glanced down at her outfit. "Thanks. It's nice to get out in something other than work blouses and skirts." He watched as she surreptitiously took in his own attire. "And, um, you look good, too."

He didn't think his navy polo and khaki slacks were anything impressive, but he thanked her and thought how ridiculous the two of them were behaving, like teenagers on their first date.

"So, what's on the agenda for the day?"

Emma seemed to appreciate the question, as though it gave her something else to focus on rather than just the two of them standing in her living room. "I thought we'd start with the basics—the Eiffel Tower, maybe some museums, that sort of thing."

"Seems like the perfect place to begin."

"And maybe we can pick up a few lunch items at the Rue Cler market and eat picnic-style on the Champ de Mars."

"You're the one calling the shots. I'm placing myself in your hands."

She laughed. "You may regret that."

He denied it, certain he would have absolutely no regrets at all.

EMMA COULDN'T REMEMBER the last time she'd experienced such a perfect day. Cole was absolutely charming, and before they'd even arrived at their first stop, she knew that if he hadn't won Avery over with the flowers, he certainly had just by the attention he paid her. It moved her to see how her daughter giggled at the things Cole said. Soon, Avery was clinging to his hand instead of Emma's and begging for him to carry her when she grew tired or wanted extra attention.

Though Emma tried to chastise her and remind her she had to walk on her own, Cole never seemed to mind picking her up when she demanded it. With Cole there to keep her entertained, she never grew whiny about their sightseeing like she might have done otherwise. Before long, Emma found herself caught up in the day as well, enjoying Cole's company and the late-summer weather of sunshine and pleasant breezes.

They hiked the stairs to the top of the Eiffel Tower, and though Emma protested, Cole willingly carried Avery most of the way, well over fifteen hundred steps. He held her up as they took in the magnificent views at the top, drinking in the skyline of the city, and he confessed that it truly was an incomparable sight. She gushed more than she should have about the monument's history—from its creation by Gustave Eiffel to its modern upkeep of being painted with six tons of paint every seven years to prevent the cast iron from rusting. She suddenly realized how Cole was staring at her, seemingly mesmerized.

"Sorry. I know a little too much about some of these landmarks. I'll try not to go into boring tour guide mode."

"I'm not bored," he said, and though she didn't entirely understand the way he looked at her, she believed him.

After the Eiffel Tower, they wandered for a bit, and she chose to bypass a few of the museums since she didn't think Avery's attention span would hold long enough for them to spend much time there. She couldn't resist a visit to the Musée Rodin, however. Instead of paying the fee for the museum portion, she took them to the gardens, where she and Cole paid a euro each to enter, and Avery was admitted for free. Fortunately, the sculptures captivated Avery, her little head cocked as she studied several of the statues along the grounds. Cole seemed to be enjoying himself, especially when Avery would grab his hand and pull him in the direction of another statue. The three of them stared for some time at the famous sculpture *The Thinker* until Avery pronounced it "boring" and asked if they could leave.

They moved on, and Emma prayed for Avery's patience when she insisted they visit Le Musée des Égouts de Paris for an hour. The underground museum on the sewers of Paris always fascinated her with its history and the connections to Victor Hugo's *Les Misérables*. Besides, she hoped such an unusual tourist attraction would help Paris stand out in Cole's mind, and its unique setting kept Avery interested, at least for a little while.

After that, Emma continued their tour of the seventh *arrondissement* by stopping at the open-air market, Rue Cler, to gather items for lunch. After the dank air of the underground museum, it was refreshing to get back out onto the cobblestone street and breathe in the more diverse smells of the city—baking bread and pastries, fuel exhaust, damp and musty stones from old fountains, and flowers from cart vendors on every corner.

They made their way to the Champ de Mars with Cole carrying Avery on his shoulders. Somewhere along the way, perhaps when she'd been distracted with selecting some Brie for their lunch, Cole must have bought Avery a yellow balloon to match her buttercream-and-white-striped sundress. It bobbed in the air above her head, seeming to dance along with her laughter.

Avery basked in this attention, constantly calling for Emma to look up at her and then throwing her arms wide, the balloon firmly secured to her wrist by a length of string. Emma's chest tightened at the sight of her daughter's joy. Brice had never carried his daughter on his shoulders like that, had never taken the time to perform many fatherly actions at all.

When they at last arrived at the long stretch of green that was the Champ de Mars, Emma settled on the grass and spread out the food she'd purchased. Avery was still bouncing with energy, so Emma took her balloon and tied it to one of the bags from the market, and Avery soon settled down long enough to look over the lunch offerings, choosing the Brie, a cluster of grapes and a large chunk of the fresh bread to nibble on. Cole helped Emma lay out the items, but before he got very far, Avery settled herself in his lap.

Emma watched as he looked down at the top of her daughter's head in surprise; and then, he brushed a palm over her hair before situating himself more comfortably and reaching for a roasted pepper.

They each munched quietly, allowing the sounds of tourists and native Parisians to flow around them as they devoured sections of rotisserie chicken, Mediterranean olives, sugared almonds, Brie and Camembert, in addition to other delicious finger foods.

When they had finished, they lay back on the grass and watched thin swirls of clouds make shapes in the sky. Avery kept asking Cole to tell her what shapes he saw, and his suggestions grew ever more outrageous until she giggled and told him he was silly before giving up on the game.

Avery noticed a pair of twins working at flying a kite and jumped to her feet to move closer and watch. Emma sat up to keep an eye on her, and Cole followed suit.

"So, how am I doing?" she asked him. "Have you fallen in love yet?"

He clicked his tongue. "Patience, Aquitaine. I'm not some cheap date. I have to be wooed here."

She laughed and realized that such a reaction was something she was experiencing more and more when Cole was around. He always found something to say that amused her.

"I guess I fell in love with the city at first sight, so I can't understand why you wouldn't."

"You're doing just fine," he confessed. "I am sufficiently awed by everything we've seen. But in love? Not quite yet. You're going to have to keep it up."

"Not a problem. I could keep touring this city forever. There's always something new to discover, even after you think you've seen it all. Could you say the same about New York?"

He leaned back, stretching his arms out and resting his weight on his palms. "I don't know. It's different. Paris has centuries of history behind it, but New York has more of an undercurrent of energy, something almost frantic, running through it, I think. Have you ever been there?"

"No," she confessed.

He eyed her with new interest. "You mean all this time you've been telling me how wonderful Paris is, and you haven't even been to New York?"

She shrugged.

"Oh, Aquitaine. I think you've been playing me all along here."

"I wouldn't take it personally." She pretended to look at her fingernails, blew a breath on them and then acted as if she was shining them against her scarf. "I'm just smart that way."

He laughed and reached out to tickle her in the side. She squealed and rolled away on the grass. Avery took notice of the laughter and came to join them, vaulting herself against Cole, who fell onto his back.

They lay like that as Avery began singing in French, her voice filled with happiness. Emma was stretched out several feet away, where she had rolled when Cole tried to tickle her. She turned her head and saw him grinning up at her daughter, trying to hum along in snatches to the song.

When he moved his head and caught her eye, she felt as though everything inside her rose up in a swell of happiness and realized that this was what Jacqueline would have called "a perfect moment."

THEY STAYED IN the seventh *arrondissement* for the rest of the afternoon, sightseeing, shopping and then eating dinner together at a little restaurant along the Seine. When the sun finally dipped below the horizon, they visited the Eiffel Tower again so that Cole could see it lit up at night. It was an incomparable sight, a beacon of brilliance visible for miles beyond, and the view of the city from its observation decks after twilight had fallen was an entirely new perspective.

By that point, Avery was done in with exhaustion, and Cole carried her in his arms as she sagged with sleepiness. Emma led the way toward the RER train lines that would take them back to Batignolles and her apartment. They didn't speak much on the ride home, but the silence was much more relaxed than it had been when they'd stood in her apartment together that morning. Cole felt completely comfortable in the quiet with her, and he sensed she felt the same.

They didn't get back to her apartment until almost eleven o'clock. Cole still carried Avery, and rather than place her into Emma's arms, he offered to carry her to her room. Emma opened the door for him, and he laid the sleeping child on top of a bedspread printed with fairies and flowers.

He took one last glance at Avery's face, smiling as she worked her little cheeks in slumber, and wondering if she was talking in her dreams. He fondly brushed aside the sweep of dark hair that fell over her forehead as Emma removed her shoes and socks. Then they moved toward the doorway.

"She had a great time today. Thanks for being so patient with her."

"It was my pleasure. She's a sweetheart. You should be very proud of her."

"I am," she said as she eased the door closed, and they went back toward the living area.

It made him curious about Emma's ex-husband. What sort of man didn't take an interest in his own daughter, especially one as sweet and adorable as Avery?

"Can I get you anything before you go?" Emma asked, but he declined with a shake of his head.

"No, I'll let you get some rest."

She showed him to the door, but he lingered, as did she, on the threshold.

"You still up for all this sightseeing?" he asked her, not wanting to leave just yet. He wanted to spend just a few minutes more in her company.

She leaned against the doorway. "I am if you are. Am I convincing you, about Paris's worth?"

She was, but he didn't want to give in too soon. He wanted more days like this one, more time with her and Avery. He hadn't known this feeling before, of being part of a family unit, of belonging. His own childhood had never given him that, and despite his relationship with Ophelia, it hadn't been the same experience as this.

"We'll see," he offered, and she reached out to nudge him slightly with her finger.

"You're already hooked, and you know it."

He shifted forward after she pushed him, looking into her face. Hooked. Maybe he was.

He leaned in, and the amusement faded from her expression as she grew serious. She eased off the doorway, shifting toward him. Their faces came within an inch of each other, and they stood like that, somehow frozen. He was unable to move, forward or back, caught in her presence. Her hair still held the faint traces of her perfume, something with notes of lavender, along with the scent of grass. He hovered there, his hand reaching out to touch the side of her neck, his palm drawing her a little closer. He waited for her to pull back, but she didn't. He could see her eyes resting on his lips.

As if testing her willingness, he ran the tip of his nose along hers, and she exhaled so softly that he felt just the barest whisper of breath against his cheek. He took that for assent and tilted his head so that his lips brushed ever so slightly along hers. When she still didn't resist, he touched his lips to hers once more, lingering a little longer this time, and then he pressed deeper until she responded, and they were kissing fervently. Her back was pressed against the doorframe, and he shifted, trying to give her room to keep her from being uncomfortable. She didn't move, but she kept responding to his kiss, her fingers tracing along his jaw so that his skin tingled wherever she stroked. Her lips were soft and sweet beneath his, and he thought he could go on kissing her like this forever… until a quiet cough at his back caused him to stiffen.

Emma jerked and peered around him, but he turned more slowly at the interruption.

Melanie stood a few feet away, her face flaming a bright red to the roots of her hair.

"I, um, went back downstairs and came up again, but you were still, er…here."

He felt a ripple of amusement run through him and nearly laughed out loud until he felt a rush of cold air and turned back, realizing Emma had stepped away from him. She was beginning to flush the same shade as Melanie.

"I'm sorry, Melanie. Here." She moved back from the doorway so Melanie could enter.

The girl moved forward and gave him a quick glance.

"Sorry, Melanie," he offered.

If possible, her face reddened further. "It's okay. I'll just..." She quickly ducked past him and into the apartment, glancing at Emma before hurrying inside.

He and Emma were left staring at one another, and he could tell by the expression on her face that he never should have kissed her, even if she had seemed willing.

"I'm sorry, Emma," he apologized for the second time. But then he decided that wasn't the truth. "No, I'm not sorry. Not for kissing you anyway." He was sorry she seemed to be regretting it.

"That can't happen again," she said, her voice so low he had to move a little closer to make out the words.

She took a step back when he came near, and he stopped. "Why?" he asked. "Did I make you uncomfortable?"

She licked her lips as though testing the memory of his touch. "No, not at all, but...I can't get involved with you."

He felt a little relieved that she had at least seemed to like kissing him. Leaning against the doorway, he folded his arms, hoping she would see he wasn't going to reach for her again if she didn't wish it.

"You don't date people you work with, is that it?"

She nodded, looking a little pained. "I can't. It would make things too complicated, especially since you're my boss, and with this merger and everything..." She trailed off, and he felt a sinking disappointment. Kissing Emma had been a new experience, unlike the perfunctory kisses he'd known with Ophelia. Was it simply that Emma was someone new, a fresh possibility? He didn't think so. Emma stirred him in ways he hadn't thought possible.

Not that it mattered. She had made her preferences clear.

"It's all right. I understand," he offered. "We need to maintain a professional relationship."

"Yes, exactly." She appeared relieved at his agreement. Not exactly the reaction he would have wished for, but maybe she was right. Things could become complicated very quickly if they took their interest beyond friendship.

"You're not going to hold this against me, are you? Back out of our bargain?"

"No, of course not," she hastened to assure

him. "There's so much more to see in Paris. It would be unfortunate for us to stop just because of this…misunderstanding."

Misunderstanding? That was how she was going to label it? "Good. I'd hate to lose the best tour guide I've ever had."

She nodded, the gesture a little too abrupt, he thought.

"I better let you get some rest." He automatically moved toward her, just to brush a kiss against her cheek, but she stepped back again, as though she didn't trust him. Or maybe herself.

"I'll see you in the office, Aquitaine."

"Yes. I'll see you then."

He left, feeling slightly awkward with this goodbye, and trying not to let his disappointment get the better of him.

CHAPTER TEN

AFTER THEIR KISS, Emma worried that things would become strained between her and Cole. It was the very reason she disdained office relationships—the fear that it would affect her ability to do her job. But she needn't have been apprehensive where Cole was concerned. He behaved the same as always while they were at the office, as though nothing had happened between them. She found herself almost disappointed over the following weeks as things continued with nearly insulting normalcy between them.

Outside of work, matters were slightly different, however. Though they never mentioned the kiss, and Cole made no attempt to embrace her like that again, they still kept up their regular excursions throughout the city. Most of the time, Avery was with them, but occasionally, she would stay home with Melanie, if the au pair volunteered to babysit. Those times were some of the trickiest for Emma, when she didn't have the buffer of her daughter between her and Cole. It was more difficult to keep from leaning into him when they would walk the streets, more challenging to stop from reaching for his hand. A part of her would feel drawn to him at the most inopportune times—their heads close together as they read a map or looked through a shop window.

She firmly resisted any temptation. Cole was her boss, and she made every effort to view their outings as part of her role as his cultural liaison. Maybe that wasn't how things had started initially, but she was determined to keep it that way.

Some days were harder than others, though. Such as when he was awed by the Notre Dame Cathedral, and she wanted to slip her hand into his and whisper the magnificent structure's history into his ear. Or at the Louvre, when his brow furrowed in concentration at the sight of Da Vinci's *Mona Lisa.* She thought about teasing him and telling him how a girl might get jealous. They visited all the well-known tourist spots from the commercial luxuries of the Champs-Élysées to the ostentatious interiors of the Sacré-Cœur. And through it all, Emma worked to maintain her focus, forever reminding herself that Cole was her boss, nothing could happen between them and that he hadn't shown any interest since the night they'd kissed.

But hardest of all was trying to hide her emotions when Solene asked about him at their next lunch date. She had avoided her friend for several weeks after the incident with the candidate lists. No more of their placements had been poached, but still, Emma had come up with excuses to avoid Solene for a time. It wasn't so much a punishment, as Solene suggested after the third week of Emma dodging her, but rather uncertainty. She didn't know what to say to her friend, and she certainly didn't know how she felt about the job Solene had offered. She feared she didn't have the fortitude to resist her developing feelings for Cole in addition to Solene's hounding her for an answer.

But after a month of these games, she knew that if she wished to keep Solene as a friend, she'd have to give in and meet with her sometime. So they set up a lunch date for the last week in September. The air had turned cooler by then, the final days of summer having gradually shifted into autumn. Solene first asked about Avery, and Emma explained how she was back at nursery school now that summer had ended. Solene commented that she couldn't believe Avery would be old enough to begin *école primaire,* France's primary school system, the following year. They chatted about the change in seasons and items in the news, neatly avoiding discussions of work for a few minutes. But as they sipped from their coffee cups, the conversation turned as naturally as the weather.

"I understand you've been sightseeing with your new boss."

Emma straightened, as though preparing for battle. "Who told you that?"

"I called one night when you were out and spoke to your au pair."

Emma recalled several different times when she had returned home to find messages scribbled down by Melanie, more than a few of which had been from Solene. But the younger woman had never mentioned that she had told Solene such a thing.

Emma forced a shrug and sipped at the espresso she had laced with cream. "I've been showing him the city, as part of my job as his liaison."

Solene raised an eyebrow. "That is not part of your job, Emma, and you know it."

"Of course it is," she protested. "He wants to appreciate the city, but he didn't know where to begin."

"Hmm."

"It's true," Emma declared, knowing she sounded defensive.

"And what all have you shown him?"

Emma began listing the places they had been, her voice growing quieter as Solene's eyes widened. "Emma, you've shown him more than I have ever seen, and I am a native Parisian."

Emma shrugged again. "You know I love this city. There's so much to see and do here."

Her friend's eyes narrowed in consideration. "You like him, don't you?"

Emma dodged her glance by looking into her demitasse cup and swirling around the dwindling espresso.

"Oh, Emma."

She looked up to find Solene watching her with pity in her eyes. "You're falling for him, aren't you? I've heard he is very handsome and quite charming, but I never thought you'd succumb to those things, not after Brice."

"Don't be ridiculous. I am not falling for my boss."

"Ah. So that's it." Solene leaned back in her seat and continued to scrutinize her.

"What's it?"

"You can't fall in love with him because you work with him."

Emma toyed with the handle of her cup and

refused to look at Solene. She didn't want to think about these things. She couldn't be falling for Cole. It wasn't possible—she hadn't known him long enough, she didn't know enough about him. But secretly, she had to confess the signs. Her heart beat faster when he was nearby, her stomach turned with happiness every time he entered a room and her knees grew weak when he smiled at her. But these were simply signs of attraction, certainly not love.

Attraction could be mastered. Love would undo her.

"Does he feel the same way about you?"

Emma tried to laugh, but the sound came out choked. "Solene, please. I am not falling in love with my boss."

She had been avoiding looking directly at Solene, but when her friend's hand fell over hers, stilling its movements, she couldn't help looking up. She saw both sympathy and understanding and suddenly felt as though maybe it was okay to confess it out loud.

"We kissed. He kissed me."

Solene's frown deepened.

"I don't know that it meant anything," Emma rushed on, "and I told him it could never happen again. It hasn't. He doesn't even look at me that way now. He hasn't touched me like that since it happened. It was a one-time thing." She looked away and back again. "Just the once and never again."

"What was it like?"

Though she tried to stifle it, she felt the smile stretching across her face. "It was… wonderful. I felt…wanted."

"And you told him it could never happen again?"

She felt her smile shrink. "Yes. Because it can't. I can't get involved with him. It would make things too difficult, if it didn't work out. Especially because he's my boss."

Solene gave a thoughtful sigh and leaned back in her chair again. "There is a solution, you know."

Emma waited.

"Come and work with me at Léon Professional. Then, you will be free to pursue Cole without any concerns. If things do not work out—" she lifted one shoulder in an artful shrug "—you will face no awkwardness at the office."

"I don't know." She was still uncertain about leaving Aquitaine for their rival despite the offer of a raise and greater opportunities for advancement. What would Julien think? And what if Cole saw such an act as a betrayal? "I'm not even sure how Cole feels."

"Find out," Solene pressed. "Give him the opportunity you took away. Let him know you might be interested in seeing where things could lead."

"I'm not like Giselle. I can't just inform a man when I'm attracted to him."

Solene laughed, having once known Giselle as well as Emma. "Perhaps not, but Cole does not sound like the sort of man who needs to be told that sort of thing. He will understand the cues well enough if you present them the right way."

Emma felt a ripple of excitement pass through her at the possibility. But she still hesitated. "I don't know, Solene."

Solene tapped a finger against her cup. "Does Avery like him?"

Emma knew the answer immediately. "She loves him. She's always asking about him, and he's perfect with her. He's gentle and sweet and charming. He makes us both laugh. It's like he fills up all the holes that Brice leaves in Avery's life." As she spoke those words, Emma knew that she'd truly begun experiencing deeper feelings for Cole when she'd seen him with her daughter. He treasured Avery. Wasn't that exactly what every child deserved? But of course, she'd want to take it slow. She didn't want to weave

Cole into their lives and then have to unravel it all later. Although, without intending to, she knew she had done just that. Avery had come to expect their outings together.

Cole was already a part of their lives. This realization alarmed her. "What if this isn't a good idea?"

"*Chérie,* how will you know if you do not give it a try? Your heart has been closed up since Brice. You have avoided all forms of romance since then. If this man has found his way in, then you should not hold him at arm's length."

"I don't even know if he feels the same way," Emma protested again.

"Then find out. And if he does, talk to him about the possibilities, and come work with me at Léon."

Emma didn't say anything. Solene sighed.

"Do you remember how you were when you first came to Paris? You were brave and romantic, moving here and marrying Brice, pursuing a job with Aquitaine and beginning your career. Be that girl again, Emma. Be the woman who takes a risk on someone. Just because Brice let you down does not mean this man will, too."

These words stirred her. It was true. She had lost part of that girl when she and Brice split up. She remembered how Cole had called her a romantic. And she had been… once.

She wondered if she could be that same romantic, brave girl again.

WHEN EMMA RETURNED to the office after her lunch with Solene, she found her floor abuzz with energy and whispered conversations. The normally relaxed after-lunch hour was replaced with frantic movement and an air of heightened anticipation. She watched as Marc strode down a hall at a clipped pace, knocking into Aurora, who dropped the sheaf of folders she'd been carrying. Marc kept walking while Aurora gasped in dismay and fell to her knees to gather up the scattered files. Emma moved to join her.

"What's going on?" she asked as she assembled the papers into a tidy pile.

"You haven't heard?" Aurora asked.

"Heard what? I just got back from lunch."

"*She* is here."

"She?"

"The American boss. Lillian Reid."

Emma sat back on her heels. Lillian Reid was here? Had Julien or Cole known she was coming? If they had, neither man had bothered to inform her.

"Where is she?"

"In the conference room with Julien and Cole. I think..." Aurora trailed off and then met Emma's eyes, her own wide and ringed with the same tension that seemed to have everyone at the office on edge. "I think they are waiting for you."

Emma blinked. "Me?"

She felt a moment's panic at the same time she heard her name.

"Emma." She looked up to find Cole approaching. She searched for signs of uneasiness, but he appeared completely relaxed. He was even grinning with amusement, as if finding her on the carpet beside Aurora had made his day. "There you are. You're needed in the conference room." And then, belatedly, "What are you doing on the floor?"

"Marc ran into Aurora, and she dropped these files. I was helping her gather them up." She began to struggle to her feet, but he came and offered her a hand and then another to Aurora.

Aurora thanked him, gave Emma an almost pitying look and moved on. "What's gotten into everyone around here? They act almost...frightened."

Cole laughed. "Lillian can have that effect on people, I'm afraid."

This statement caused Emma to hesitate when Cole tried to place his hand on her back to move her forward.

"You have nothing to worry about," he assured her. "She's brought good news."

"Did you know she was coming?" She tried to keep her voice from sounding accusatory, but she hated being left out of the loop.

"I didn't," Cole admitted, "but apparently Julien did. He picked her up from the airport this morning."

"Shouldn't he have told us?"

Cole shrugged. "I guess he wanted it to be a surprise."

Emma didn't much like this sort of surprise.

She allowed Cole to rest his palm at her back and guide her along. She knew she shouldn't have dwelled on how comforting it felt to have the reassurance of his touch, but she couldn't seem to help herself. Since they had kissed, he rarely placed a hand on her. Feeling his steady touch, she realized how she had missed it. He led her in the direction of the conference room and, once they were over the threshold, dropped his arm. She felt a physical ache at the loss of it.

All such longings were soon forgotten as she stepped into the room, and Julien rose from his seat while Lillian looked up at her entrance. If the woman brought such good news, as Cole said, why was her expression so cold?

Emma moved toward the table, her hand extended. "Ms. Reid, what a lovely surprise. It's a pleasure to see you again."

Lillian inserted her fingers briefly into Emma's, and the touch was every bit as chilly as her expression.

"Likewise, Ms. Brooks."

"Please, call me Emma."

Lillian nodded but gave no such offer for Emma to do the same. She shifted her gaze to Julien, who was smiling rapturously in the older woman's direction. Huh. Well, that was interesting.

"Emma, why don't you take a seat?" Emma did as Cole suggested and felt a small throb of disappointment when he took the seat across the table instead of the one beside her.

Lillian consulted her watch and cleared her throat. "Well, now that we're all finally here, I'll proceed."

She leaned down and pulled several brochures from the briefcase Emma spied resting on the floor. She slid them toward her and Cole.

"The Twenty-third Annual Corporate Recruiting and Sourcing Conference," she announced.

Emma picked up the glossy paper and scanned the same words Lillian had just read. The title of the conference, along with the dates and a photo of professional businessmen and women, graced the cover, superimposed over the conference venue. Her eyes moved down the page to see it was being held at the Towers International Hotel Suites in Manhattan, New York City.

She slid a glance at Cole, who had turned the brochure over and was reading the back. She looked to Julien, but he was still staring at Lillian, so she swiveled her gaze in that direction to find Lillian eyeing her.

"You want us to attend?" She glanced at the dates again and then back to Lillian. "But it's in two weeks. We can hardly make arrangements—"

"I already have," Lillian informed her.

"Excuse me?"

"I've already made arrangements. You and Cole will be featured as guest speakers at a seminar on the topic of company mergers and cultural executive relations."

Emma knew she must have been staring and sensed that maybe her jaw had sagged in her surprise. She tried to gather her wits and say something, anything, but she was too stunned to reply.

"That's fantastic, Lillian."

Emma managed to turn her head in Cole's direction when he spoke these words. She finally found her voice. "But it's in two weeks. We can't come up with a presentation in two weeks' time."

"Of course you can," Lillian said, her tone condescending. "Julien assures me you're a most capable woman, Emma, and I can certainly vouch for Cole's abilities. Between the two of you, it should be no problem."

Emma knew better than to protest further. She also recognized it would do no good to point out to Lillian just how uneasy the idea of speaking at a conference made her.

"I've already had my assistant book your flights and hotel. You'll be staying at the Towers Resorts, where the conference is being held. Of course, Cole is already familiar with the city, so you should have no issues in that regard."

"With all due respect, Ms. Reid, perhaps it would be better to send one of the senior recruiters. Cole and I have our hands full running—"

"I am fully aware of what all has occurred on this side of the ocean, which is precisely why I pulled some strings to arrange your presence at the conference. Those leaked candidate files made us look incompetent, at best. Your presence as speakers at the conference will reinforce our reputation, remind the corporate world that we are still the best at what we do."

Emma couldn't argue with this logic. Lillian had a point. Her mind began planning the details, wondering if Melanie would be amenable to watching Avery while she was away. She certainly couldn't leave her with Jacqueline after last time. Her former mother-in-law had only recently been discharged from the hospital and was back home, recuperating in Le Mans.

"Well." Julien pushed back from the table. "I am sure Cole and Emma have much to plan concerning their presentations at the conference. And I believe you promised me a few hours of your time, *madame*."

Emma watched in awe as Lillian shifted from her somewhat haughty demeanor to a much softer one as she looked at Julien.

"I believe that I did."

The two stood and offered their farewells as Emma worked to catch Julien's eye. He hadn't looked at her once since she'd entered the room, and though she didn't expect any sort of coddling, it was still aggravating that he hadn't even acknowledged the enormity of the task Lillian had presented. He left the room with barely so much as a nod in her direction.

She watched him exit the glass doors of the conference room with Lillian's hand on his arm. When she turned back, she saw Cole watching her.

"So, it's going to be just you and me, Aquitaine. You still have my back?"

And that's when the full weight of it hit her. It would be her and Cole, together for almost five days, just the two of them on a trip across the ocean to New York.

She wondered what Solene would have said about that.

CHAPTER ELEVEN

THAT NIGHT, EMMA tossed and turned until the early hours of the morning. She felt uneasy about speaking at the conference, unsure of her own abilities. The thought of an auditorium full of expectant peers caused her stomach to twist unmercifully. She had managed to arrange things with Melanie and was surprised to find that Avery was more disappointed in not seeing Cole for several days than she was about her own mother leaving. She teased her daughter about this, but Avery made her reasoning clear.

"Cole is fun. He makes you laugh, Mommy. And I laugh, too."

Emma certainly couldn't argue with that logic, but it made her think about her conversation with Solene from earlier in the day. Could working for Léon Professional be the answer? Could she really turn her back on Julien and work for his rival? What would Cole even think of her for doing such a thing? But the promise of a promotion within a year's time and the possibility of dating Cole tempted her. She wondered if Cole was even still interested after she'd rejected him.

She'd called Solene briefly to tell her the news. Her friend wasn't attending the conference, but she said there were a few others from her office who were. She suggested Emma take the opportunity to meet with them while in New York. Emma had made no promises since she wasn't sure how she'd explain such a thing to Cole.

She spent that night in fitfulness, finally dozing for a couple of hours in the predawn light before waking and deciding to head into the office early. She might as well get a jump on her presentation. Maybe that would help with the jitters she was experiencing.

She rose and showered, decided she'd grab breakfast from the building cafeteria later in the morning, left a note for Melanie and snuck into Avery's room to kiss her goodbye before leaving for work.

She arrived at the office far earlier than the rest of her coworkers but was grateful for the quiet permeating the floor. Hopefully, she could work without distraction and lay down an outline for the topics she and Cole would be speaking on at the conference. Then, when he arrived, she'd ask him to review what she had so far. The very thought of speaking in front of hundreds of people still left her faintly nauseated, but at least she had a plan in place. She walked toward her office, anxious to get her thoughts on paper, and noticed that the light was already on inside. She frowned and moved closer before she relaxed, noticing Henri in the interior of the room.

Of course, she hadn't thought about Henri being in the building, doing his regular janitorial tasks. Hopefully, he was finished with her office, and then he'd have no need to disturb her as she got to work.

But as she stepped closer, she noticed him bending over her desk. She watched as he settled himself in her office chair and positioned his hands over her keyboard, swiftly running through the keystrokes to access her computer. She frowned. She kept a password on her computer, and she rotated it every three months; but she realized, to her dismay, that the last time she'd changed it, she'd been in a hurry and had simply used Avery's name and age as the key word. That was easy enough for anyone to figure out, especially Henri, since Avery was a common topic of conversation between them. But what could Henri possibly want on her computer?

Her mind skipped over a variety of possibilities as to what Henri could be doing. Checking his email? But why invade her privacy and crack her password just for that? He seemed comfortable enough in his actions that she doubted this was the first time he'd used her computer. She felt a ripple of unease, seeing this man, whom she had always thought of as a friendly acquaintance, taking such liberties. If his actions were innocent, why hadn't he just asked her if he could have access?

She watched as his hand reached toward the mouse, clearly clicking through several screens. Her sense of betrayal deepened. What could she possibly have stored on her system that he would want? She kept very few personal files on her work server. There were only items relating to Aquitaine, such as the merger documents, client profiles, and… She drew in a sharp breath.

The candidate name lists. They were all stored on her computer, for every single recruiter in the firm. Files with background checks, personal profiles, skill sets—all of it right there for the taking. Was that what he was after?

She watched as he typed a bit and then reached toward her desk's printer, which was spewing out several sheets of paper. Indignation rose in her, and she moved forward, entering her office and waiting for Henri to notice her. He was so intent on his task, however, that he didn't look up.

"Did you find everything you needed?"

The question startled him, and he jumped, his head jerking toward the door. A mixture of relief and chagrin flooded his features.

"Emma," he murmured with regret. "You're here early."

"Good thing, too." She stepped farther into the room and held out a hand, palm up. "Please give me the papers, Henri."

He hesitated for only a fraction of a second before turning the printouts over. She glanced down, scanning the information there. She had been right. These were more potential names, complete profiles for candidates in the technology sector. Some of the information was even labeled as confidential. This was a nightmare.

She looked up. "Why, Henri? Why would you do this?"

Henri swallowed. "I needed the money. I did not think it would matter too much."

"You didn't think it would matter? Henri, we spend months grooming these candidates, learning their background and skills, making every effort to pair them with the right company and career. How could you think it wouldn't matter? This is what we do. It's what Aquitaine is all about."

He looked at the floor, and she could see the top of his head, where the hair was beginning to thin. "There are always more opportunities for people like that, the ones in those files. There will always be more chances for them. But someone like me, for my family, there are not as many choices."

"Oh, Henri."

"I am on the verge of losing my children, Emma. Can you not understand how desperate I am?"

"Henri, I offered to loan you money. You didn't have to resort to this."

He gave a swipe of his head. "I refuse to bring my friends into this. I wanted to handle it myself. It is for my children, Emma. I would do anything to be able to see them, but the fees for a good lawyer, especially in my case, are considerable. If anyone understands this, surely you can. If someone tried to keep you from Avery, would you not pay any price, do anything, to be with her?"

Emma felt a knot rise in her throat. If only Brice had shared this man's passion to be in his child's life.

"Your love of your children is admirable, Henri. But you should want them to be proud of you. This is not the way to earn that."

He gave a curt swipe of his hand. "I do not care about pride! I only care about keeping my children."

She didn't respond to this impassioned statement but rather considered the situation. Solene had known Henri, when she worked at Aquitaine. Perhaps she had never been as friendly with him as Emma was, but she had joked with him on occasion. "Did you approach Solene with this information? Or did she ask you for it?"

He shrugged and avoided her gaze.

"Henri," she pressed. "Whose idea was it?"

He looked up. "Both of us," he confessed. "I contacted her—it was easy to find her phone number on the Léon website. I asked if she knew of any way I could earn some extra money, to pay for the lawyer fees. She said her candidate files were thin and suggested there would be recompense if I provided her with some from this office. She told me what sort of files to look for when I logged on to your computer."

Oh, Solene. She had probably seen it as the perfect way to strike back at Julien. Convincing Emma to switch companies would simply be icing on the cake.

"It was only the one time," Henri went on. "This—" he gestured toward the computer, "—was just in case she needed more."

"How much did she pay you for the first list of files?"

"Fifty percent of whatever commission she earned on the placements."

Fifty percent. Half her commission on each recruitment. With all the candidates combined, it would seem like a fortune to someone like Henri, more than enough to afford the lawyer he needed. Solene hadn't done this for the money, though. She'd done it to hurt Julien. Emma was disappointed but not surprised. Solene's bitterness toward her former employer ran deep. How much of it leaked back onto her? Did Solene resent Emma for staying with Aquitaine, after she had left? Did she begrudge the attention Julien had bestowed on Emma, treating her as his protégé as she moved up the ladder at this company?

"Emma." Henri's voice had become pleading. "No one can know about this. If my ex-wife found out, she would use it as leverage to make sure I never see my children again."

Emma felt a weight settle itself in her stomach at what he was asking. "Henri, it was my job to find the source of the leak. I can't just ignore this, pretend like it never happened."

"I'm not asking you to," he responded. "I'm only asking for a little time, until the custody trial is over. After that, I will come forward myself and confess what I've done."

"Why not make a clean break of it and tell Julien now? I'm sure he'd be sympathetic to your situation—"

But Henri was already shaking his head. "I cannot risk it. After the custody is determined, matters can be handled more quietly. I will admit to what I've done and seek employment elsewhere. My life will no longer be, how do they say, under a magnifying glass."

Emma felt the twist of indecision. If she spoke up now and told Julien what she had discovered, she would very likely be responsible for Henri never getting to see his children again. Was that something she could live with?

On the other hand, if she did as he asked, she betrayed Julien by not coming forward. But it would cost the company no more than had already been lost. It would only delay things for a little while. Henri would take responsibility for his actions, and matters would be set right. Just in the future instead of immediately.

As long as he learned of the discovery, and appropriate action was taken, she could keep this to herself for a while longer.

She nibbled her lip raw as she weighed these options.

"It cannot happen again, Henri. We minimized the fallout this time, but you cannot sell any more names to Solene. I mean it, nothing."

"I will not. No more."

"And you have to promise me that you will come forward as soon as the custody battle is finished. If you don't tell Julien at that point, I will."

He gave another swipe of his head. "I give you my word. As soon as things are decided, I will confess and resign, if that is what Julien requires."

She held his gaze, searching to see if she could take him at his word. When he didn't turn away, she nodded.

"All right."

"You will say nothing, then? You won't tell anyone, not even the American boss?"

"Cole?" She faltered. She didn't like the idea of keeping secrets from Cole.

"I know you are close to him, but I beg you, please do not tell him it was me."

She frowned. "Why do you think I'm close to him?"

"Because I have eyes. Anyone can see how he watches you when you don't think he's looking and how your face lights up when he comes into a room. The two of you talk to each other as though you understand one another."

Had her coworkers noticed this? Or was it simply Henri, who had more opportunity to observe them as he went about his tasks around the office?

"He should know," Emma spoke, her voice soft. "I don't like not telling him."

Henri took a step toward her, his expression desperate. "Please, no. He would not understand, Emma. You know that he would not."

She didn't know any such thing. Cole had proven himself more kind and compassionate than she could have imagined. But he had no children of his own. Despite his affection and care for Avery, would he be able to sympathize with Henri's situation?

"Just a few more weeks," Henri pressed, "and then I will speak to both Cole and Julien myself. I promise. Please, Emma. Think of what you would do, if it was Avery at stake."

She hated how Henri knew exactly where her weak spot was, but he was right. For Avery, she would do anything.

"Fine," she agreed, though she felt a stab of guilt at keeping this to herself. "I won't tell Cole, so long as it doesn't happen again."

Henri's face split into a smile of relief. "*Merci,* Emma." He reached for her hands, and before she could pull away, he had raised them to his lips, dropping kisses across her knuckles. "You have always been the kindest of everyone around here."

Embarrassed, she tugged her fingers from his. "Thank you, but remember what I said—it cannot happen again."

"It will not, I assure you."

She nodded. "All right, then. We won't speak of it anymore. Now, if you'll excuse me, I need to get some work done."

"Of course. Certainly." He moved to the door, and she waited until she heard it click shut before she sank into her chair and released a sigh.

Her conscience still prickled with uncertainty, and she could only hope that she had done the right thing.

COLE KNEW HE was in trouble when he began counting the hours until he and Emma left for the recruiting conference. The prospect of five whole days, including travel time, with her pleased him far more than he would have liked to admit. After all, Emma had made her position clear on the night he'd kissed her. She didn't want to pursue a relationship.

Since that night, he had been vigilant in guarding his heart. He had no plans to fall for another woman who didn't want to be with him, so he reined in any feelings he might be experiencing for Emma and kept things friendly without making any attempt at something more.

But the more time he spent with her and Avery, the more difficult he found it to limit his emotions. When he was with the two of them, he had a sense of belonging that he'd never experienced before. And when Avery would reach for him or place her tiny hand into his, he found himself melting with tenderness. He felt a protective instinct where Emma's daughter was concerned, one that had begun to extend to Emma herself.

Cole had never been much of a protective sort. He had grown up in an environment where he had only himself to look out for, and if he didn't watch his own back, no one else would. But for the first time in his life, he had the urge to watch over another, to shelter and care for someone else. He wanted to be there for Emma and Avery, to shield them from whatever might come their way. To put it simply, he wanted to be a more permanent part of their lives.

But he was not foolish enough to confess such feelings to Emma, for fear she would shut him out like she had the night of their kiss. He kept things easygoing, exerting a tremendous amount of effort in maintaining a facade of camaraderie instead of genuine caring.

So he'd known he was in trouble when Lillian had announced their spot at the conference, and his heart had tripped over itself in his chest. Just him and Emma, all those hours working together on their presentation, then in each other's company on the plane and during their time at the conference. He could barely contain his excitement and had to work doubly hard not to appear absolutely giddy at the idea.

Emma's unease over their seminar helped him to keep his own reactions in check, at least. He watched her fret and fuss for the two weeks leading up to the conference, eyed her with amusement as she kept reviewing her notes on the plane and had to resist touching her in reassurance when they arrived at the Towers Resort in Manhattan and her hands trembled as she accepted the key to her room.

They spent the first night in the city at the orientation and reception for the conference, mingling with fellow colleagues in the recruiting field before calling it a night and heading to their respective hotel rooms. He called Lillian, who had remained in Paris with Julien, to let her know they had arrived safely and were all set for their presentation. The next day was filled with networking and seminar events, a catered lunch and an evening's entertainment—a well-known stand-up comedian who specialized in corporate humor.

Emma begged him to forgo the show in favor of reviewing their presentation once more. Since he'd barely had five minutes alone with her since their arrival, he was more than happy to agree to this suggestion.

They each gathered their notes and settled into Emma's room to review the talking points. As the hour dragged on, he watched Emma's anxiety rise. He did his best to reassure her.

"There's nothing to be nervous about," he said.

"But what if I freeze up there? What if I can't remember which PowerPoint slide goes with which topic? What if someone asks me a question, and I don't have the answer?"

She fanned through a sheaf of papers while he stared in disbelief. He had never seen Emma so rattled. "You've given presentations dozens of times, to clients, to employees."

"I know, but not like this. Not in an auditorium full of peers. It's different."

He couldn't help being slightly amused at her insecurity. "Emma, you're going to do fine. You're very capable, and I don't have a single doubt that you can do this."

A faint relief entered her eyes. "Really?"

"Really." He didn't normally allow himself to touch her, but he told himself that just this once wouldn't hurt. He reached for her hand and drew it into his, smoothing the pad of his thumb across the ridges of her knuckles. Her fingers tensed and then relaxed under the soothing ministration. "I wouldn't let just anybody share a podium with me. Lillian may be tough, but she's also smart. She knew you could handle this, and I know it, too. You're good at what you do, Aquitaine. You might as well show it off."

She laughed softly, and the sound made him happy.

"I guess I do make you look good."

His heart lifted. "You make me look very good. We're an effective team." He locked eyes with her, his thumb still running over her hand. He watched as her expression shifted and then let go of her hand.

"We know this presentation front to back. Let's take the night off."

She frowned. "I'm not really interested in seeing that comedian."

"That's not what I meant. Let's go out. You've spent the past few weeks showing me everything there is to love about Paris, so why don't you let me return the favor? You've never been to New York, and I only have a couple of days to show you what you've been missing."

She hesitated. "I don't know. Shouldn't we make sure everything is ready for tomorrow—"

"Emma." He grabbed her hand again. "You're going to do just fine tomorrow. But who knows when you'll get to the city again? Come on. Let me take you out. Just this once."

He tried not to sound too pleading, too desperate for some one-on-one time that didn't involve spreadsheets and talking points. He could see her wavering.

"We can look for a souvenir to bring back for Avery."

At the mention of her daughter, she relented. "All right. That's a good idea."

HOURS LATER, EMMA couldn't help marveling at how different she felt from earlier in the day. Most of her tension had dissolved, and she was feeling relaxed and carefree. It amazed her that Cole had known exactly what she'd needed to feel better. He had taken her to dinner at one of his favorite Manhattan restaurants followed by dessert at the infamous Serendipity 3. They'd stopped in a few shops, where Emma had picked up a couple of trinkets for her daughter. Cole had insisted on buying Avery a teddy bear wearing a sparkly tutu and T-shirt that said Broadway Star. They had wandered the Museum Mile and ended up at Central Park, where the autumn air had tinted the leaves' edges with color.

He compared it to the Square des Batignolles, discussing which features he liked best about each place. They talked about all the places in Paris she had taken him to in the past month, and she realized, quite unexpectedly, that Cole knew this was the way to still her uneasiness about tomorrow, to remind her of home and the places she loved best in all the world.

As they walked through the park, it occurred to her that Cole had come to know her far better than she would have expected. He had seen her at her best and at her worst, and he still seemed to genuinely like her. More than that, she had the sense that he wanted to spend even more time with her. There would come a point when she would have shown him everything in Paris she thought he should see, and then what? There were the surrounding cities, day trips and the countryside, but eventually, she would have to make a decision on just how she was going to keep Cole in her life, outside of work, if she didn't want to pursue a relationship. Could they be just friends? Did she want to be just friends with him?

She knew the answer before she'd even considered the question. She wanted to know Cole better, to keep him in her life, and in Avery's life. But it dawned on her that for as well as he knew her, her likes and dislikes, she still knew relatively little about him.

She spotted a bench up ahead and walked toward it. Without asking any questions, he followed, and they settled onto the bench before she turned to him.

"Cole, why haven't you ever told me more about yourself?"

He didn't quite meet her eye. "What do you mean? I've told you plenty of things."

"No, you haven't," she argued. "I know about how you came to Paris, about how things ended with you and Ophelia. But I mean before all that. Like, where did you grow up? Where are your parents? What do they think of you moving to Paris? Who did you leave behind in the States when you moved abroad?"

He stared at her for a long moment before he looked away. "It's not important."

"What do you mean? Of course it's important." She drew a breath and then released it. "You matter to me, and I want to know."

She watched him carefully as he stared straight ahead as if debating how much to tell her. "No one." When he finally spoke, his voice was low.

"What?"

He looked at her, his hazel eyes darkening to a caramel-brown. "There was no one I left behind."

She frowned. "I don't understand."

"I don't have anyone," he explained. "I was a foster kid, shuffled from home to home growing up. I was in and out of so many places that I can't even remember most of them. They became a blur after a while, an endless routine of boxed macaroni meals and packing my bags for the next house. I changed so many high schools that I can't tell you the names of more than half of them. I was just one more kid in the system, one more mouth to feed, one more number in a long list of them.

"When I was old enough, I began looking into my records, curious about my background. Every kid in foster care had a story, but I didn't know mine. When I finally tracked down the original paperwork on my case, I knew almost less than when I started. My mom was fourteen when she had me, just a kid herself. She was a runaway living in New York, and there was no information on her real name or where she'd come from. She died of a heroin overdose a year after I was born. There was no father listed on my birth certificate, so the trail went cold from there. Even my name isn't my own. I chose Dorset because I thought it sounded more sophisticated than my own background. I had it legally changed when I turned eighteen."

A lump rose in Emma's throat at these confessions. She never would have guessed these things about Cole. It amazed her how much of himself he'd been able to keep hidden from her. She felt the full weight of what he must have experienced as he relayed his story and longed to reach for him but didn't in case he would stop speaking.

"I learned a lot growing up in foster care, about people and the way they think. When I graduated high school, I decided I would take what I'd learned and use it to make myself better, to make sure I never had to rely on anyone else again. I never went to college. I just began applying to recruiting firms as soon as I could. Eventually, one of them took me on, and I worked hard to learn everything I could about this business. From there, I joined a bigger firm and then a bigger one until I had a strong track record behind me. That's when I applied at Reid Recruiting. I don't know what she saw in me, but Lillian was impressed. After she took me on, I had nowhere to go but up, and I never looked back."

Emma digested the rest of this brief history. "Then, you really have no one? No siblings, no parents?"

He shrugged. "No one. And you know the saddest part?" He caught her gaze with his. "I told myself it never mattered to me…until I met you and Avery."

Emma's eyes burned with suppressed tears.

He sighed and looked away. "Listen, Emma, please don't be freaked out by this, but I want you to know that these past weeks in Paris, with you and Avery, have taught me more about family than I ever thought possible. I never knew what it was to belong somewhere, to feel a part of someone else. But when I'm with the two of you, I feel like that. I know it will never be anything more," he rushed to assure her, "but for what it's worth, I'm really grateful to you. You've given me a new sense of hope that maybe I can find that feeling again someday."

She felt emotion rising up in her at his honesty. Cole always seemed so confident that she had never guessed about this particular vulnerability of his. He wanted a family of his own; he had just never known it before this.

Her silence must have made him uncertain because he moved away from her on the bench. "I'm sorry. I shouldn't have said all that. I promise you, it's not going to interfere with our working relationship." His hazel eyes burned with desperation, his need to convince her. His golden hair fell across his forehead, and without thinking, she reached forward to brush it back. When she touched him, he stopped talking, frozen in place.

Awkwardly, she pulled her hand away and placed it back into her lap. "It's all right. I'm…glad you told me. That's a lot to keep to yourself."

"I've never told anyone before," he admitted. "Not even Ophelia. She knew I was an orphan, but I never told her the rest of it."

Her lips parted in surprise, and she realized then just how much she must mean to him, if he could share with her a past he had never even told the woman he'd been prepared to marry.

"Cole, what if—" she started and then stopped.

"What if—?" he prompted.

"What if something changed? What if it was possible for us to…you know."

Her blood coursed faster as he smiled. "I'm afraid I don't know. You're going to have to enlighten me."

He inched closer on the bench, closing some of the distance between them. Her breath hitched in her chest. "What if it was possible for us to…see each other?"

His lips twitched with what she assumed was amusement. "It's perfectly possible. I see you right now."

"No, not like that."

"You mean, as in dating?"

She knew he was enjoying this, her difficulty in finding the right words. But his enjoyment didn't bother her in the least. "Yes. What if I said I'd like to consider a relationship?"

"Aquitaine, are you asking me out?"

She rolled her eyes, and he laughed. "If your ego needs to hear it, then I suppose... yes. I'm asking you out."

He closed the final gap between them, his hip coming to rest against hers. He shifted and moved his arm around the back of the bench so that she could feel his fingers playing along her shoulder. She felt a surge of nervousness at the close proximity, at the subtle scent of his aftershave and the warmth of his body beside her.

"I—I mean, I'm not sure about how things would work, since y-you're my boss, and I'm the managing director, and...you know."

She had the offer from Solene. She was opposed to accepting after what she had learned from Henri, but if things didn't work out between them, she could still consider working for Léon Professional instead. At the moment, feeling heady with his nearness, she decided it was an acceptable plan.

He moved his face closer, his mouth resting near her ear. "I don't think we'll have any problems," he murmured.

His breath tickled her earlobe, and she shifted her head, only to find her lips perilously close to his.

"And maybe you could tell me more," she quietly offered, "about your past. About... anything."

"I'll tell you whatever you want to know."

But just then, they didn't do any more talking on the matter.

CHAPTER TWELVE

WHEN EMMA AWOKE the next morning, she was filled with both a light happiness and a weighty sense of dread. She sat up in her bed at the Towers Resorts and tried to sort through these emotions until she pinned down the reasons behind them.

The conference presentation. Cole. She felt a wave of anxiety mixed with giddiness roll through her.

She had to speak at today's seminar, but at least Cole would be by her side. Cole, who had talked with her long into the night, about his past and the possibilities for the future, his protectiveness toward Avery and his feelings for her. She hugged her pillow to her chest and squeezed. She hadn't known she could feel like this. When she had first met Brice, she had been young and idealistic and had expected love to be like something out of a fairy tale—exotic locations and handsome princes. As she had grown older, she'd never anticipated experiencing that sort of thrill again and chalked her previous assumptions up to her naïveté. But now, with Cole, she realized she'd been somewhat wrong. Love didn't need everything to be perfect in order to bloom and grow. Her feelings for Cole were the prime example of that. They had gotten off to a poor start, and they'd had a few hiccups along the way, and she still felt uneasy about dating her boss, but none of it mattered.

Cole cared about her. And about Avery. She treasured that thought and held it tightly to her as she rose and readied for the day.

When he knocked on her door, she felt a surge of joy and ran to answer it. He stood on the threshold, his smile causing her own to widen.

"Are you ready for this?"

At first, she thought he meant the two of them, exploring the possibilities of the future, and she nearly gushed a "Yes!" until it dawned on her that he meant the presentation. A bit of her excitement ebbed.

"Um…as ready as I'll ever be."

He reached for her hand. "I'm going to be right there with you, the entire time." This thought helped reassure her, but some of her doubt must have still showed because Cole released her hand and placed his palms along the sides of her neck instead, forcing her to look into his face.

"You are one of the very best at what you do, Aquitaine. Don't doubt yourself now. I certainly don't."

He leaned down to drop a kiss on the tip of her nose. Her heart swelled and warmed with affection. His words helped steady her, reminded her that she wouldn't be alone in front of the audience.

"Let's show them how successful Reid and Aquitaine is going to be."

IT HAD ALL gone perfectly. Emma's nervousness had dissolved the moment she stepped to the podium. It was as if Cole's presence had banished it. Standing beside him, she'd felt confident, every bit the professional he had told her she was. From their opening remarks, which related some of the cultural land mines one could expect in international dealings, to their closing summaries, which emphasized the success of their companies' merger, they had held the audience's attention and received due applause at the end.

When they opened the session up for a Q & A, the inquiries were smart and showed just how much the attendees had garnered from what had been shared. Even in this portion, Emma marveled at how well she and Cole worked together. Their responses were in sync, they deferred to the other when necessary and delivered flawlessly.

When their time was finally up, and they dismissed the auditorium, it was all Emma could do to keep from rushing into Cole's arms, bubbling with success. They lingered a few minutes with the conference coordinators, who had slipped in when the Q & A started, and then they were free.

Emma felt too restless and excited for networking or sitting through a workshop, and Cole must have felt the same because he suggested they play hooky for the rest of the day. There was so much more he wanted to show her in the city, he said.

So that's what they did, changing clothes before setting out. They ate lunch at a pizzeria, and then Cole took her to the Met. They strolled among the paintings, hand in hand, occasionally whispering an opinion or sharing a comment. The artwork passed by in a blur; Emma was far too aware of the feel of Cole's hand in hers, warming her.

After the Met, he took her to the Empire State Building, and they compared views from the American structure to those from the Eiffel Tower. He kept his arm around her waist as they talked, and she leaned into him, resting her head against his shoulder when they fell silent after a time.

Later, he took her to a Broadway show, and they finished the evening with a quiet dinner in Little Italy. She couldn't remember the last time she'd been so relaxed.

They finished out the last day of the conference in much the same way—attending a couple of events in the morning and then sneaking out into the city for the remaining hours of the afternoon and evening. Emma checked in at home and listened to Avery talk about all the things she and Melanie had been doing, then related a little bit of what she was experiencing in New York.

It wasn't until the flight home that she looked over at Cole, who had fallen asleep, and let the full measure of her happiness fill her up. In his slumber, he was still holding her hand, as he had been in every spare minute they had together. She studied his features, the fall of blond hair across his forehead, the sandy-colored lashes that darkened at the tips, the clean-shaven jawline. Her eyes found his lips, recalling how they felt on hers.

She felt something stirring deep within her, and it was then that she realized.

She loved him. Somewhere between that

first frustrated encounter and the moment he had opened his heart to her and shared his past, she had fallen in love with him. Whether it was his gentle way with Avery, his ability to charm a laugh out of her or simply how he had tried to support her in the midst of the company's transition, he had stolen his way into her heart. She had only known him for a couple of months, but she couldn't imagine life without him anymore.

They would make things work, she decided. She would tell Solene she had no intention of abandoning Aquitaine now. She would stay, for Julien and for Cole, because she wanted to be wherever he was, no matter the consequences. She would even learn to like Lillian, she decided, feeling expansive. It all made so much sense when she looked at Cole, sleeping so peacefully. Perhaps it was merely the optimism of her inner romantic, but as long as she loved him, she didn't see what could possibly go wrong.

WHEN IT CAME time to return to work on the Tuesday morning after they arrived back from New York, Cole found himself looking forward to heading into the office more than he had in years. The reason, he knew, was because he would get to see Emma again. As if their time in New York and a phone call the evening before wasn't enough, he couldn't wait to see her face.

He hummed snatches of some nameless tune as he entered the office building and headed for the elevators. He was just pressing the button when he felt someone step up beside him.

"Good morning."

He felt a tingle of anticipation as he turned and saw her smiling up at him.

"Good morning, Emma," he greeted her in return.

He knew his own smile matched hers. They faced the elevator doors together, waiting for them to open.

"I wondered if you're free for lunch today?" he asked.

"Hmm, I don't know. I'll have to check my calendar."

"I'm your boss—I could always demand you clear your schedule."

"You wouldn't even try," she replied, and he chuckled.

The elevator doors opened, and they stepped inside. As soon as they were away from prying eyes, he reached over and took her hand.

"Would it be too cheesy if I told you I've missed you, even though I just saw you yesterday?"

"It's definitely cheesy, but a girl still likes to hear it." She looked up at him. "I'm free for lunch. I didn't mean to tease you about it."

"Then it's a date."

As soon as the elevator doors slid open, they released hands. Exiting together, they made their way toward their offices, shifting the tone of conversation to business-related matters. They greeted a few of their colleagues, who congratulated them on the success of the conference, having already heard that their presentation was well received.

Louis came out of his office to welcome them back, and Aurora and Giselle each found them to share excerpts from the conference website, highlighting Cole and Emma's seminar as one of the best at the annual event.

They rode the tide of such happy commentary down the hall until they reached Emma's office. Cole had his hand on the small of Emma's back, guiding her along, until he felt her spine stiffen. He followed her line of sight past the doorway.

Marc and Julien stood inside; the former's expression was smug while the latter's was grim. And beside them, seated in the guest chair and looking equally forbidding, was Lillian.

EMMA KNEW, AS soon as she saw the trio in her office, that she was in trouble. If Marc's smirk and Julien's grimace weren't indication enough, then the thundercloud on Lillian's face certainly was. She felt an unexpected calm come over her. Cole's hand remained in the small of her back, and she drew strength from that touch as she squared her shoulders and entered the room. She placed her purse on a table just inside the door as Cole entered behind her.

"Why, hello. What a wonderful way to be welcomed back. This is a pleasant surprise."

Of course, it was anything but pleasant, but she would never say so. They weren't here to congratulate her and Cole on a successful conference. No, whatever they had come to say, it was bad news.

"Cole, you won't be needed in this meeting." Lillian's voice was cool and dismissive, and Emma's heart sank at its tone.

"If it's all right with you, Lillian, I'd like to stay."

Lillian shook her head. "I think it's best if you go."

Emma steeled herself for his departure, but he moved toward the small love seat against the opposite wall and sank into it.

"As CEO, I think it's in the company's best interest if I sit in."

Emma felt a surge of relief at this but waited for Lillian to contradict him. The older woman ignored him, however, and focused on Emma once more.

"There have been some disturbing revelations in your absence, Ms. Brooks."

Emma didn't suppose there was any point in once again reminding Lillian to simply call her by her first name. She glanced at Marc, who was positively puffed up with pride. She looked back at Lillian, bypassing Julien completely.

"I'm sorry to hear that. Perhaps it's something I can assist you with?"

Emma thought the chill in Lillian's words could practically freeze water. "I don't think that's likely, given the circumstances."

Emma needed to establish some sort of edge here. Lillian had ambushed her, and Julien was entirely too silent. Marc's attendance puzzled her since he'd never before sat in on any meetings with the senior leadership. Cole's presence helped buoy her, but she knew she needed more than that for whatever bomb her employer was about to drop. She moved to her desk, easing around it and settling herself into the chair. At least, in that position, she had the benefit of the power seat. She feared, however, that it wouldn't do her much good.

"What are these circumstances that we're facing?" She figured Lillian was the sort of woman who'd want her to come straight to the point. "It must be formidable if all three of you had to come to see me."

Though she felt little of the confidence she tried to exude, she still leaned back in her seat and rested her hands together. She hoped she appeared far more in control than she felt.

She saw Lillian look at Julien, who finally met her eyes.

"There has been another stolen placement in your absence," he informed her.

Emma's stomach twisted. Solene. Her friend had broken her promise. And Henri? Had this new candidate been from his original theft or had he lied to her as well, selling more names to Solene and her company?

"I hardly need to remind you that Emma and I have been tied up with this conference," Cole pointed out. "We haven't had time to track down the source of those leaked files."

"We already know the source," Marc

chimed in, clearly eager to make his presence known.

Cole fell silent, and Emma looked his way to catch his eye for a second.

"Marc, perhaps it would be best if you step outside," Julien suggested.

Marc hesitated, looking from Lillian to Julien and back again. When no one suggested otherwise, he moved toward the door, some of the triumph fading from his posture.

"Please, close the door behind you, Marc," Lillian called.

He looked over his shoulder one last time and then did as he was told. When it was just the four of them once more, Cole leaned forward in his seat.

"What exactly is going on here?"

Lillian had turned to look at Emma.

"Ms. Brooks, would you care to enlighten him?"

"How can I?" she replied. "When I haven't been enlightened myself?"

Lillian narrowed her eyes. "All of those stolen candidate profiles were placed by the same recruiter."

"Yes, I'm aware of that."

"Solene Thierry. It's my understanding that she is a friend of yours?"

Emma wondered just what sort of picture

Marc must have painted for Lillian, to make the older woman look at her so distastefully.

"Emma tried speaking with Solene, to find out who gave her the files," Cole reminded them.

"And did she tell you?" Lillian directed the question to Emma, who shook her head.

"No. Solene refused to incriminate anyone."

"Convenient."

Emma looked at Julien, willing him to speak up, but he was utterly silent, his gaze fixed elsewhere.

"If you would like to accuse me of something, I'd prefer it if you go ahead. Evasiveness is a waste of time," Emma stated, hoping none of them noticed how her hands had begun to tremble.

"Very well, if that's what you prefer. Marc pointed out that those candidates came from a variety of recruiter files at the firm. But the only person who had every single one already stored on their computer is Aquitaine's managing director."

Of course. Emma had realized that when she'd caught Henri. While the files kept on each recruiter's computer were for their specialty alone, her computer held all of the candidate lists. A buffet of information for someone looking for easy access to names. In her desire to protect Henri, she had never really considered how his actions incriminated her.

"You cannot honestly find me culpable with such weak evidence."

"Marc told us your opposition to this merger is well known. Julien confirmed it. I did some investigating myself and spoke with the CEO at Léon Professional. It seems you are in talks with that company concerning the possibility of employment."

It was one thing to be accused of something she felt somewhat responsible for, like the candidate leak. But she had not followed up on Solene's offer, and the shadow such an allegation cast on her in this situation was too much. She spoke without thinking her response through.

"That wasn't me. Solene was determined that I should interview for a position there. She was the one setting things up."

The instant the words left her mouth, she knew she never should have spoken them. Three sets of eyes rested on her, but Julien's were the ones she locked on to. His gaze positively burned with betrayal. She had always been very careful where her friendship with Solene was concerned. Even though there was animosity between Solene and Julien, Emma cared for them both and hadn't wanted to make an enemy of either. But by naming Solene, by indicating she knew what her friend was up to, she had caused herself to look guilty in Julien's eyes. She felt the blood draining from her face as he stared at her, his expression turning cold.

"I wasn't necessarily going to go through with it," she whispered, but she recognized the culpability in those words. There were too many strikes against her.

Drawing a slow breath, she shifted her eyes in Cole's direction. He was staring at her with an expression somewhere between shock and disappointment. When she tried to meet his eyes, he looked away. A weight settled on her shoulders. She looked back at Lillian and found her stare even frostier than before.

"I believe it's best if you pack up your things."

She lost the slippery grip on her composure and jumped to her feet. "I didn't do it. I did not sell those candidate files to Solene."

Lillian scoffed. "So, they were *sold* to our rival? My, how the plot thickens."

Emma's eyes slid closed. How deep would

she dig this hole before she realized there was no way out of it?

"I would never do something like that to this company." She opened her eyes and looked at Julien. "I would never do that to you. I swear it, Julien. I wouldn't betray you like that."

Lillian clicked her tongue in disgust. "The candidate files were all stored on your computer. You are clearly good friends with this Solene, a woman who obviously has a vendetta against Julien. You were opposed to the merger of my company with this one. You had plans to interview for a position with our rival. And you just inadvertently admitted those files were sold off, making the entire situation even more sordid. Exactly why should we believe you?"

At this list of sins, Emma slowly swiveled her attention back in Lillian's direction. It was apparent to her, from both Julien's silence as well as Cole's, that she would lose this battle. All that remained to be seen was how much dignity she could take with her when she left.

"You know, Julien once told me that I should admire you, given the similarities between my situation and your own past. Both single mothers, both trying to make better lives for ourselves and our daughters through our careers. But I don't see as much to admire as he does. I hope I am never as cold and unfeeling as you are."

She moved from behind the desk and headed for the door. She wanted to look in Cole's direction, to try to read his expression once more, but she couldn't bring herself to do it. She had just picked her purse up from the table when Lillian spoke.

"I trust it goes without saying, Ms. Brooks, that you will not be welcome in this office again."

She swallowed and didn't bother to turn around as she left the room. She would ask Giselle to box up her belongings later. Right now, she needed to get away. She caught sight of Marc, hovering nearby. She glared at him, and at least he had the decency to look abashed.

She was sorry Lillian had confronted her when the day was just beginning. Too many of her coworkers must have sensed what had happened because she felt their stares as she headed for the elevator. She rounded a corner and caught sight of Henri. He, too, must have realized because his eyes conveyed apology.

She still didn't know who had broken their promise—whether it was Solene or Henri.

She supposed it didn't matter anymore. She held Henri's stare for the length of time it took her to reach the elevators. Only then did she look away and turn her back on them all.

COLE SAT FROZEN, unable to move, as he tried to process the evidence Lillian had presented against Emma. It seemed unbelievable. He began to experience a sinking feeling. Just how well did he know Emma?

"We'll need to begin interviewing for a new managing director," Lillian announced. "Do you have any acceptable candidates for promotion, Julien? I know Marc has already put in his bid, but we should at least consider a few others, for the sake of formality."

Cole looked at Julien. The other man appeared heartsick. He'd mentored Emma for years. Why hadn't he come to her defense? Lillian seemed oblivious to their mood. She continued.

"Perhaps I should bring over someone from New York, as I wanted to do in the first place. Someone whose loyalty is secure—"

Cole stood abruptly at this. He couldn't listen to another word. He had to talk to Emma himself. He moved toward the door.

"Cole. Where are you going? We have a lot to discuss, including how we're going to spin Emma's departure after your session at the conference. This couldn't have come at a worse time," Lillian muttered.

But Cole didn't answer. He exited the office and ignored her calls for him to come back. He headed for the elevator, avoiding the stares from his employees and hoping he could catch Emma before she left the building. He pressed the elevator button multiple times until it opened, and then he hurried inside, hitting the button for the lobby. He tapped his foot impatiently as the car descended. The minute the doors chimed open, he rushed out.

His gaze fell on Emma as she exited the front entrance, and he ran to catch up with her.

"Emma!" He kept calling her name, hoping she'd stop. "Emma!"

Her clipped pace meant she had already made it down the steps and halfway across the plaza by the time he reached her.

"Emma!" He hurried past her and blocked her path. She moved to step around him, but he matched her movements and hindered her progress again.

"Emma, please. Talk to me for a minute."

Her gray eyes were darker than he'd ever seen them, shaded in charcoal. They were also slightly red, as though she was holding back tears.

"We'll find a way out of this, all right? I'll stand by you. If you still want to work for Aquitaine, I can talk to Lillian and maybe negotiate a trial suspension…."

She was staring at him wordlessly.

"And if she won't agree, well…at least we don't have to worry about you dating your boss anymore, right?" He knew it wasn't the right thing to say, but he had never been all that good at consolation.

She scowled at him. "That is the least of my concerns at the moment. I just got fired. For something I didn't do."

He hesitated, uncertain how to approach her in this sort of mood. He had seen her angry, of course; their first meeting had shown him how mad she could become. But this was different. He cared for her now. Loved her, even. He didn't know what to say to make things better.

"You know that I didn't do this, right?" she asked.

He looked at her, saw the frustration building in her face. He willed himself to answer, but he couldn't. Slowly, her features fell.

"Cole, you do believe me, don't you?"

A cold wind cut sharply, as though a curtain of ice had descended between them.

"I'm sure you had your reasons," he forced out. "It doesn't change how I feel about you, about Avery."

She took a step back, widening the space between them.

"You think I'm guilty. You believe them. Even after what happened with Marc at the retreat. You know he's been out to get me, that he wants my job—"

"Then tell me the truth. Did you know about this, about any of it? Did you know how those files got into Solene's hands? You said they were sold to her. By whom, Emma? If not you, then tell me who sold them. Did she tell you? Did you lie to me?"

Her face had grown stony, hardening with each question he asked. Now he took a step back, the gap growing even wider.

"You can't keep those kinds of secrets, Emma. Not from me. If you're as innocent as you claim, you have to tell me what you know."

She opened her mouth and then closed it. "I can't. I made a promise."

"A promise that you can't even share with me?" He shook his head. "That's not a very good way to start a relationship."

"I don't know what kind of relationship we can have after this."

Maybe she had spoken the words in truth or maybe she'd been trying to wound him. If her goal had been to cause him hurt, she'd succeeded. He had trusted her, had shared more with her than he had with anyone ever before.

At least she looked as miserable as he felt.

"How can we build on something when you can't even believe in my innocence?" she asked.

"Because you're not giving me all that much to go on," he argued. "I want to believe you. But I need to know what you're holding back."

She seemed to be wavering, shifting her weight from one foot to the other as she considered. "Can't you just trust me?" she finally asked. "Don't you know me well enough to believe me if I tell you that I didn't do this?"

His frustration spread, fanning into anger. "I'm beginning to think I don't know you at all."

He felt a flicker of guilt as tears finally filled her eyes. "Maybe you're right. Maybe you don't know me. Maybe I don't want you to."

She began to brush by him, but he grabbed her hand. She jerked it out of his grasp.

"Emma, we're not done yet."

"I'm afraid we are. I don't have anything more to say to you." He could tell she was battling herself, not wanting him to see her cry.

"I can talk to Lillian, ask her to demote you instead of firing you." He was growing desperate, bargaining to keep her from just walking away.

"No. That would be the same as saying I did this. Julien will never look me in the eye again. It's better if I leave."

"But what will you do? You can't go work for Léon Professional."

"Why not?" Her tone was bitter. "If I'm going to be accused of seeking a position there, I might as well do it."

"You don't mean that."

She sighed. "I don't know what I mean, Cole. I just want to go home. I just want everyone, including you, to leave me alone."

He knew she was right. She needed time. "Can I call you later, to see how you're doing?"

She looked away. "I think maybe it's better if we don't talk to each other for a while."

He felt an ache begin in the center of his chest. "Oh. I see."

"It's probably better if you don't associate with me right now anyway. You wouldn't want my guilt to rub off on you."

He didn't reply. They stood there for a few seconds more.

"Can you tell Avery I'll miss her?"

She blinked rapidly, but even so, a single tear escaped. She quickly dashed it away.

"I will."

"Okay. I guess this is goodbye, then."

"Yes. Goodbye, Cole."

"Bye, Emma."

He watched her walk away, the whole way across the plaza and toward the *métro* station until her figure blurred in amongst the commuters and tourists, and she faded completely from his sight.

CHAPTER THIRTEEN

EMMA BROKE DOWN as soon as she entered the CNIT building that housed the *métro.* She quickly made her way to the bathroom, locked herself in a stall and had a good cry for the next thirty minutes. After that, she felt marginally better and exited to splash some cold water on her face, trying to reduce the puffiness of her swollen eyelids. Then she left the building and headed in the direction of Léon Professional Services, on the other end of the business district.

She drew on the last dregs of her self-confidence as she approached the receptionist and asked her to page Solene Thierry. She waited, her anger rising as she replayed the morning's events. When Solene finally appeared, Emma met her halfway across the room.

"You broke your promise."

Solene frowned. "Emma." She didn't deny it, didn't even ask for clarification. "Why don't we take a walk outside?"

When her friend moved as if she would take her arm, Emma stepped away. She saw the woman at reception and other bystanders eyeing them curiously. Solene was right. This was no place for a scene. She turned on her heel and headed for the door. Solene followed her out into the morning sunshine. Emma kept walking, moving away from the building until Solene asked her to stop.

"What is going on, *chérie?*"

Emma faced her. "Come on, Solene. You know exactly what's going on. You went back on your word."

Solene seemed to be considering keeping up the pretense and then must have realized the futility in it. "He was a perfect match for my client. I had a deadline to place someone, and he was interested."

"You *promised* me."

"I know, and I am sorry. Truly, I am, Emma. But I didn't think one more placement would matter."

Emma's emotions overflowed. "How can you possibly be so selfish? When did you start to believe the world only revolved around you? Julien gave you chance after chance, and you burned through them as if he owed them to you. And when he stopped handing out chances, you decided your own shortcomings were his fault. Did it ever occur to you that you had simply let him down one too many times? Have you ever thought about how often you let people down?"

Solene's face remained blank at this litany of accusations. "Something has happened."

Emma threw up her arms in disbelief at this response. "Of course something has happened. I was fired from Aquitaine."

At this, Solene's jaw went slack. "What? Truly? Julien fired you?"

"Lillian did. But Julien sat there and watched it happen and never said a word."

Solene's face hardened. "I told you that he would turn his back on you, as he did to me."

"No." Emma put the full weight of her disgust behind that single word. "You won't blame Julien for this. At some point, you need to start taking responsibility for your own actions."

"But, Emma, what did I do? I used another name from the first list that I had gotten, but I didn't arrange for any more since I spoke to you. It was just one more name. I didn't think it would matter."

"But it did. It matters not just because it caused me to lose my job but because you were supposed to be my friend. I trusted you. I knew about Henri. I caught him logging on to my computer, and he told me everything—about his custody battle, and the lawyer fees, and the arrangement you two made. I could have turned him in, revealed what I knew, but I didn't. He said he'd confess once his personal matters were settled. I wanted to give him a chance to be with his children. Because I believed you both when you said it wouldn't happen again."

Solene seemed dumbstruck by this. Emma sighed. They stood together in silence for several moments as the hum of the business district continued around them.

"Emma, I'm sorry," Solene finally said, "but this is not as bad as it seems. My boss is still interested in interviewing you for the managing director position. I know you're angry right now, but once you get over it, we could work together again—"

"Get over it?" Emma cut her off. "Solene, you cost me my job. And Lillian somehow managed to find out that you were trying to get me hired at your company. I think that little tidbit hurt Julien more than anything else."

"Why are you so worried about what Julien thinks? I keep telling you, he is not the saint you make him out to be."

"I never said he was a saint. But you can't keep blaming him for firing you when he did.

It's his company, and he has the right to run it the way he wants. He told you plenty of times that he didn't approve of your methods. You knew how he felt, and you went over his head and did what you wanted anyway. I thought it was just because you didn't know any better, but I don't believe that anymore. You've always known that what you do benefits *you,* and you don't worry about anyone else."

Emma realized it then. There was no place for her at Léon Professional, either. If they condoned Solene's tactics, then Emma couldn't be a part of a company like that.

"I can't come work with you. I won't."

"Oh, come on, Emma, don't be so high and mighty."

"It's not high and mighty to have a few principles." Emma was exhausted. She felt as though she had lost one friend after another today. And Cole. In him, she feared she had lost more than just a friend. "I appreciate how you took me under your wing all those years ago. I really do. But who you were then can't make up for what you did now."

She had nothing else to say, so she turned to go.

"Emma, come on."

She ignored her and kept walking.

"Emma!" Solene called after her. "You're

going to regret this. You're making too big a deal out of things!"

Emma didn't so much as look over her shoulder as she strode away. She thought her day couldn't possibly get any worse. Her cell phone chimed from within her handbag. She kept walking but shifted the purse off her shoulder to reach inside. A part of her hoped it was Cole, despite what she'd told him about not speaking for a while. Her stomach sank as she saw the name on the caller ID. Brice.

She tapped the screen to accept the call and held the phone to her ear.

"Hello?"

"Emma, it's me."

"Brice, now is really not a good time—"

"I am afraid I have bad news."

Her steps faltered, and she paused, waiting.

"Jacqueline, my mother, she's had another heart attack."

She was stunned when she heard him sob on the other end.

"She did not make it, Emma. She's gone."

LOSING JACQUELINE WAS the worst blow of them all for Emma. Jacqueline had been like a surrogate mother to her when she married Brice. And even after the divorce, Emma had looked forward to visits with her. Avery adored her, the only grandmother she had ever known since she'd been too young to remember Emma's mother coming to visit them before she had passed away. Explaining Jacqueline's death to her daughter that evening was far more difficult than anything she'd experienced already that day.

Avery's response to the news was somber, with a few questions about the afterlife, but mostly, she wanted to know if her grandmother had been in pain. Emma hugged her close at these words.

"She's not in pain anymore, Avery. I promise."

The funeral was scheduled for that Friday, at Jaqueline's church in Le Mans. Since Emma's schedule was now clear, she had no trouble arranging the one-hour train ride through the Gare du Mans railway station. She gave Melanie that day off and tried not to think about the problem her au pair now presented. She had no idea how she would continue to pay for a live-in nanny in the upcoming weeks, especially when the girl's services were not necessary at the moment.

In the face of Jacqueline's death, however, Emma put off such concerns, focusing instead on her own grief and that of her daughter. They attended the service at the church, which was filled with Jacqueline's friends and family. Emma knew about half of the funeral goers, family members and acquaintances she had met during her marriage. Brice sat near the front with his girlfriend, Christine, at his side. Emma and Avery sat in a pew halfway back. The service was simple, just as Jacqueline would have preferred it. Avery leaned into her, nestling her head in Emma's lap several minutes into the eulogy. After it ended, they hung back, allowing the rest of the family to proceed to the church's cemetery, where Jacqueline's body would be interred.

Avery was listless as they waited, but Emma did her best to keep her daughter's spirits up. She seemed deep in thought, however, and finally voiced what was on her mind.

"Why doesn't Daddy ever come to see me?"

This question added to the grief Emma already carried.

"Well, he's very busy with his job." It was the weakest of excuses, but it was all she had to offer her daughter.

"Does he love me?"

Emma didn't know what to say. She'd tried to reassure Avery on this matter before, but the girl could obviously tell something was missing. If Brice did love his daughter, he rarely did much to show it.

"I love you, Avery. Very, very much. More than anyone else in the world."

"Even more than you love Cole?"

She jerked in surprise. Because of Jacqueline's death, she hadn't had to answer too many questions from Avery concerning Cole. When Avery asked why he hadn't come by to visit them that week, Emma had said that he was busy at the office, and Avery hadn't asked again.

"I don't love Cole like I love you," she said, brushing the hair back from Avery's forehead.

"But you do love him," Avery countered.

Emma had no reply to this. She did love Cole. The past week without him had been the most miserable she could ever remember spending in France, even worse than the week after she and Brice had decided to divorce. She'd told herself it was because of her grief over the loss of Jacqueline and her job. And even though it was true, she suspected she was grieving for losing Cole, too.

"Maybe you and I should go away for a while, hmm? We could take a trip to Oregon. Wouldn't you like that? You could finally meet your great-aunts and uncles, and I have a lot of cousins who would probably love to get to know you."

Avery looked up at her with eyes that had aged just a little bit more than Emma would have liked in the past week. "I miss him."

"Who?" She knew the answer, but she asked anyway.

"Cole. He makes you laugh. You haven't laughed at all since *Grand-mère* died."

"I loved your grandmother, Avery. It's hard to laugh when I've been missing her this week."

Avery looked away, and they fell silent once again as they waited for the family to return from the graveside. After that, they all convened at Jacqueline's house for a memorial gathering. They mingled and remembered, and Emma felt out of place. She had known these people once, but she was no longer a part of their lives. It got her thinking.

She thought about her job, and the loss of it and her future. What was left for her in Paris? Why had she stayed as long as she had in the city? She loved it, true. It had become home to her, and she couldn't quite imagine leaving it behind. She supposed she could find another job. If not in the recruiting sector, then certainly in management or human resources. She could start anew in the City of Light.

But what about Avery? Would her daughter be better served spending some time in America? Emma still had family there. Her parents were gone, but she still had extended relatives she kept in touch with. Avery had never met any of them. Perhaps it was time she did.

Avery clung to her during the gathering at Jacqueline's house. She didn't mingle with the others; she knew them even less than Emma did. Jacqueline had been the one who'd stayed in touch after the divorce. She had loved her granddaughter and, by extension, Emma. And Emma had loved her. But now that she was gone, what sort of ties did Avery still have to these people? What sort of ties did she have to Brice?

She was still considering this question when her ex-husband approached. He patted Avery on the head, an awkward gesture, and she slipped away from his touch, moving toward the hall and, if Emma could guess, Jacqueline's bedroom.

"Thank you for coming, Emma," Brice said. "I know she would have appreciated it."

"She was always so kind to me," Emma replied. "I'm going to miss her very much. She made me feel welcome in this country. I don't think I ever told her that. I wish that I had."

Tears filled his eyes. "I suppose we all have things left unsaid."

"I suppose." They stood there, and though Emma should have felt uncomfortable, she didn't. "Brice, could we go somewhere to talk? Privately?"

He nodded and began to direct her to the balcony. His face was so lined with loss that she couldn't tell if he was uneasy about her request. Once they were outside, he closed the door behind them. A breeze had picked up since the services at the church, and she shivered slightly, folding her arms across her midsection.

"I lost my job this week." She hadn't intended to start so abruptly, but once the words were out, the rest came easily. "I'm thinking of moving back to the States. It might do Avery good to meet some of her family there."

There was a small bistro set on the balcony, and Brice reached blindly for one of the wrought-iron chairs before sinking into it.

"You would leave Paris?"

"I don't feel like there's much here for me anymore."

They were silent for a time.

"I'm sorry that you lost your job. You always seemed to be Julien's favorite. What happened?"

"A misunderstanding. One that can't be fixed."

"Do you need money? I could give you some."

This offer startled her. Brice occasionally provided support for Avery, even though she had never asked him to. She had always supposed he did it out of some sense of obligation, but she never pressured him about it. She had chosen to keep Avery, even when he had made it clear he didn't want a child. She didn't necessarily feel it was right to ask him for additional support.

"I'll be all right. I have some money set aside. It should hold us for a little bit, provided I tighten up my expenses. I'll probably have to contact the agency about transferring Avery's au pair to another family."

"Melanie? Avery likes her very much."

Again, Emma was surprised, both that Brice knew Melanie's name and that he was aware how much his daughter liked her current caretaker. She supposed Jacqueline had told him and wondered just how much her former mother-in-law had shared with him over the years.

"I think…" She wasn't exactly sure how to say this next part. "Maybe… I might need you to sign away any rights to custody, if I want to go back to Oregon. I didn't think it would be a problem, since, you know…you never really see her anyway."

He sighed. "Emma—"

"I'm not trying to make you feel guilty. I'm just stating the facts. You've never shown much interest in Avery, but I want everything to be done as legally as possible."

He was silent for a very long time. Emma pulled out the other bistro chair and sat, waiting for him to work through what she'd said. They didn't see each other often, but she knew the distance this move would place between them was something he probably had to think about.

"What if things…changed?" He looked at her. "What if *I* change?"

She felt a faint unease. "What do you mean?"

He looked away again. The breeze continued to blow, and she realized her nose was becoming numb. She wondered if she could be back in America by Christmas, if she and Avery could spend the holidays in the States.

"What if I wanted to get to know my daughter?"

Nothing he could have said would have surprised her as much as this question did.

"Excuse me?"

"My mother adored Avery. She was always telling me stories, about things she said or did. I ignored her. I thought she was trying to make me feel guilty, for our divorce, for not wanting to be a father." He placed his arms on the table between them and studied his hands. "And I'm not much of one. I know that. I'm not sure I ever will be because it's not something that comes naturally to me."

He slowly lifted his eyes. "But perhaps it's time to try."

She couldn't stand the regret in his expression. She stood and paced back and forth across the tiny balcony. "Brice, you can't do this to me now. I just decided to leave the country, and now you're asking something that would require me to stay."

"I know. I suppose I've always been too selfish where you are concerned. But she is my child, too."

"She shares your blood, but that doesn't make her your daughter. You weren't there. You didn't hold her when she cried. You didn't get up in the middle of the night to feed her. You didn't even change a single diaper, Brice! And now you want to be her dad?"

He looked chastened by this rebuke. "I know, Emma. And if you truly want to leave Paris and move back to America, then...I will not stop you. But, please. I would like the chance to know her. I'm asking you to stay. I will help you find another job, if you want. I will loan you money. But don't take her away. Not just yet."

She wanted to be angry with him, wanted to rail at this new hitch in her plans. But she couldn't. It was the only thing she'd ever wanted for her daughter, to know her father.

"What does Christine have to say about this?"

"I think she understands. She'd like to get to know Avery, as well."

Emma had no more reason to fight him on this. "All right. I'll stay in Paris. We'll work something out for Avery. But you can't break her heart, Brice. If you stand her up even once, I'm putting a stop to it."

"I understand."

She sighed. She suddenly missed Cole. She wished he were here with her, or at the least, she wished she could call him when she got home, tell him everything that had happened today. She wondered what he had been up to in this past week. Had they promoted Marc to her position at Aquitaine? Despite what she had said, she wished Cole would call her. She supposed she could have called him, too, but she wasn't sure what she'd say if she did.

Brice had stood. "I better get back."

She nodded. "I should find Avery. We're taking the train back tonight."

They stared at each other, a trifle self-consciously.

"I'm sorry about your job," he offered.

"Thanks. But I think your loss was greater than mine this week."

He nodded. Before they turned to go, he touched her arm. She looked back at him.

"You deserve more, Emma. So much more than I ever gave to you."

She tried to smile, but for some reason, his words made her want to cry instead.

COLE HAD STACKS of paperwork waiting to be addressed, and he couldn't find an ounce of incentive to work on them. It had been a long and frustrating week at the Aquitaine offices. Lillian was determined to forge ahead with Emma's replacement while Cole battled with her to have a couple of weeks to sort things through and consider their best options. Julien said little during these discussions, leaving Cole and Lillian to circle round and round without reaching any conclusion on the matter.

She hinted at the truth during these arguments, that Cole had become too personally interested in his managing director to be able to make the necessary decisions now that she was gone. While Cole could agree with that accusation up to a point, he also knew that it was more than his attachment to Emma that made him reluctant. She had been good at her job, and replacing her would be more difficult than Lillian realized. He and Emma had made a good team, and promoting Marc, or anyone else, was not something he wanted to rush into. If Emma needed to be replaced, he wanted to choose someone who could measure up to the standard she'd set.

He tried to explain this to Lillian, each time they debated the matter, but he feared he made little headway. Lillian wanted things settled in Paris. She wanted the Reid and Aquitaine merger to continue to take root. But you couldn't force something to happen by sheer will. He told her so, though he feared he had come perilously close to crossing the line on that one.

She had left him alone for another day, to contemplate the matter, but had informed him that she expected his decision by Monday.

He stared at the stack of files in front of him but couldn't will himself to reach for one. He was wondering about Emma and what she'd been up to in the past week. Had she interviewed for a position at Léon Professional yet? They'd be foolish not to hire her; her track record in the field was impeccable, not to mention how quickly she'd advanced. And if they had no scruples about Solene's dubious tactics then surely they'd have no issue with why Emma had been dismissed from Aquitaine. If not for him, she'd be sitting in this seat right now, CEO of the entire Paris branch for Reid and Aquitaine. Perhaps Emma's life would have been better if he'd never come to France, if he'd rejected the ultimatum from Lillian and let things play out on the other side of the ocean. Too late now for such musings, he decided. And besides, selfish though it might be, he didn't think he'd have changed coming here for anything. This city, for as much as he'd resisted it, had captured his heart. He had spent the past week viewing it through eyes that no longer held blinders. He saw it as Emma did, as Ophelia must have once seen it, a timeless blend of ancient and modern, classic and contemporary. There was no other city on earth like this one. Paris was the place he'd sworn never to accept, and not only had he learned to call it home, but he had found love here, as well.

He turned around in his chair to look out over the La Défense district with its high-rises and forecourt featuring fountains, sculptures and the Grand Arch, its symbol of hope.

Where was his symbol of hope? He had begun to put down roots in this place, had opened himself up in ways he had never dared to before, and what did he have to show for it? He had lost the two people who had begun to matter more than anyone else.

What good was it to love a city if there was no one in it who loved him back?

Before he could contemplate the answer to this question, a beep sounded from his phone's intercom. He turned around and pressed to answer it.

"Mr. Dorset, there is a woman in the lobby requesting to see you." He experienced a swell of hopefulness. Emma? "Send her up."

There was hesitation on the other end. "She's been banned from the offices here as a security risk."

Emma. It has to be Emma.

"I'll vouch for her. Send her up immediately."

"If you say so, *monsieur.*"

He stood, uncertain. Should he greet her at the elevators? Wait for her to come to his office? Better to meet her when she arrived on the floor, so she wouldn't have to face any of her former coworkers.

He hurried from his office, smoothing down his hair as he stepped into the hall. Several employees greeted him, and he nodded briefly to each, careful not to linger lest they try to engage him in conversation.

"Going somewhere, Cole?"

He halted at the sound of Julien's voice.

"Yes. Well, no. I'm…meeting someone."

Julien waited for a more thorough explanation. Cole felt a ripple of unease. How was he going to explain Emma's arrival to Julien? Lillian had banned her from the building, and Cole had just defied that mandate by telling them he would vouch for her presence.

"Are we expecting a client?" Julien prompted.

Cole shook his head. "No, it's… No. It's Emma. She's on her way up."

Julien's eyes widened, but before he could react further, the elevator door chimed. Cole turned, a smile on his face, but it wasn't Emma who stepped off the elevator. He hadn't met this woman before in his life.

The mystery was soon revealed, however, as he heard Julien say the arrival's name.

"Solene."

HE HAD EXPECTED Julien to rail, perhaps even call security. He had heard the rumors about Solene Thierry and the bitter parting between her and Aquitaine, and of course, there was her involvement in the pilfered candidate lists. But Julien made no protest, even when Solene announced she was there to speak with Cole.

Perhaps he was simply weary of seeing people dismissed from his building, or maybe he was curious what had brought Solene back to the office. In any case, he suggested they head to the conference room for some privacy. Already, prying eyes were staring in the direction of the elevators.

"The conference room is this way," Cole directed, but her eyes narrowed at this.

"I know perfectly well where it is."

"Oh. Right." Of course she would. She had worked here for years. He tried to surreptitiously study her as they made their way down the hall. She was a beautiful woman, with a classic French profile, and wore a business suit that hugged her curvaceous frame. Her posture was stiff and erect as they moved along, but it was only once they were in the conference room with the door closed that she dared to speak.

"I came to talk with Cole, Julien. Not with you."

"Despite the fact that my company has merged with another, these are still my offices, and you came here," Julien reminded. "So your business is as much with me as it is with him."

She clicked her tongue in annoyance and moved around the table dominating the room to take a seat. She swiveled it around, studying the room, and then stopped to look at them.

"You haven't changed a bit, Julien, nor has the office. You always were a creature of habit. Didn't I tell you it pays to be open to new ideas?"

Julien scowled. "I am all for keeping abreast of the latest tactics, Solene, so long as they're ethically sound."

She leaned forward, and Cole sensed they were about to wage a full-out verbal battle unless he intervened.

"Ms. Thierry, I hardly think you came here to discuss recruiting techniques with your former employer. Why is it you asked to see me?"

She smirked at him. “No wonder Emma is smitten. You really are quite handsome.”

The mention of her name caused his heart to pound a little faster. “You’ve spoken to Emma?”

The smirk quickly faded from her features. “That’s the reason I’m here.”

Julien huffed. “If you’ve come to gloat, to tell me she’s been hired at Léon, you are wasting your breath. What Emma does now is none of my business.”

“Quiet, Julien. You always think you know what someone is going to say, before they even say it. This is not about Emma working for Léon Professional.” She straightened and looked at the hands resting in her lap. “In fact, Emma has no plans to work with me again. She never did. I was the one who inquired about hiring her. I wanted us to be on the same team again, but she made it clear she didn’t want to leave you.” Her gaze rose and shot to Julien. “Even though I told her you would betray her, given enough time. You already sold out her promotion to the American here. It was only a matter of time until you turned your back on her again. I warned her, but she would not listen. Emma is utterly loyal. You should have known that.” She clicked her tongue once more. “You should have known she would have stood by your side through anything." She sagged back in her seat. "Perhaps we both learned that lesson too late."

Cole's eyes darted between the two of them, watching as Julien pulled out one of the conference room chairs and sank into it.

"Lillian said Emma planned to resign, and go work for our rival."

"Lillian obviously didn't know the full story," Solene said. She looked to Cole now. "I came to tell you that Emma was innocent of any wrongdoing. The files may have come from her computer, but it wasn't Emma who sold them to me. It was Henri."

"Henri?" Cole frowned, trying to place the name. After a moment, it dawned on him. "The janitor? He's responsible for this mess?"

Solene gave a short nod. "Henri remembered me from my time here at Aquitaine. He looked me up and asked if there would be any sort of monetary remuneration for information from this office. I told him there might be. Things progressed from there."

"Did Emma know?" Julien demanded.

"Not at first. She asked me about the candidates and made me promise I wouldn't use any more names from the list. Later, she caught Henri trying to get more names from her computer."

Cole felt a rush of anger. "Why?" he demanded. "Why did Henri do this? Was it simply greed?"

Solene sighed. "He is in the midst of an ugly custody battle with his wife. The lawyer fees were mounting up, and he needed a way to pay for them. When Emma learned the truth about what had happened, she didn't turn him in because she wanted to give him the chance he needed to maintain ties to his children. He said he would turn himself in after the custody hearing. She would have reported him at that point otherwise. And he made her a promise—we both did—that it would never happen again. But I…broke that vow."

Of course. It all made sense to Cole now. This was what Emma had kept from him, fearing what it would do to Henri's custody case if she admitted what she knew. He wished she had confided in him, though he couldn't really blame her for not telling him, especially after how they had argued. And now that Julien knew she hadn't been involved and would have turned Henri in if he didn't come forward on his own, maybe she could come back. Perhaps Lillian would let her return to her job.

"Emma's only crime is that she is unfailingly loyal. She does not betray others." Solene looked to Julien. "Unlike you and me, I suppose."

"Why come here and tell us this?" Julien demanded. "Since I know you to be as disloyal as you say, why try to undo what's happened?"

It was then that Cole saw Solene for what she really was. Beneath the layers of makeup and careful styling, she looked far older than he had initially assumed her to be. She seemed weary as she rubbed the side of her temple with a manicured hand.

"It was not easy for me to come here. You have to know that."

Julien's tone was soft when he replied. "I do. That is why I want to know what you're up to."

She sighed and dropped her hand back to her lap. "I have not had many friends in my life. I am a woman who collects only people she can use. I'm sure you will not argue with me, Julien, when I say that I do not know how to be a good friend. I know what I am. Ambitious. Selfish. Morally questionable, if you must know the truth." She straightened in her seat and placed her hands on the conference table, folding them in front of her.

"When I first befriended Emma, I had every intention of using her. She was brilliant, hardworking and perhaps had a touch of the romantic in her."

This observation caused Cole to stifle a smile. Emma the romantic. He had recognized that trait in her practically from the beginning.

"But that girl." She shook her head. "She liked me. She was nice to me. She got under my skin, and somehow, we became friends." She turned her attention to Cole. "When Julien and I began to disagree about recruiting tactics, she concurred with him, but never once did she make me feel as though she had chosen sides. When I was dismissed from Aquitaine, she did not cut off all ties with me as I expected her to."

Her gaze swiveled back in Julien's direction. "She was the only person from this company to offer me condolences for the loss of my job. Did you know that? She came to see me in the weeks afterward. She asked if I had enough money to get by. When my savings ran out, she offered for me to sleep on her couch. She would take me to the Rue Cler, pretending she wanted company while shopping, and fill up a basket with a week's worth of groceries, paying for them, and then insisting she had changed her mind and didn't want anything she'd purchased so that I would take the food home with me."

Solene swallowed. "She has been the best, perhaps the only real friend I've ever had, and I vowed I would one day return the favor of her kindness to me. That is why I tried to get her an interview at Léon. I wanted to give her something back for all the tiny things she has given me over the years. But in my selfishness, I still forged ahead with my own plans, rather than considering how they might affect her." She squared her shoulders. "And because of that, I fear I have lost her friendship forever."

Cole felt a swell of shame as Solene related all this. Why hadn't he taken Emma at her word? Did he really have to know all the details in order to believe her? Or should it have been enough to know *her?* To know that she was dedicated to Aquitaine, that she loved her job, that she loved...him.

"Julien." She faced her former boss once more. "You and I have certainly had our differences, but there was one thing we always seemed to agree on, and that was Emma. We both knew she was something special, that she had the skills to go far in this company. I still disagree with your decision to give her promotion to him—" she inclined her head in Cole's direction "—but I think we can agree that Emma has been a valuable part of Aquitaine for a very long time.

"I am not the president of a company. Perhaps you have had the experience of knowing many employees like Emma, and therefore, her loss is not significant to you. But I can tell you that as a friend, I feel qualified to let you know she is priceless." Solene pushed back and got to her feet.

"If I have lost her friendship forever, then I have no one to blame but myself. And I'm here not for you, Julien, because I don't feel I owe you anything. But I do owe her something, and it's to tell you this. Emma did not betray you. She wouldn't, not if she was offered the entire Palace of Versailles. You would be a fool to make the same mistake that I did and not see her true worth."

She moved away from the table and toward the door but not before stopping before Cole.

"And you."

He waited.

"You would be wise to take that advice, also."

She left them then, and Cole moved around

the table to take the seat she had vacated. Julien stared at the floor, lost in thought. Silence permeated the room for several long minutes before Cole cleared his throat.

"You know, I think that deep down, she likes you more than she lets on."

This statement caused Julien's fixed stare to falter, and he jerked his head up. When he saw Cole's smile, he seemed to be unable to resist a small one of his own.

"I doubt it," he replied, "but for once, she makes a good point."

"Yes, she does," Cole agreed. "Perhaps Lillian acted too hastily."

Julien didn't respond, and Cole feared he would not take Solene's words to heart.

"Bring her back, Julien. We need her. She makes this company better."

She makes me better.

"I'll consider it."

Cole shook his head. "Don't consider it. Do it. Solene was right. You never should have let Lillian demand for me to have this position. Emma earned it, and it was promised to her. It was wrong of you to let me take it."

Julien blinked, as though stunned by this declaration.

"She could have gone to Léon at any time. It sounds as though Solene was practically begging her to. And she stayed right here. For you, most likely."

"Yes. Perhaps...perhaps you're right."

"Convince Lillian to bring her back. If you don't, then you'll lose me, too. I can't work for someone who doesn't know the value of loyalty."

Julien nodded. "I will consult with Lillian and see what she has to say."

"Why don't I go with you?"

Julien appeared skeptical. "Are you sure you want a piece of that battle?"

"You may not realize it, but I know Lillian pretty well. I think the two of us against the one of her might even the odds a bit."

Despite the challenge still facing them, Julien laughed at that.

CHAPTER FOURTEEN

LILLIAN COULDN'T UNDERSTAND what had gotten into Cole. She had always admired how reasonable he could be. It didn't usually take any great effort to convince him to see her point of view. But since Emma's dismissal, he had become far more stubborn than she liked. And now, after this Solene person had stopped by the office, both he and Julien were suddenly determined to absolve Emma Brooks of any wrongdoing. It took more than a friend's heartfelt plea to change Lillian's mind, however. Emma had likely put the other woman up to it, trying to play on their male sympathies. She suppressed a sigh.

"If this was such an eye-opening exchange, I'd like to know why I was left out of it," she remarked.

These words brought the two men up short.

"It wasn't consciously done," Cole finally said. "Solene took us by surprise. We certainly didn't intend for you not to be there."

Lillian looked to Julien, who frowned apologetically. "Solene came to speak with Cole, and I just happened to be there when she arrived. It was not an intentional exclusion, I assure you."

"Even so, it must have been quite a performance. I'm sorry to have missed it." She turned her attention to Julien's desk. She didn't have her own office in Paris yet but, rather, shared one with Julien while she was in town. She sensed the two men exchanging glances while she looked away, and when she quickly lifted her head, their guilty expressions confirmed it.

"Emma Brooks no longer works for this company," she declared.

"But that's the point," Cole said. "She was unjustly dismissed. We need to get her back."

"We *need* to?" Lillian tried to temper her tone, but Cole was becoming almost obsessive on this tiring point. "I hardly think we need Ms. Brooks to help run this company."

Cole fell silent, but he turned his gaze to Julien, who leaned forward, drawing her attention.

"Lillian, Emma has been invaluable to me the past few years. It was foolish of me to so hastily dismiss her without delving further into matters."

"All the evidence pointed to her," Lillian

reminded him. She couldn't believe she was having this discussion. The two of them had been privy to the same information she had, proof enough that Emma was responsible for the leaked files that had threatened the company's credibility.

"She didn't do it."

Lillian's head swiveled back toward Cole. His face was hard with determination, and she couldn't remember ever seeing such an expression on him before.

"She didn't do it, Lillian," he repeated. "At most, she's culpable for finding the cause of the theft, Henri, and then not bringing it to my attention immediately. Nothing else was her fault."

"And how do you suppose we can trust her after that, after keeping such crucial information to herself?"

He leaned forward in his seat. "Because *I* trust her," he said. "She has been instrumental in assisting my transition to this office. She may not have approved of the merger initially, but she has committed herself to its success. She has worked as tirelessly as you would have to be sure the Reid and Aquitaine name is the first on everyone's lips when it comes to executive recruiting. And if she can place so much faith in us, even after her promotion was taken away, and she had her doubts about this move, then can't we afford to place just a little bit more in her?"

Lillian stared. She had never seen this side of him before. What had caused such passionate eloquence? What had the loss of Ophelia done to him? It was almost as if he… She leaned back.

It was almost as if he were in love with this Emma. Her eyes narrowed.

"Cole, you wouldn't be letting any personal affection you might have for this woman color your decision, would you?"

"I would," he fired back without hesitation. "It's because of those affections that I know her better than you do. If you let her go, Lillian, you'll be making a mistake. You asked me— No, you insisted I take over this company in your name, that I become your CEO in Paris. If you trusted me in that, you're going to have to trust me in this. You want Emma on your team."

"Because you want her," Lillian replied, rankled that he was defending the woman so zealously.

"Because I want what's best for this company."

She scoffed. When had her best employee become so blinded by emotion?

Julien cleared his throat. "Cole, perhaps you could give Lillian and me a moment alone?"

Cole hesitated and then slowly nodded, getting to his feet and leaving the room. Julien stood and held out his hand. She resisted him; she was in no mood to be wooed at the moment, but he insisted. She placed her hand in his and allowed him to lead her to the small leather couch in a corner of the room.

"It is difficult, is it not? After a time, you begin to feel responsible for them, as though their feelings and choices are something you can control."

"Julien, I don't have a single idea what you mean by that."

He enveloped her hands in his larger ones, and she allowed herself to look at him. He wasn't a very handsome man. His face was too fleshy, his stomach too wide. But he had a presence that couldn't be denied. She had noted it from the moment she met him, how he exuded an air of capability. Perhaps that was what had initially attracted her. Maybe, despite all her beliefs to the contrary, she really did want someone who would take charge, or at least, share the burden. She wondered if that was why this merger had held so much appeal—she wanted a partner, both in business and now, it seemed, in life. She had come to rely on him, on his steadiness, and though she couldn't remember feeling such things in a long time, she suspected she might be very much in love with this man.

"Lillian, when will you learn to trust the people you've chosen?"

She shifted, trying to remove her fingers from his embrace. "Trust is one thing, naïveté is another."

"Why would taking Cole's advice make you naive? You placed him in this position because you believed he would make the choices you would want him to make. If he feels Emma should be given her job back—"

"He's speaking from infatuation. Can't you see he's in love with her?"

"And what is so wrong with that?" Julien pressed, his fingers still holding hers. "I am in love with you, after all."

She went still and stared at him. He had never said those words before. Out of dozens of conversations, during hours of being in each other's company the past few weeks, he had never spoken them out loud. She suddenly realized how much she'd longed to hear them.

"Are you?"

"*Oui.* Madly in love with you."

Her heart fluttered in a way she hadn't experienced since she was much younger. "And if our roles were reversed, and I was in Cole's position and you were in Emma's, I would fight with everything I had to keep you in this company. It is because I love you that I know you, that I see what the rest do not always see."

"And what do you see?" she asked, feeling just a little breathless.

"I see an extraordinary woman, dedicated to her job and her company, but perhaps a bit vulnerable, as well."

She shifted uncomfortably. "I'm hardly vulnerable."

"But you are, *chérie.* You are proud and vulnerable. It is, somehow, an intriguing combination."

She couldn't understand how he made such traits sound like something he cherished.

"Do you really believe she's innocent in all this?" she asked him. "Even if we brought her back, how do we know she wouldn't betray us, just out of spite?"

"Because I know her. And Cole knows her. And we both believe in her. And because you know us and trust our judgment.... You do trust our judgment, don't you, Lillian?"

She considered this and then nodded.

"Then you can trust her, too."

Perhaps he had a point.

"Is she really as invaluable as Cole claims?"

Julien brought her hand to his mouth, his lips hovering over her fingers. "Why don't you give her another chance and find out?"

EMMA WRAPPED HER sweater a bit more tightly around her frame. The weather was turning cooler by the day. She kept a watchful eye on Avery and wondered if she should have insisted her daughter wear more layers for this afternoon outing to the park. She couldn't bear to suggest they go back to the apartment, not yet anyway. She had just been reviewing her finances last night and decided that she and Avery would have to move within the next month or two. While her apartment in Batignolles was not as expensive as most in the seventeenth *arrondissement,* it was still more than she could afford without her wages from Aquitaine. So she decided to let Avery enjoy the park for as long as possible. After all, she would likely be saying goodbye to Melanie this week, as well. The au pair agency was already working on finding another family for the young woman. Once she left them, Brice had offered to help out however he could, by watching Avery if Emma had a job interview or if she just needed time to sort through things. She was still a little skeptical of her ex-husband's desire to get to know his daughter, but she had to admit that so far he seemed committed. Upon his return from Le Mans, they had arranged for him to spend a weekend with Avery, who was, Emma could tell, both wary and excited at the idea.

Emma didn't even want to consider how she would feel when that weekend rolled around. She found herself missing Cole more and more, but somehow managed to stave off the worst of the longing by lavishing attention on Avery. She feared these attempts at distraction were slowly wearing her daughter down. Last night, when Emma had suggested they bake cookies, Avery refused, saying she was sick of cookies. Belatedly, Emma realized that this had been her standard suggestion for several nights in a row. They had so many cookies piling up that, instead, she'd decided they should offer them to their neighbors in the building. That idea had been met with more enthusiasm, but she knew she couldn't rely on Avery to distract her forever.

She might have talked to Solene about things, but of course, they still hadn't spoken since the day she'd been fired from Aquitaine.

She regretted telling Cole they shouldn't speak to each other for a while. She missed him and wished he were around to cheer her up and make her laugh. She wanted to tell him about Brice and hear his thoughts. She wondered how things were going at the office and what sorts of new positions needed filling with their clients. She pictured Julien and pondered whether he ever thought about her at all since her dismissal. His opinion had meant so much to her over the years, and it felt strange to know she would probably never speak to him again.

And then, as if this very consideration had summoned him, he appeared, stepping up to the bench where she sat. She could only blink at his arrival, speechless.

"She is growing up fast," Julien remarked, looking toward Avery as she ran circles around the playground. Emma watched in surprise as he settled himself on the seat next to her.

"Your au pair, Melanie—such a lovely girl—told me you were here."

She was too flabbergasted to respond. Why had he come?

"The weather is turning cooler so quickly.

I fear we will have snow on the ground well before Christmas." He shifted his gaze around the park. "You know, I don't think I have ever seen the Square des Batignolles when it is covered in snow. It must be a delightful sight."

By this time, she had regained some of her composure. "Julien…what are you doing here?"

He shifted his rather hefty weight, and the bench squeaked in protest.

"I came to apologize."

She felt another ripple of shock. "Apologize?"

He nodded. "I did not give you enough credit, Emma. You are not Solene. I forgot that. You must forgive me."

She turned away from him, keeping one eye on Avery as she held out her arms and pretended to flap them like a bird.

"What are you trying to say? That you realize I'm innocent?" She could only wonder how Julien had come to that conclusion. Had Cole been involved?

"Solene came to see us."

Her head jerked around. It seemed this conversation was going to stun her at every turn. "Solene? She came to Aquitaine?"

"She did, to proclaim your innocence. And

I have to admit, she must feel quite strongly about your friendship to have entered those doors again. She made it plain that there is still no love lost between the two of us."

Emma gaped at him. "You and Solene were in the same room together? And you both walked out alive?"

He laughed at this, and the sound warmed her. "Cole was there as a witness, if you do not believe me."

Cole. She felt her nerve endings come alive at the sound of his name. "So then...Cole was there, to hear her say I wasn't responsible for those leaked files?"

Julien eyed her speculatively. "You are as in love with him as he is with you, aren't you?"

This pointed question caused her to turn away. She didn't want Julien to see how much she wanted this to be true.

"I thought as much," he said.

"How is he?" she questioned, unable to resist asking about him.

"Much better, now that Lillian and I have decided to ask you back. I fear he was at loose ends without you, quite distracted. How he managed before he met you, I have no idea."

Though all of these words caused a lightening in her spirit, she chose to focus on only the first few. "You're asking me back to Aquitaine?"

He looked down. "I am ashamed I let you go at all, Emma. I was perhaps not as understanding as I should have been. You have proven your dedication to this company a thousand times over, especially when I denied you the promotion I had promised and worsened the blow by assigning you as Cole's liaison."

She was quick to reassure him on that score. "That's okay. I enjoyed assisting with Cole's transition."

A faint smile tugged at Julien's lips. "Yes, I daresay you did."

She fought the blush she felt heating her cheeks and looked for Avery once more. Her daughter was oblivious to the conversation taking place several yards away.

"And you said that Lillian agreed to my return, as well?"

He inclined his head. "Not without a bit of persuasion, but then, she does not know you as well as I do." He turned on the bench, and it groaned at the movement. "Will you forgive me, Emma? For doubting your integrity? And will you return to Aquitaine? I cannot promise an immediate promotion, but hopefully, in the future, something can be arranged."

"Not if it means losing Cole," she stated. "I think he's going to do wonderful things for our company."

"Our company? Then you'll come back?"

She thought about hesitating, trying to punish him a little bit longer. But that wasn't her style.

"It will be just like I never left."

She knew by his smile that it was the answer he'd been hoping for.

EMMA COULD NOT understand Melanie's insistence. Now that their au pair would be staying with them through the school year, she didn't see why they had to visit the Champ de Mars tonight, of all nights. But Melanie kept saying she wanted to see the Eiffel Tower lit up against the evening sky, and she couldn't wait. She insisted it would be a celebration, now that they could stay together for a few months more. Avery backed her up on this, pleading with Emma to take them.

Emma pointed out that since they would be together for a while longer, they'd have plenty of opportunities to view the Eiffel Tower at night another time. But Melanie and Avery protested mightily at this, insisting it had to be tonight.

She hedged for a bit, repeatedly checking the screen of her cell phone. She had spoken to Solene earlier, thanking her for what she'd done. They'd made plans to get together next week to talk through everything that had happened. But Solene's wasn't the number she kept hoping would light her screen.

After her news from Julien, she had expected Cole to call and speak to her himself. Wasn't he happy about the decision for her to return? Perhaps their last exchange had changed his feelings for her. Maybe she wouldn't hear from him at all but would have to face him when she returned to the office in a few days' time. She was embarrassed to admit that rather than going out and viewing the breathtaking magnificence of the Champ de Mars at night that she would prefer to stay in and wait by the phone for him to call.

Ashamed of these feelings, she finally caved and told Melanie to dress Avery warmly for their evening excursion. With one last glance at her cell phone's screen, she pocketed it and grabbed her own sweater to guard her against the chilly autumn air.

THE CHAMP DE MARS was not as crowded on a weeknight as it might have been on the weekend, but still, there were several dozen people spread out along the stretch of green fronting the Eiffel Tower. Emma paused to take in the glittering beauty of the iron structure. Lamplights lined the avenue and illuminated the strip of grass that stretched to the tower's base. The monument glowed with hundreds of light projectors and several thousand strobe lights, casting a golden radiance. Emma's breath caught in her chest. How had she thought she could leave this place? She loved Paris, the city that had somehow come to be home more than any other. She reached for Avery and drew her daughter against her side.

"You guys were right. This was a good idea."

She didn't care who called her a romantic. There was something about that beacon of love that made her feel all would be right with the world.

She reached into her pocket and withdrew her cell phone, checking it one more time. No calls. A bit of her romantic optimism deflated. Perhaps Cole had forgotten all about her already.

"Come on, Mom."

Avery began tugging on her arm, so she reluctantly slipped the phone back into the pocket of her jeans.

"Slow down there, kiddo," she begged as Avery's grip became more insistent. She practically dragged Emma across the lawn in the direction of the Eiffel Tower. Melanie laughed and kept pace beside them. She could hear the joy in that sound and wondered if the younger woman would learn to love Paris as she had when she was an au pair.

"Avery, what's gotten into you?"

But her daughter just kept moving, and when Emma looked to Melanie for help, the girl could only shrug. The excitement of Emma's return to Aquitaine must have lifted their spirits even more than it had raised hers. Of course, her own happiness was tempered by no word from Cole.

What would she do if he no longer wanted to see her? How would she mend together a heart that he had claimed, if he now released his hold on her? She couldn't begin to think in those terms, didn't even know where to start.

And then, her attention was arrested by a sight that made her sigh. Someone had set up a table in the middle of the Champ de

Mars, directly in the center, with the Eiffel Tower shining down. It was lit with candles, and it appeared as though a dinner had been laid. How lovely. Some woman was extraordinarily lucky to experience such thoughtfulness. She looked around, wondering just who the happy couple was, and that's when she saw him.

Cole. He was dressed in his office attire, wearing black pants and a white button-down shirt with his vest over top. His hair was styled as though he'd just come from work, though a blond lock had fallen across his forehead. He stood, a single rose held in his hand. She looked from the candlelit table to him and found his expression serious.

"Go, Mom."

Avery went around and pushed her forward from behind. She glanced at Melanie.

"Avery and I are going for a walk. We'll see you back home later on, okay?"

Emma felt a flutter of nerves take over. "Maybe you guys should stay."

"M-o-o-m," Avery protested. "Go talk to Cole."

She grabbed Melanie's hand, and before Emma could protest further, they were skipping away, back across the green. She turned back to Cole, who offered a tentative smile and then took several steps forward. He met her halfway and held out the rose.

"Would you like to join me for dinner?"

Her stomach was doing so many somersaults that she didn't see how it would be possible to eat a thing. Still, she wasn't about to turn him down. She took the rose in her hand.

"Yes, I'd like that."

He gestured toward the table, and when his hand touched the center of her back to guide her forward, she felt her knees grow weak. He pulled out a chair, and she sank into it, laying the rose beside her. She wished she'd had some sort of warning so she could have dressed a bit more elegantly than her T-shirt, jeans and sweater. From the corner of her eye, she noticed several couples stopping, taking note of the scene Cole had created, before sighing and leaning into each other as they moved on.

"How did you do all this?" she asked, as he took the seat across from her.

"A gentleman doesn't reveal his secrets," he said and then pulled the covers off their plates to reveal a simple dish of soup and sections of baguette along with several slices of cheese. In the center of the table rested a small plate with half a dozen *macarons* in varying flavors. She knew they had to be from Ladurée.

"Cole, this is..." Inexplicably, she felt tears fill her eyes. "No one has ever... I've never..."

"What's more romantic than dinner in Paris with a view of the Eiffel Tower?"

She looked at him, her chest expanding with love. "I can't think of anything more wonderful," she whispered.

He placed his arm on the table, reaching toward her with his palm up. She placed her arm there, as well, putting her hand into his.

"Emma, I'm sorry for any doubts I had, about things at Aquitaine. I know you better than that, and I should have spoken up for you, should have trusted in you more than I did. I'm asking you to forgive me and making a promise that if anything like this happens in the future, I'll put more faith in you."

She swallowed at these words but couldn't find breath to speak.

"You are the most loyal person that I know, and I...I am completely in love with you. Can you forgive me and agree to work with me at Aquitaine again? Will you consider restarting a relationship with me?"

She was overwhelmed by this declaration and found her chest so full that she still couldn't force out a reply. He must have mistaken her silence for hesitation because he continued.

"If you still have doubts about dating someone you work with, and especially your boss, I'll resign my position at the company."

"No." The idea of Cole leaving forced the word out. He jerked back slightly, his fingers losing their grip on hers.

"No?" he asked, and she realized how her reply had sounded.

"I meant, no, I don't want you to resign from Aquitaine, but, yes…I want us to be together."

She watched as a smile broke over his features, lighting his hazel eyes with happiness. "Then it's a yes?"

"It's a yes," she confirmed, feeling her own grin widening with joy.

He stood, moving his chair around the table and setting it beside hers before taking his seat once more. He reached for her hand again.

"When I came here, I never thought I could learn to love this city, but I have come to adore it, all because it brought me to you."

She moved her free hand to touch his face, running her fingers along his jaw and down to his chin.

"When I was younger, I just knew I'd find

love here. Maybe it's why I never left, after my marriage to Brice ended. Maybe, deep down, I knew I had to stick around until you found your way here."

"Then thank you," he said softly, "for waiting."

"Thank you for giving me a good reason to." She leaned in to nudge her nose against his. "And for reminding me I'm a romantic at heart. I had almost forgotten."

"I won't ever let you forget again."

And that, she knew, was a promise.

EPILOGUE

EMMA WAS IN awe of the church sanctuary, each pew draped in swaths of silk and an abundance of orchids stationed at every end. There were ultrafeminine touches of lace and trailing ivy and more candles than she could begin to count. She turned to Cole, his hand wrapped loosely around her waist as he guided her forward.

"I always pictured Lillian and Julien's wedding as a simple affair."

Cole shrugged. "It appears that Lillian's idea of a wedding is much more ostentatious."

Emma couldn't believe it. She'd been privy to many conversations between Lillian and Julien over the past eight months as they planned the event of their nuptials, but she hadn't paid close enough attention to realize just how extravagant it all would be. After all, Julien had always been a bachelor, and Lillian had been a widow for over twenty-five years. Who knew the two would go all out on the occasion of their marriage?

The usher stopped and directed them to enter a pew. Cole gestured for her to go first, and then he slid in beside her. His arm immediately went around her back, his palm running over her other arm. She leaned into him.

"Oh, by the way," she said, "I wanted to ask you what you'd think if I threw a goodbye party for Melanie. She's scheduled to return to the States in another month, so I'd have to pull something together rather quickly, but Solene's already agreed to help."

He leaned over and pressed a kiss to her temple. "I think that's a very thoughtful idea. Just make sure you pick a weekend when Avery isn't scheduled to spend time with her dad."

"Oh, good point."

She turned her attention to the front, where she spotted Julien in his tux. It had been specially fitted for his wide girth, but she had to admit that he was a commanding figure.

"Julien looks happy, doesn't he? I never imagined Lillian would be the one to wrangle him into matrimony."

"Really? I always thought they'd make a great couple."

She rolled her eyes. "You did not."

"You wound me, Aquitaine. Have you already forgotten what I know?"

"What's that?"

"I know that the heart wants what the heart wants."

These words, murmured in her ear, caused her to shiver, and Cole noticed the goose bumps rise on her arm.

"Are you cold?" he questioned. "I can give you my jacket."

He started to shift away from her to remove it, but she grabbed the end of his tie and pulled him back into position. He ran a hand over her arm, and she shivered happily.

"Oh, look, there's Ophelia and Dane, up near the front." She had met Lillian's daughter and her husband when they flew to Paris from Hawaii after the announcement of Lillian's engagement. "It's a good thing Lillian and Julien scheduled this wedding when they did. It doesn't look like Ophelia will be able to fly much longer. That's quite the baby bump."

When Cole didn't respond, she slid him a glance out of the corner of her eye. "You're not jealous, are you?"

"Of Ophelia's baby bump? That was never a good look for me."

She nudged him in the side. "You know what I mean."

He moved his arm and cupped her chin,

turning her face to look at him directly. "I'm happy for Ophelia, and I wish her well. But I don't miss her. Not even the tiniest bit. Let her and Dane keep their island paradise. You and I have the City of Light."

She thrilled at this reminder just as the music began to swell. The guests all moved to stand, and the sound of rustling fabric filled the sanctuary. Emma turned toward the back, along with the rest of them, and waited for Lillian to appear.

She entered the auditorium in a cloud of tulle and satin, a stylish little hat cocked on her head with a thin veil of netting covering her face. Her gaze swept by them all and went to the front of the room. Emma couldn't help following her line of vision to see how Julien's face brightened with pleasure at the sight of Lillian. She suppressed a sigh of contentment.

She loved weddings. And though she and Lillian had experienced a few ups and downs on her return to Aquitaine, it was obvious the older woman made Julien happy. So Emma had gradually learned to put aside her occasional annoyance with the way Lillian handled things and decided to like her.

Besides, she wouldn't be seeing as much of the company owners in the future. Lillian and

Julien had informed them that they would be turning over an even greater amount of control to Cole and Emma in the days ahead. The newlyweds planned to travel and spend a considerable amount of time in Hawaii once Lillian's grandchild was born.

All the talk of babies had made Avery curious, and she had begun asking Emma if there might be a sister for her one day soon. Emma kept putting the question off, but she knew a secret that she'd been holding close. It was the discovery of a velvet ring box from a jewelry shop she had admired some months ago during an outing to the Champs-Élysées with Cole. She had been dropping off several of Cole's suits at his apartment, placing them in his closet after picking them up from a dry cleaner's, when it fell from its hiding place and knocked her gently on the head.

She had picked it up, hesitating, and wondering if perhaps it was from Cole's failed proposal to Ophelia from the year before, when she'd finally opened it up. If she hadn't recognized the jewelry shop's name, she wouldn't have immediately realized it was for her. She had quickly returned it to its hiding place and hadn't breathed a word of her discovery to Cole or anyone else.

But she was waiting, eager to see what sort of proposal scheme he'd come up with. For someone who had been so opposed to Paris in the beginning, Cole had proven himself a romantic of the highest caliber. He was forever offering up little unexpected surprises, making her fall in love with him all over again each and every day. Like this morning, when she'd gone into her kitchen to find the words "I love you" spelled out in grains of French lavender across the counter. She still wasn't sure when he'd snuck into the apartment and set that one up. Perhaps Avery had helped him. She was often his accomplice in that sort of thing.

By now, Lillian had reached the altar, and the guests all resumed their seats. The minister began the ceremony, discussing love and its importance, how it knew nothing of age nor time, that it was eternal.

Cole reached for her hand, and she felt a rush of happiness at the warmth of his fingers around hers. As Lillian and Julien began their vows, she turned her head and looked at Cole, letting everything else fade away save for his face. He met her gaze, and she saw exactly what she'd been looking for in his eyes. Then she nestled into him, placed her head on his shoulder and let his arm come around her as she turned her attention toward the front of the sanctuary and her heart toward the future.

* * * * *